THE GAMES

Patricia McLinn

Dear Readers: If you encounter typos or errors in this book, please send them to me at Patricia@patriciamclinn.com. Even with many layers of editing, mistakes can slip through, alas. But, together, we can eradicate the nasty nuisances.
Thank you! – Patricia McLinn

"Patricia McLinn wins gold with this sparkling romance! **The Games** is your ticket behind the cameras and inside the hearts of the winter Olympics."

— Carla Neggers, New York Times bestselling author

"Fast-paced, vivid and true-to-life, Patricia McLinn's **The Games** captures the personal drama and compelling stories of the greatest sports event on earth. It's a gold-medal winner any fan of the Games will love."

— Christine Brennan, USA Today sports columnist

"**The Games** accurately portrays the emotional roller coaster an athlete rides . . . The pride, excitement, disappointment, relationships, doubt, relief, joy and all of the pressures . . . all come to a head at the Olympic Games."

— Michael Weiss, U.S. Olympic figure skater and three-time U.S. Men's champion

"**The Games** is a wonderful book! All of the characters are so dynamic, so believable. The tension of the various competitions is nerve-wracking. The romance going on behind the scenes is explosive. . . . a story you won't be able to put down, and one you'll not soon forget."

— RomanceJunkies.com

"If the aim of **The Games** is to give readers a vicarious Olympic experience that is lively, entertaining, and emotionally satisfying, it hit its mark dead center."

— Romance Reviews Today

"I delighted in the 'real world' look at some Olympic heroes. . . . Ms. McLinn's knowledge added the excitement of the Olympics to her wonderful book."

— CataRomance

"Written with invigorating, breathtaking passion, I found myself jumping up and cheering for the wins, and sobbing out loud during the defeats. . . . The sensual romance . . . will also have you cheering, sighing, and all choked up throughout this wonderfully compelling read. This is an exceptional read, a winner worthy of the gold, and one I highly recommend!"

— Romance Reviews Today

✧ ✧ ✧ ✧

ACKNOWLEDGEMENTS

The Author gratefully acknowledges:
First, those athletes who demonstrate the grit and grace of striving.

In particular, I am extremely grateful to the following people for answering so many questions and for giving such wise answers (any errors are mine, not theirs):

Nancy Johnstone, U.S. Olympic biathlete; Joan Smith Miller, U.S. Olympic biathlete; Wendy Fisher, U.S. Olympic Alpine skier; Robert Kyle Wieche, U.S. Olympic Alpine skier; Kirsten Culver, U.S. Olympic speed skier; Jenny Stone, U.S. Olympic Committee sports medicine and training; Maurice W. Stillwell, past-president U.S. Figure Skating Association; Jeff Cravens, U.S. Olympic Committee media relations at Albertville; Jim Johansson, U.S. Olympic hockey team; Rocky Marval, U.S. Olympic figure skater; and Rachel Mayer Godino, U.S. Olympic figure skater.

They were invaluable in bringing The Games alive.

Dave Shultz, who sent a rookie reporter out to cover figure skating, cross-country skiing and ski jumping – and got me hooked.

Scott Hamilton, who even all those years ago at the Wagon Wheel in Rockton, Ill., was a gracious champion.

Christine Brennan, who was always encouraging. And colleagues in sports departments at the Rockford Register-Star, Charlotte Observer and Washington Post, who let me handle lots and lots and lots of winter sports stories. Especially Mike Doyle, Sherri Winans Glennon, and Kay Coyte.

Athletes and coaches from the Rockford, Ill., area, who taught many lessons about competition, sportsmanship and people.

My family, who got me started on sports in the first place.

A long list of writing buddies who heard about this story. You know who you are because now you're hearing about new stories. A special thanks to Pat Van Wie, Ann Majors and Debbie Pfeiffer, who gave me a stern talking to in a bar in New Orleans.

Fran Baker, who turned belief into reality.

Thank you all. Let The Games begin.

✧　✧　✧　✧

OPENING CEREMONIES

*"**MESDAMES ET MONSIEURS,** l'equippe Olympic des Etats Unis!"*

"Ladies and gentlemen, the United States Olympic team!"

Red, white and blue, they marched through an archway that vibrated with their eagerness, then burst into the open floor of the oval stadium. A roar rose, the sheer volume of it enough to set a sea of hand-held flags fluttering. All for them.

In return, they spilled into the frosting night the essence of themselves. Youth, exuberance, skill, endurance, dedication, determination, hope, anxiety, excitement. Stirring and stirred.

Energy crackled through each movement as voices admonished them to "Keep those lines straight!" with little effect. Lines? Lines sat as static, dull things. This burned with motion and emotion.

A culmination of years distilled into the first of a handful of moments. Moments that would flash past at speed beyond sound, yet would cover a world, and last a lifetime.

Emotions.

Rikki Lodge figured some scientific machine ought to exist to chart the waves of emotion swirling around her. Maybe the gadget that measures electrical flow. Lord knows, she felt the current. The Olympics! At last. If she wasn't the grand old lady of her contingent, she might give into the urge to do a cartwheel just for the joy of it. Come to think of it, that might be the only way the TV cameras would zero in on a biathlete. Even at the Olympics.

The Olympics.

A shiver skipped up her backbone, and she grinned at herself.

You'd think someone who'd competed as long as she had and at as many dots on the world map wouldn't react to one more. But how could anyone ignore all the reminders that this was different, this was special. If the hometown sendoff and the team outfits hadn't reminded her, there'd still be these other athletes from all the other sports and countries. She wasn't even rooming with biathletes, so how could she possibly pretend this was just another meet?

The American team curved around the track's first turn. Behind her, and to the left she caught sight of the men's hockey team. A few faces she'd recognized from newspaper and television coverage when she saw them two days ago while they all got accredited and outfitted. The dark, intense face that stayed well behind the youthful group of players mugging for a TV camera, belonged to Lanny Kaminski.

They'd never met, yet from what she'd read, Rikki Lodge felt an affinity with him. Like her, he was the oldster on a team of youngsters. A man who'd clung to his dream long after most his age – *their* age – embraced more ordinary lives. And now here they were with one, final, shot. *Good luck, Lanny Kaminski*, she thought. *We're both going to need it* . . .

Luck.

It came to those who touched the Olympic flag. Even non-believers didn't scoff at the superstition. As the rippling field of white with rings of yellow, blue, green, red and black passed just above the athletes' section, they stood. Stretching arms, straining fingers, climbing on seats, for a touch before the flag rose out of reach.

Kyle Armstrong's arm dropped to her side; her fingertips' contact with the silky material had been so brief she doubted it had happened.

She had always counted on luck as her companion. Now, she felt deserted. Not alone, no never alone. Not as long as other members of the ski team surrounded her. She didn't even have to think about where she was going, she could just go follow the force of their flow. Kyle had skied with these people, traveled with them, eaten with them, lived with them. Even when she wanted to she couldn't be alone. Never alone with Rob Zemlak watching her.

She looked up. And slammed directly into Rob's stare. His mouth smiled at the exuberance around him, but his eyes scowled. At her. *He knows. Oh, God, he knows!* She sat abruptly, but controlled the fear with will-power honed through years of hurtling down mountains. He couldn't know. No one here did except her. And he didn't watch her any differently than he watched the rest of the skiers he coached.

Keep it in perspective, Kyle. If she could get through the next sixteen days. . . .

Sixteen days.

The flame, brought from Greece by hand in honored stages, would burn over the stadium for sixteen days, as it had over another stadium so long ago.

From her spot in the stands, Tess Rutledge watched this Olympic flame flare to life. Memories of another one flowed into the present seamlessly, dangerously.

Remember your reason for being here. No longer Tess Rutledge The Skater, she had come here to coach Amy through her first Olympics and to help the team. She searched the section where the American athletes sat. She recognized the distinctive auburn hair of Rikki Lodge and a momentary shifting of the crowd showed her Kyle Armstrong's straight back. Tess sat taller, looking over heads, and there sat Amy Yost – as bright and vivid and alive as the red, white and blue she wore. She was the reason Tess once more sat in a stadium watching the Opening Ceremonies, listening to the pomp, and forming a minute part of the pageantry. The reason she had come back to all the reminders. Had come back, after years of meticulous avoidance, not to a place, but to a moment in her life.

That's what she had to guard against. She'd known he'd be here. If they should meet – and they would – she had to have a firm control on all this. To keep the years and the memories clearly separated. Because if she saw him –

Fate could be as cruel as people. She learned that anew in the instant she caught sight of the man staring at her. A man from another world, another time, sitting close enough now that she could see the winter night's breeze ruffling his blond hair, his too-long-remembered blue eyes piercing into her. Andrei Chersakov.

Let the Games begin.

THE DAY BEFORE – FRIDAY

"ISN'T THIS GREAT? When they said we were in a pod I thought gross, but this is just like an apartment."

At the sound of the youthful voice, Rikki Lodge straightened from folding newly washed clothes into the dresser in her room. Across the hall, the voice was accompanied by thumps of luggage hitting the bed and floor. That had to be Amy Yost.

Three nights ago Rikki had found a namecard "Rochelle Lodge – Biathlon" tacked to a room door and moved in. Alone in the apartment, she'd wandered from door to door and checked namecards.

A large room with a double bed, a desk and an arm chair had a single name on its card, but when Rikki read "Tess Rutledge – Ladies Figure Skating/Asst. Team Leader" the special accommodations didn't surprise her. Tess Rutledge had been a familiar name for close to two decades, first as the darling of figure skating, then as a pro and most recently as an emerging coach.

What was surprising was that she was staying in official housing at all. Rikki would have figured Tess Rutledge for luxury hotels.

The other large room had two beds and two names: "Kyle Armstrong – Women's Alpine Skiing/Nan Monahan – Women's Alpine Skiing." More familiar names, at least to a winter sports fan – that duo had ranked as among America's best on the international ski circuit for several years now.

Across the hall the final card read "Amy Yost – Ladies Figure Skating."

Rikki had heard that name, too, but only in the past month as U.S.

figure skating's surprising third Olympic qualifier in ladies singles. The media had loved the story of the late-comer to skating bursting onto the scene while remaining what so many referred to as fresh. She supposed that might explain Tess Rutledge's presence in these pedestrian surroundings, since Amy Yost was her protégé, and this was her first Olympics. Give the kid another four years and she'd probably be like most of the top figure skaters, who jetted in before competing, stayed in luxury accommodations, and departed immediately afterward. Their Olympic experience was almost entirely what happened in front of the cameras.

Amy had a mirror image of Rikki's train-compartment room. Rikki didn't mind the size. For the luxury of a private bath she would sleep in a closet. Come to think of it, she'd slept in spaces the size of the closet *without* a private bath.

After reading all the cards, Rikki had whistled to herself and wondered how she'd gotten into such exalted company. Women's biathlon had only reached the Olympics in 1992 at Albertville; the United States didn't rank among the top teams and Rikki Lodge couldn't even claim to be the top U.S. competitor. Just the one with the most longevity.

Now, after two days of wondering, she was about to meet the people behind the names on those cards.

As Rikki reached the hall, Amy Yost disappeared through another door. She reappeared almost immediately.

"That's a double room." Amy tossed the news over her shoulder without looking back as she plunged deeper into the apartment. At first she seemed a blur of long blonde hair and even longer limbs, but Rikki saw the teenager couldn't be more than five-three, her slenderness creating the illusion of height. "Oh, and Tess, there's a living room with a big window and a fireplace!"

Rikki looked back toward the hall door, and saw Tess Rutledge emerging from the room marked with her name.

"Amy – Oh. Hello. You must be Rochelle Lodge. I'm Tess Rutledge."

Even caught in surprise Tess Rutledge's voice flowed as smooth and graceful as the woman did on ice. A clip held dark hair drawn back at her nape, the style's severity a counterpoint to the soft lines of a face that hadn't seemed to age in the fourteen years since it had captured the world as Olympic champion.

"Rikki. Everybody calls me Rikki. It's an honor to meet you."

"Tess! There's – Oh, hi! I'm Amy. You're one of our pod room-mates? Pod! Can you believe they call it a pod? Pod roommate sounds like something from a sci-fi flick, doesn't it? Which one are you? What event are you in? Have you been to the Olympics before?"

"Amy –"

"Rikki Lodge. Biathlon. First Olympics."

"Biathlon? That's cross-country skiing and, uh. . . ."

"Target shooting." Rikki grinned. "You're ahead of most people. Just the other day someone said, 'Oh, that must be hard with swim-ming and running.' "

Having won a laugh from Amy and smile from Tess Rutledge, Rikki went on. "What I don't understand is how we got put together. I thought they assigned housing by sport. And in dorms. Not apart-ments like this."

"They usually do, but –"

The entry door swung open with enough force to hit the wall and bounce back on its way to reclosing.

"Damn!" A U.S. team suitcase was propelled across the threshold to prop the door open. "Where are the bellhops?"

"It's the Olympics, Nan, not the Ritz."

Rikki identified the second voice as well-bred Eastern boarding school, no doubt well-accustomed to bellhops and other considera-tions. From what she knew of her two remaining roommates that had to be Kyle Armstrong, of the Delaware Armstrongs, discreetly moneyed and influential for generations. A most unlikely gene pool to produce a world-class skier.

"Here, let me." Amy flew past Rikki and Tess, tugging the suitcase.

"Thanks! Here."

Amy took a second bag from the curly-haired woman who'd la-mented the lack of bellhops and passed it to Tess. Rikki received another and in seconds suitcases, overnighters, oddly shaped totes, bulging shopping bags, a wrapped tray of cheeses and fruit and five women clogged the narrow hallway.

"I guess you're right, Kyle, I am a pack rat," said the curly-haired woman, not much taller than Amy, but considerably more compact. She had the high-contrast coloring of Irish ancestry – black hair, fair skin, blue eyes, bright cheeks. She reached across to shake hands. "Hi, I'm Nan Monahan."

Rikki grinned back, then turned to meet the last of her roommates. Kyle Armstrong brought together subtle variations on a theme, light brown hair tinged with red, honey skin, pale brown eyes flickering to hazel.

Names and introductions came in a flurry. All the while, Rikki watched the faces. Amy was thrilled. Tess was classy. Nan was a dynamo. Kyle was . . . what? Maybe an enigma. The same as the rest, she yet seemed separate, the smile never reaching her eyes.

"I've been *dying* to get here," pronounced Amy with full dramatic emphasis. "I can't *wait* to meet everybody. C'mon, the living room's great and –"

"Slow down, Amy."

"But, Tess –"

"We've all just arrived – all except Rikki and it looks as if she's in the middle of something, too. Give us time to get organized, then we'll get to know each other."

"THEY SAID WE'RE an experiment within an experiment," Tess told the rest of them after they'd settled in with mineral water and Nan's cheese and fruit basket.

"They're housing some athletes in these 'pods' that will become apartments after the Games. With us, the idea is to see how it works mixing people from several sports in one pod instead of dividing up by team. Even though that will mean longer trips for practices and events for everyone except Amy."

She looked at the people who would share these rooms for the next sixteen days. Not only had the organizers mixed sports, they'd mixed ages, looks, backgrounds, circumstances and, unless she missed her guess, personalities.

Lord, please, no problems. She'd been promised her title of assistant team leader was strictly nominal.

For no reason she could name, Tess's gaze went to Kyle Armstrong, silently looking out the window, her face expressionless. Despite experts' cautions that Kyle needed more experience, great things were expected of her at these Olympics. Kyle looked almost too delicate to carry that expectation much less the physical demands of her sport, tall but quite slender and with less color in her face than Tess would have expected from someone outdoors so much.

"In other words, they ran out of room to keep the various teams together and we're the leftovers, so they threw us together." Rikki Lodge's dry voice held amusement as well as a clear-eyed realism.

Tess liked that. Rikki Lodge impressed her; she felt almost a kinship with the biathlete. Maybe because the information sheets listed Rikki as the one closest to Tess's age, thirty-one to her thirty-six. "Exactly."

"Then I'm glad to be a leftover, because this is great," said Amy. "The whole thing's been like a miracle."

"That's what the papers called it, too," said Rikki, interest glinting in her blue-green eyes. Tess had always heard a temper went with red hair, but she suspected curiosity went with Rikki Lodge's auburn. "One writer called you a miracle of enthusiasm on the ice."

Amy giggled – thank God, she still giggled at compliments. Her impish grin appeared. It was one of the things Tess most loved about Amy – that she was satisfied to remain a girl at fifteen, and only rarely lapse into sophisticated ennui. Having spent most of her youth playing rowdy team sports with her brothers definitely helped. "That's not what Tess called it when she was making the arrangements for all this after Nationals."

Tess shook her head. "You can laugh. But it was a month of unadulterated craziness. Then, on top of the arrangements to come here and the interview requests for Amy, plus keeping a practice schedule, they pressed me into service to help the team leader."

She hadn't really minded. There'd been less time to think that way. Less time to remember.

"The first person who'd agreed to help had a car accident last week and broke *both* legs," said Amy, brutally cheerful. "So they needed somebody fast, somebody already coming. Everybody knows Tess won't play favorites even though she's my coach. And everybody likes her."

"I've always said it was dangerous to be likable." Rikki shook her head. "See what happens? They ask you to be a team leader and when you're too likable to say no, they put you in a pod with a bunch of strangers. Why are they calling these things pods instead of apartments, anyway?"

"These aren't the final apartment layouts. After the Games they'll reconfigure them," Tess said.

"Ah, I'd wondered about four bathrooms per apartment."

"Well, at least they picked a fun group for our 'pod,' right?" Nan Monahan lifted a chunk of cheese in salute.

"Absolutely." Amy's response reminded Tess how certain a teenager's certainty could be. And how wrong.

"I intend to have all the fun I can," Amy added. "I don't get to skate until the Olympics are practically over – and there's no way I'm going to spend all that time sitting around worrying when there's all this fun stuff going on."

"My sentiments exactly," Nan said. "I've got to wait ten days to ski the GS – giant slalom," she interpreted for the non-skiers. "Then three more days before the slalom. Kyle gets to start Tuesday, with the combined – that's half downhill, half slalom. So, Tuesday she'll do downhill for the combined, finish up with the slalom run Wednesday, and she'll already have an event under her belt. Probably a medal, too."

Tess watched for Kyle's reaction, but her gaze out the window didn't waver.

"That's another reason I intend to have all the fun I can this time." Amy's enthusiasm nearly covered Kyle's lack of response. "If I get to the Olympics again, I'll want a medal. Everybody'll expect a lot. So this time is to have fun. And if there's a next time, that's to be serious."

Nan shook her head slowly, but her lips curled up. "This kid is frightening. Truly frightening."

"Sounds wise to me," said Rikki.

"That's what I mean."

Kyle had stared out the window so long her voice startled Tess a little. "She must have had a good teacher," she said to Tess.

Memories of her own painful lessons, learned when she was not all that much older than Amy, telescoped into a blink, and for a moment, Tess couldn't answer.

Nan covered the silence, by design or accident, Tess didn't know. "Yeah, boy, I wish I'd had somebody who'd told me those kinds of things. I sure could have used that kind of wisdom when I was fifteen."

"You could use that kind of wisdom now," said Kyle, affection, truth and teasing braided in her voice.

And then she smiled, and Tess understood why the media had dubbed Kyle Armstrong the sweetheart of skiing.

Before that smile faded, Rikki raised her glass, saying, "Here's to wisdom for all of us, then. That would be my idea of a most successful Olympics."

Tess looked at the faces of the others, the three women she'd just met and the girl she knew so well. Would these Olympics bring them success of that kind or any kind? Would they bring them happiness? Or would they return some day to the Olympics, as she was returning, trying not to be defeated by the memories?

"Right," piped up Amy. "Here's to us. The five peas in the pod."

DAY 1 – SATURDAY

AN HOUR AFTER the Opening Ceremonies ended, the main Olympic Village recreation center was a babble of languages and laughter. Colors splashed it like confetti, adrenaline frothed the air.

Tables and chairs filled the center, retrofitted into an industrial area made over for the Olympics. Through an arch to the left, they could see an open area with couples dancing to international rock and pop songs. Opposite their spot at the entrance another arch opened to a food court. And to the right flashes of light and occasional whoops of triumph promised a video arcade.

Yet, amid all that confusion, Rikki became aware of the prickling sensation of being watched, once removed. One pair of eyes had zeroed in on Tess Rutledge, who sat next to her.

Rikki picked out the watcher easily – blonde, blue-eyed, probably in his late-30s. By age, he was probably a coach or an official, but as well-built as the athletes. She'd seen him before. But no name came to mind.

She scanned his companions and recognized two as Russians, including the male half of the pairs figure skating team she'd heard called a medal favorite. Nobody else at that table showed interest in the newcomers, but this man's eyes hadn't left Tess. Sure, Tess was recognizable, but this seemed extreme.

Curious, Rikki turned to question Tess. And shut off the words immediately.

Tess's smooth skin had turned a shade paler. Her wide brown eyes tightened in strain. Her graceful body was stiff. She stared sightlessly in the opposite direction from where the man sat.

"Oh, look, there's Vladimir Metroveli. Gorgeous," Amy announced, pointing to the skater Rikki had already recognized, the one sitting next to the man Tess so carefully ignored. Tess was so taut, Rikki thought the older woman might hum any second.

Nan bustled in behind them. "Oh, good, I caught you before you got lost in the crowd."

"Where's Kyle?" Amy asked.

"She decided not to come. She wanted to rest. She's been feeling a little punk the past week or so."

"Maybe I should go check on her –"

"No need, Tess, she said she wants to be alone. She's just fighting a bug of some sort." Nan's tone dismissed anything more serious, but Rikki thought she caught uncertainty in the skier's eyes.

Was she getting imaginative in her old age, or were there really all these undercurrents in this small group?

"Somebody's waving to you, Rikki."

Rikki looked in the direction Amy indicated and saw several members of the biathlon team, who had come into the main Village for the Opening Ceremonies. With the biathlon venue among the farthest away, the rest of the team was headquartered in a smaller Olympic Village near the course. She waved back, but didn't respond immediately to their gesture to join them.

"They want you to go over there," Amy pointed out.

"Yes," she said slowly. "But I thought I might stick with you guys for a while, if you don't mind."

Odd to feel protective of Tess, a woman who'd been in the spotlight more than half her life, yet Rikki did.

"Please do." Under Tess's politeness, Rikki thought she heard real relief.

"Sure, stick around, we'll show you a good time," added Nan. At twenty-five Nan Monahan had a reputation for having a good time. Also a reputation for letting that interfere with her skiing.

"Good. Let's try that direction." Rikki gave a final wave to her teammates, then started Amy and Nan weaving between tables, in the opposite direction from the unknown watcher. At least unknown to her. She'd bet the ranch – if she'd had one – that he was known to Tess Rutledge, and that it wasn't her imagination that he was staring, that Tess knew it and fully intended to ignore it.

"Baby Amy! Amy Yost!"

Before they could do more than turn in the direction of the bass shout, a burly figure engulfed Amy in a bear hug that nearly eclipsed her slight figure.

"Mikey! Mikey Sweet! How are you?"

"Mikey Sweet?" Nan's astonished murmur echoed Rikki's reaction to the incongruity of that name for a young man with the face and build of a barroom bouncer. And perhaps a not entirely successful one, since his nose looked as if it had done some bouncing.

She met Nan's eyes, looked away to try to avoid laughing, connected with Tess's equally amused look and lost the battle.

Amy excitedly performed the introductions, filling them in that she'd known Mikey Sweet since she really *was* a baby, and he and her older brother had attended hockey camps together. But the hockey player saw their reaction.

"With a name like Mikey Sweet, I started playing hockey in self-defense," he said with a shrug and half smile. "I didn't hear you'd made the Olympic team until I called home last night, Amy. We've been training and playing exhibitions for weeks and I kinda forget there's another world outside. C'mon, sit down, meet the guys," he invited them all, pulling out two empty chairs from a rectangular table, "while I catch up with the half-pint here."

Leaving Amy and Tess to take those seats, Rikki and Nan took the only other empty chairs, which were at the far end of the table and bracketed a pair of men bent over a paper napkin where one diagrammed something. Rikki recognized the diagrammer as Lanny Kaminski.

He barely looked up when she sat next to him. His younger companion showed considerably more interest in Nan's arrival.

If Rikki's ego had been the type to feel that as a slight, it would have quickly been salved by the reaction of the player to her right.

Flirting for all he was worth, he introduced himself as Dan Christopher and made his admiration obvious. She supposed that could be considered something of a coup since he was attractive and a good eight to ten years younger than her. But she found his attention more sweet than exciting.

I must be getting old.

With a mental sigh, she answered his questions – what's your name, where are you from, what's your event – though a slice of her attention lingered on the oblivious man to her left.

Kaminski kept his head bent, the thick, slightly wavy hair masking his expression. He spoke only to the player next to him, too low amid the din for Rikki to hear anything more than a murmur.

"You want something to drink?" asked Dan, her right-side companion.

"Thanks. A mineral water would be great."

He disappeared on his mission, and with the blank wall of Lanny Kaminski's indifference on her other side she was left to look around.

At the other end of the table, Amy's hands moved in animated accompaniment to her conversation, while Mikey Sweet grinned indulgently. Tess's lips also curved, but without any meaning behind the smile.

Rikki slued around in her chair and leaned to the side. Just as she thought, the blond, blue-eyed man still focused on Tess. His face expressionless, almost wooden. The very lack of emotion seemed to indicate an intensity that prickled Rikki's backbone.

Now what was that all about?

Straightening, she glanced again at Tess. One look, and she concluded that she wouldn't be getting the answer to this mystery from that source any time soon, so there was no sense fretting about it.

Her gaze skimmed the faces of the other hockey players at the table. How young so many of them seemed.

If that thought brought a twinge, it disappeared as she focused on the vignette down the table. Nan had the full attention of the player to her left. She also had a good portion of the attention of the player to her right, though Lanny Kaminski doggedly hung on to the rest as he continued diagramming.

His blunt-tipped fingers guided a pen tip into emphatic lines and arrows. A broad palm dwarfed the shaft of the pen. Without looking away from the other player, Lanny reached his right hand to grab a napkin off the top of the stack next to his drink. Dark hair sprinkled the back of his hand, then disappeared under the cuff of his Team USA shirt. Veins and knuckles strained against the tough skin. Joints on his middle and little fingers were misshapen, preventing the little finger from straightening completely. The white line of a scar sliced across two knuckles then slipped out of view around the softer web of skin between the thumb and index finger.

Looking away from that evidence of hard use, Rikki saw that the player being tutored had taken advantage of Kaminski's second of interrupted concentration to turn to Nan.

Kaminski reared back slightly, as if taken by surprise, then spoke a single, stern word.

"Tonetti."

The player named Tonetti frowned, but turned back to Kaminski.

"Here you go."

Dan placed a glass in front of her and one in front of his spot. Rather than pulling his chair out, he swung one leg over the back and slid down into the seat. He'd almost made it when his solid thigh connected with the underside of the table. The resulting earthquake set off tidal waves in the two full glasses, slopping over the sides.

Instinctively, Rikki snatched from the napkin stack and started mopping.

"What the fuck –!" Lanny Kaminski's outrage from her left drowned out Dan's mingled curses and apologies from her right.

She grabbed more napkins, containing the flood within a circle of soggy paper.

"Hey, I need those napkins." Kaminski's voice, with a distinctive thread of Boston, came as stern as when he'd called Tonetti to order. Maybe he didn't know any other tone.

She slanted a grin at him, just to annoy him. She tucked away the observation that his eyes were a soft, deep brown.

"My need was greater. And more immediate." She made a third raid on his dwindling cache despite the frown that drew his dark brows into a straight, uninterrupted line. Out of the corner of her eye, she saw Tonetti had wasted no time in turning to Nan. Rikki's grin widened. She drew the circle of wet napkins smaller. "You can get more later."

His frown tightened, but before Kaminski said anything, Dan scraped back his chair. "I'll get more for you, Kam. It was my fault. I'll be right back."

With Kaminski busy frowning at Rikki, Tonetti and Nan stood up and started away. Happy to be an accomplice, Rikki took the last of the dry napkins and put them to use.

"Want my shirt, too?" Kaminski muttered darkly, moving the already diagrammed napkins out of her reach.

"You think I need it?"

He ignored that, turning his shoulder on her in preparation for reeling Tonetti back in.

But all that was left of Tonetti was an empty chair and a glimpse of his retreating back as he and Nan headed for the dance floor.

Rikki laughed, and Kaminski spun back to face her. His gaze – with the softness gone – slammed into hers. Her laughter hitched, then mellowed to a chuckle.

"Looks like your captive audience went over the wall."

"Think that's funny?" The Boston in his voice grew wider. "So will the Czechs when we play them tomorrow. Yeah, they'll get a real kick out of it when they go against Tonetti, because he's nowhere near up to speed on this. They'll think it's a damned good joke all right."

"Oh, come on. It's not as if Tonetti catching a dance instead of looking at one more napkin diagram is going to decide the fate of the world."

"How about the fate of a team."

His dourness rubbed her as raw as criticism. "These are supposed to be games, you know. Olympic *Games*. Or aren't you –"

"Oh, I see you've met Kam."

Dan's return snapped her strangely testy mood. "Not officially," she said sweetly, because that seemed most likely to irk Kaminski. She held out her hand. "Hi. I'm Rikki Lodge. Biathlon."

He looked down at her hand, then into her eyes. "Lanny Kaminski."

He met her hand, but didn't shake it. Just engulfed it with his big, rough one. Letting her own unpampered, no nonsense hand absorb the sensation of heat and the friction of calluses and scar ridges.

She swallowed, trying to clear the way for words that would be light, funny. Nothing came. She was grateful he didn't look up from where his hand enclosed hers.

"Well now that the introduction's official, you want to dance with me, Rikki?" asked the voice behind her. She turned to the younger athlete.

"Sounds great." Gratitude to Dan for the unintentional excuse infused extra warmth in her voice.

Lanny Kaminski released her hand and turned back to the fresh pile of napkins Dan had provided, apparently content to dismiss her with a mumbled "See you."

But as she danced with Dan, then with Mikey Sweet, Tonetti and other members of the team, she did notice Kaminski watching her once.

She hadn't counted how many times she'd glanced at him.

DAY 2 – SUNDAY

EVEN BEFORE THE descent, the mountain brought Kyle Armstrong peace.

Enclosing herself in the familiar armor against the cold. Contemplating strategy, reviewing what had already been learned that day, anticipating the course's next lesson. Being conveyed sedately up the incline she soon would make her private domain for one final time today. Beneath the babble of voices, listening to the silence of stretching nerves, even now, when it was only a training run.

It was her haven, always.

Even tomorrow when she would forfeit the relative privacy of this workout with her team. When the official training run for Tuesday's downhill half of the combined would bring a U.N. of television cameras to cause confusion as they jockeyed for set-up shots they would use to explain Alpine skiing to viewers in Tampa and Taiwan, Boston and Brazil, Albuquerque and Australia.

Kyle Armstrong loved it all.

Each mountain was different, individual. Yet this was the same. She loved her moment in the start shack, totally alone, inside herself, with only herself and the mountain. She loved the jangle of the bell that released her with a heart-jolting burst of adrenaline. She loved the twist and flow of the movement. She loved the calm reason of the notations and reminders her mind issued. She loved the undertow of fear.

And it was almost as if it all loved her back.

"Okay, Kyle. Course is clear."

Now. Her moment. The second of release. The pushoff. The first, clean swoop down the mountain like a bird diving after prey.

Speed. She felt it. The wind her own body stirred, the spinning away of the snow she slid over.

Fear. She didn't mind this kind of fear. It was the other fear, slow and gnawing that rattled her. What am I going to do?

Ski. That's what she was going to do. Just ski. And not think.

Last year, in a World Cup, she'd skied well on this mountain, on courses set by the same designers, but there would be changes since then. Minor, true. But a hair's-breadth of balance split disaster from victory. So the coaches had set up this training run as close as possible to what they expected the race courses to be, so every nuance could be traced, noted, filed as she sped through the curves, scanning the turns so they would be recorded in her muscles' memories.

And then it was over. In a blink. Less.

Frowning, she started tugging her goggles off even as she curved to a stop.

No huge electronic scoreboard flashed her time at her as it would on the race course, but she didn't need one to tell her. The run had gone by too fast. Way, way too fast. Never a good sign. In some perverse rule of skiing, when she was really on, really concentrating, really flying, every ridge of snow, every inch of mountainside seemed to linger in crystal clear slow motion.

She flicked loose her skis, automatically propping them against her shoulder with the brand name forward, even with no TV cameras to focus on her. Turning, she came face to face with Rob Zemlak, holding the clipboard he never seemed to be without despite its almost nostalgic old-fashionedness.

"What was that?" His dark brows clashed over the bridge of his straight nose in a frown that turned his gray eyes steely.

She turned so she didn't look directly at him. "Training run. Didn't you read the day's schedule you're always yapping at us about?"

He glared, but said nothing about her tone. Still, he got his digs in.

"Pretty shitty training run."

"Thanks for the support, Coach."

His jaw tightened. That seemed to be the only way his jaw operated. Always tighter. Never looser. As tight as she'd seen his jaw get over the past fifteen months, he'd never let loose.

"Your start was barely acceptable, but you could have made it up if you'd had your head on. Instead, it looked like you took a side trip to another planet. I thought you were heading off the side of the mountain. And the end —"

"A training run. I simply used it as a training run. Checking the course, working on sections, honing technique. You know, all those things we're supposed to do on training runs."

He ignored that too – ignoring her was one of Rob Zemlak's best honed techniques – and finished his sentence. "The end looked mechanical. Like some expensive windup doll."

That jerked her back to face him.

Standing toe to toe, she stared at him, too angry to fully realize it was probably the first time in more than a year they'd made direct eye contact. And too angry to wonder about the change in his gray eyes. But he went on, as always.

"That's not going to get you a medal. Nowhere near. And combined's your best shot, much better than GS or slalom. You used to want a medal more than anything, Armstrong. Don't you want it anymore? Have you gotten bored with all this? Tired of working so hard for a bit of precious medal you could have bought with a week's allowance when you were eight years old? Want to leave all this behind and run away to Daddy's Caribbean hideaway and —"

She shoved him in the chest with enough force to make him take a step back and started past him.

"Kyle! Rob! Just who we were looking for." Nan hurried up to them with a man in tow. Her mouth smiled, but her brows knit in warning. "This is Benton Harbor of the Washington Observer. You know, a reporter."

The color-coded tags hanging around the zipped up collar of the man's painfully new parka gave that away.

"How do you do, Mr. Harbor." Automatically Kyle extended her hand and smiled, pushing down the sudden clutch deep in her belly.

"Actually, it's Harrison. No relation to the town in Michigan." He smiled as they shook gloved hands. He wasn't one of the regulars they encountered on the ski circuit.

"Oh, I'm sorry. Harrison. I'm really sorry. I'm always getting names mixed up."

Kyle looked at Nan, who rarely confused names or faces. But even as she continued the introductions, Nan's attention focused somewhere over Harrison's shoulder.

Kyle shifted to see what Nan was looking at. Another man stood about six feet away, his shoulder to them but the wind flipping around tags to match Harrison's. Oil, natural or artificial, darkened his hair. He didn't look at them and his posture was of complete nonchalance. He was trying his damnedest to eavesdrop.

How long had he been there? Had he heard her dispute with Rob?

"And this is Rob Zemlak, our coach. He's the one you should ask those questions about today's training runs."

"Of course. I just wanted to ask Kyle —"

"Nan's right, you really should ask me," interrupted Rob, firm but with the anger gone. *That* he saved for her. He took the reporter's arm and turned him toward one of the buildings at the base of the run. "I think I saw Stephen Carlisle, our head coach, just go inside over there, so we can get warm and you can hit both of us at the same time."

Benton Harrison didn't protest, but he did glance at Kyle again as he let Rob lead him away.

The other man darted a look toward Kyle and Nan. They looked back. He displayed a momentary intense interest in the mountain, then sauntered off behind Rob and Benton Harrison.

Nan watched them go and gnawed on her lower lip. "That's not the last of him. Harrison's going to be back."

"So?" Abruptly, Kyle felt exhausted. And the grip on her lower belly tightened.

"So? So, he got a good look at you and Rob going at it and he'd have to be blind and stupid not to see you two were pissed at each other, and I don't think he's either. And that other guy — who knows what shit he heard. He was busy sidling closer to you two when we came up."

Kyle started to shrug, then stopped when it threatened to turn tightness into outright pain.

"Do you want to be asked a lot of questions about why you and Rob Zemlak don't get along?" Nan demanded. "What is with you two anyway? You've never been buddy-buddy, but it looked as if you'd like to put poles through each other's hearts."

"I don't know what you're –"

"Don't lie to me, Kyle." Nan's sharpness brought Kyle's head up in surprise. It was so unlike Nan. By her next words it had disappeared. "You don't want to tell me what's going on with you and Rob, fine, don't tell me shit. That's your business. But don't lie to me, Kyle. Not if you want me to stay your friend."

Kyle looked away, to the top of the mountain, where she'd left her peace.

Nan sighed, but said with her usual cheer. "C'mon. Let's head back for hot showers, massages and some food. And forget about that pile of rock and ice."

✧　✧　✧　✧

"**DON'T WORRY ABOUT** the triple lutz, Tess. I'm gonna land it from now on. I can feel it." Amy grinned at her with utter confidence. "Just like at Nationals. Those falls in practice were a fluke. I'm gonna nail it. I can feel it."

"I know you will." Tess smiled, wishing she could bottle that confidence and feed it back to Amy whenever the girl needed it down the road.

Although this wasn't a bad time for a dose of confidence.

They stood in the "Kiss and Cry Area," to one side of the entrance to the ice where, in a few days, Amy would wait for the scores from her first Olympic competition. Although today's skate officially qualified as practice, it was different from sessions at the practice rink. Amy wore full competition warpaint – costume, matching tights, hair styled, makeup – because the scores that flashed on the electronic

She met his eyes, trying to bleed everything out of her own – the memories, the pain, the warmth where his hands touched her.

"There is nothing to say," she repeated.

"There is much to say. But you will not listen. Not now. But I will be there when you will listen. I will be there, Tessa."

He released her and she moved away, pulling a smile from somewhere for Amy as she came off the ice, bubbling and panting.

"Did you see that? Did you see that?"

"I saw. You were great."

As she hugged Amy, she saw Andrei standing where she'd left him, watching her once more.

"TESS! THANK GOD!" Ron Sheffield, the team leader, caught her as she followed Amy to the women's locker room.

Used to his dramatics, and perhaps grateful for the distraction from her own thoughts, Tess took things in order. "Go on ahead, Amy. Get your shower. I'll be in soon. Hello, Ron. How are you today?"

"Now that I've seen you, I might survive. Finding you is an absolute godsend. You've got to take over for me in the interview room."

"But, Ron –"

"It's not arduous duty, I swear. One pair's done. there's just two more to go. We wouldn't need anybody, but this is the big interview session for the pairs before they start competition tomorrow, and we don't want anyone upset. It used to just be the American media that wanted this and we could get the kids in and out. But now all the reporters want access and it's getting bigger and bigger, so we have to ride herd on them. It's just to have someone there, making sure there's water in the glasses, helping out our kids if they get asked a real doozy of a question. And, of course, whisking them away if they start chanting Satanic rites and making hex signs."

"But Ron –"

"I know, I know. I promised you I'd handle everything. But honest, Tess, I need your help. Unless. . ." His crafty smile immediately roused Tess's instinct for self-preservation. "Unless you want to handle this other little matter."

"What other little matter?"

"A small scheduling snafu. Just a tiny —"

"Oh, no. No way, Ron. I don't do scheduling snafus. I didn't think I did interview rooms, either, but I definitely don't do scheduling snafus."

"Wise choice," he said with a sigh. "I'm trying to convince the organizing committee official that putting up a notice at noon that the ice dancers' practice time has been moved to two this afternoon instead of nine o'clock tomorrow morning is not fair, conducive to good feelings or even practical since the whole crew disappeared into town for a free afternoon. At the same time I'm trying to stop the various coaches from having hysterics or starting an international incident by assaulting a member of the organizing committee. If I can just find the French and Japanese team leaders. . . They're in the same predicament, and if we present a united front. . ."

"All right, I'll take the interview room —"

"Bless you, Tess. Here —" He shoved a schedule sheet printed in four languages into her hand. "It should only be another hour or so. Thank you, thank you."

"You're welcome," she called out to his back in the crowded hall. "But I can't guarantee I'll recognize Satanic chants if I hear them."

She could tell who among the skaters, officials, coaches and technicians littering the hall understood English – they were the ones who turned around and stared at her. A couple laughed.

An hour and a half later, remembering Sheffield's "or so" tacked on to the promise of another hour, she could have used the laugh. Amy had come in, freshly showered and dressed, and departed to watch another practice session, and still the interviews droned on. Leaning against the back wall listening to the international media question a pairs team from France she wanted to tell them all to lighten up.

My Lord, this didn't concern nuclear war or an assault on the environment or human rights. Although maybe there should be an international commission to study cruelty to skaters. The first people investigated should be the reporters. Not the ones who asked questions that revealed they didn't know the difference between an axel and an edge – they were merely ignorant. It was the ones who asked skaters such as this stiff-jawed young man and his big-eyed partner what it felt like to have the world watching their every move and a nation counting on them to perform better than they ever had before for the greater glory of France – those were the dangerous ones.

A merciful fate saved the young skaters – time was up.

An organizing committee member and their coach shepherded the slightly dazed pair from behind the linen-draped table forested with microphones.

Uh-oh, were Americans next? Tess belatedly scanned the schedule sheet. No, the final American pair came second-to-the-last, damn Ron's hide. Still two to go. First –

"Ladies and gentlemen, Radja Rastnikova and Vladimir Metroveli of Russia, reigning world champions and bronze medalists in the last Olympics. *Mesdames and Messieurs. . .*"

As the introduction continued in the languages of the Olympics, Tess spotted Andrei.

He stood at the front, broad shoulders braced against the door frame to the hallway, unobtrusive but situated so he could survey the field of journalists, yet make eye contact with his skaters if they sought him out.

So different from that interview she'd seen him give eighteen years ago.

He'd sat next to his partner, Tatiana Serginova, flanked by their coach and three members of Soviet officialdom. She'd stood in the back, as she did now, listening to Andrei's voice, so devoid of life she'd hardly recognized it, and catching glimpses of his wooden face between the shoulders of journalists and hangers-on. She'd seen life in his eyes only once, for an instant, when he'd caught sight of her, and then it had been gone.

That night, when he'd escaped all his handlers and they'd slipped off alone together, he'd told her never to come to one of his interviews again. At first, she'd thought he didn't want her to see that side of him, the cold, public face she thought of as his Soviet identity. Later, she'd wondered if he'd already known he was going to choose that identity and betray her trust, her heart.

"Oooh, isn't he gorgeous?"

Tess started, disoriented for an instant before she realized Amy had returned and that she didn't refer to the Andrei Chersakov who existed only in Tess's memory, but to Vladimir Metroveli.

But Amy hadn't needed an answer. "Look at those eyes. And that smile." She paused to contemplate each attribute. "And that hair."

Vladimir pushed back a thick lock of hair from his forehead and Amy let out an appreciative breath. Tess thought he needed a good haircut. God, she *was* getting old.

"And of course he's a fantastic skater. Nobody does lifts like he does. Though his footwork could be smoother leading up to the side-by-side toe loops in their short program."

Maybe this infatuation didn't run as deep as she had feared if Amy could be dispassionate about his skating.

No sooner had that hopeful thought crossed Tess's mind than Amy gave an odd little giggle and added, "But he does look great in that costume."

"Amy –"

"Shhh!"

They'd been talking softly, but not softly enough for some of those trying to listen to the interview. Tess started steering a resistant Amy toward the rear door to the hallway. They really had to talk about this.

When Amy's resistance abruptly evaporated, Tess looked back and saw the interview had broken up. Vladimir said something to Andrei, who put his arm casually around Radja and walked between his two skaters, through the door and out of her sight as the next pair came in. He had not glanced once in her direction.

"C'mon, Tess."

Now Amy tugged her into the hallway. They arrived in time to see Andrei and his two skaters turn a corner and go out of sight.

"Amy —"

"What?"

But they couldn't talk about this here, with journalists exiting and entering the interview room, skaters and coaches crossing paths as one practice session ended and another began and officials going every which way.

"Uh, what are you going to do this afternoon?"

"How much longer do you have to stay here?"

"A couple more interviews. But you don't have to stay. We can go into town another day. You could go back to the apartment and rest if you'd like."

"No, that's okay. I'll wait." Amy sighed, but Tess didn't mind that sound of impatience. She was too grateful Amy wasn't lobbying to go into the unfamiliar city by herself. "But I'm gonna watch some more practice. That's not as boring as this. . . ."

Tess was unprepared for the elbow that dug into her side, and gave a soft "oof." "Amy, what —"

"Shh. Don't look, but that man right there, the one coming this way, that's Vladimir Metroveli's coach, isn't it? If I could meet *him* then maybe . . ."

Amy wouldn't make much of a spy. She never took her eyes off Andrei's approach as she whispered to Tess. But in this case she didn't need subterfuge. Vladimir Metroveli's coach stopped directly in front them. "Hello, Tess. This must be your pupil, the celebrated Amy Yost."

Amy turned rosy. More amazing, she seemed tongue-tied.

Tess gave in to the inevitable. "Yes. Andrei, this is Amy Yost of Dayton, Ohio. Amy, this is Andrei Chersakov of St. Petersburg, Russia."

"It's very nice to meet you, Mr. Chersakov."

"It is a pleasure to meet you, Amy Yost. Please, call me Andrei."

"I didn't know you knew Vla —" Amy turned even rosier as she bit back what she'd almost blurted to Tess. "I didn't know you knew each other."

Tess didn't look at Andrei. "We met when we were both competing." Less easily she added, "My first Olympics."

"And my last," Andrei murmured. Those soft words brought Tess's eyes to his face. But he looked at Amy. "Did you know that your coach and I once skated together?"

"You did? But she was always a singles skater."

"Not for that one night."

I want to skate with you. I want to hold you on the ice, and kiss you. And then, every time I skate, I will hold you again. In my heart.

But what if someone sees us. What if they tell —

It won't matter. I will have you in my heart.

Amy saved her from the memories.

"I didn't know that." Her eyes opened wide, the way they did when she wanted to get something. "I thought it was really different back then, when there used to be the Soviet Union and skaters weren't allowed to even talk to Americans. Not like now, when we can meet each other and get to know each other, even the really top skaters like you coach and newcomers like me."

Andrei looked at Amy, who looked back at him, transparent. Tess detected no visible sign of the amusement she was certain he felt.

"You are right, Amy. It is very different. Would you like me to introduce you to the really top skaters I coach?"

"Would you?"

"I would be honored. Perhaps tomorrow morning when there is the brief practice for the pairs before they have their first competition in the evening. I am sure Vladimir and Radja would be most interested to meet the lovely Amy Yost."

"Great! That's great! Thanks. Thanks a lot, Andrei. I'll see you in the morning." She edged away, as if afraid the promise might be retracted, or Tess might object. "I'll be back when that interview's done, Tess. 'Bye."

Tess frowned, watching her rapid retreat through the mostly emptied hallway, yet clinging to Amy as a distraction from the man who faced her. "Oh, great."

"You do not want her to meet Vladimir and Radja?"

"It's not Radja I'm worried about." Dryly, she added, "She likes the way Vladimir fills his costume."

Andrei made a noise, a sort of muffled bark, and she could see him struggling not to laugh out loud.

She remembered that laugh. A deep-throated sound that had once swamped her senses. The skin at the back of her neck prickled.

"Do not look so worried, Tess. It is a girl's crush."

"Sure, you can laugh." Pretending annoyance was better than that prickling awareness. She crossed her arms at her waist. "You didn't promise her parents you'd look out for her. She's fifteen years old."

"And Vladimir is twenty-four years old, accustomed to young girls adoring him, generally most kindly to them and about to marry a woman he loves very much–" He touched his fingertips to the back of her hand. Warmth. "–Radja, his partner."

Tess flinched.

Andrei jerked away, not just his hand but his whole body tensed at her instinctive reaction. His eyes seemed to go blank, his face immovable. As if a switch had been thrown and the human being inside had evaporated.

She remembered that face from eighteen years ago. The face he'd worn at that interview. The face he'd worn around anyone from his country. The face she'd come to think of as his public face; the gap between them in visible form. She'd forgotten how much she'd hated it.

It struck her now – she'd been able to forget that because she hadn't seen it these past few days. She'd been so ready to fight off the memories he stirred she hadn't noticed the changes in him. Not until she'd caused this retreat behind his old facade.

Her breath came out in a hiss of pain. Squeezing her eyes shut, she wished with all her might that it wasn't so, even as she accepted that she still couldn't bear to see Andrei Chersakov like this.

She opened her eyes and said in as normal a tone as she could manage, "A crush? A girl's crush, that's all you think it is?"

Life returned to his face, though not the laughter.

"For your Amy, now, yes. A girl's crush only."

She let herself be reassured, not acknowledging any distinctions he might be implying.

"Your English is very good."

"I have had a long time to practice it. And I have worked hard at it."

"And you've had a lot of opportunities to use it these past few years with your skaters doing so well."

He met her breezy tone with brief solemnity. "Yes."

"From eighth at the worlds just five years ago, to the Olympic bronze, and then last year world champions . . . that's quite a climb."

"Worlds, Olympics, other competitions – I looked for you always, Tess."

"Oh, I haven't had any international caliber skaters before Amy. Since I retired from the pro circuit, I've been very content to be a small-time coach. Amy's the one who's pulling me back into all this. And Amy's far ahead of where I thought she would be at this –"

"Not Amy, you. I looked to see you. Everywhere I went. Always."

"Don't –"

It hurt to breathe, each draw into her lungs a burn right down to her heart. How could he expect to open the door he'd slammed so resoundingly? Didn't he know how hard, how painfully she'd worked to build the brick wall that covered it on her side?

She looked around, through the half-opened door she saw the two skaters behind the table start to rise, and went light-headed with relief.

"I have to go. I have to be there when Americans are interviewed to – Well, just in case. I have to. Goodbye."

He allowed her to go.

It worried her to know that it was a matter of allowing.

"SOME LAZY SUNDAY brunch, huh?"

Rikki and the two other biathlon team members at their cafeteria table groaned at Sharon Wagner's comment.

They'd been out by seven to school the loops, a twice-a day exercise of covering the course to learn its idiosyncrasies so well that they

we're going over."

"Kyle, too? Where is she?"

"She's in the room, getting ready."

✧ ✧ ✧ ✧

KYLE ARMSTRONG HAD made the biggest mistake of her life four weeks ago tonight.

She'd made mistakes on the course; no skier hadn't made a mistake or two. You tried to keep those to a minimum, though, because the wrong one could kill you.

This mistake hadn't come on the course. And it couldn't break her neck or leg. Just her life.

She was pregnant.

She couldn't even claim she didn't know what had possessed her to sleep with Brad Lorrence, darling of the men's downhill. She'd always been fond of him. He was easy to be with, because he never demanded anything of her and accepted whatever surface she chose to present. And he made her feel desirable – something she'd sorely needed of late. He'd chased her, in his desultory way and with frequent distractions for other conquests, for years. Despite the media casting them as America's Olympic sweethearts, though, she'd had no inclination to let him catch her.

Not until that night four weeks ago at the party to celebrate being named to the U.S. Olympic team. She could still taste the blended exhilaration and despair.

She was headed to the Olympics. A dream realized.

Rob Zemlak was her direct coach. A nightmare to be lived through.

Of course Rob had been around before; he'd been an assistant ski coach for the U.S. women's team for nearly two years. But not in such close quarters. And not when she should have felt only the thrill, without this rock of hurt in her gut.

She'd needed warmth that night, and Brad had offered it. She hadn't made a conscious decision to let what happened happen. But she *had* let it happen.

And she could rail at the fates all she wanted that it was only one time, and she had insisted he use a condom so how could she possibly have gotten pregnant? It didn't change that she was.

And now she had the consequences to face.

The door banged open and Nan entered talking. "Hey, Kyle. C'mon. Let's go. The Austrian team issued invitations left and right, there won't be room left to breathe if we don't get there soon. Let's go."

"I think I'll stay here after all, Nan."

"Oh, no you don't. You said you'd go, and I'm holding you to it."

"I'm really not in the mood."

"You haven't been in the mood for weeks. I barely got you to go to the Opening Ceremonies and you missed out last night when we all went to the rec center. C'mon, this is the Olympics! You only get one go-around unless you're Alberto Tomba."

"No, really –"

"Are you sick?" The sharp look more than the question raised Kyle's defenses. "I heard you in the bathroom this morning."

"Oh, that." Kyle tried to make it sound like nothing. "You know I react that way sometimes to jet-lag. And nerves."

"Jet-lag? We've been in this time zone for weeks. That would have to be the longest case on record. But for the nerves, a little partying is just the cure Dr. Monahan prescribes."

She wanted to refuse, Lord, she wanted to refuse. To be left alone, to slip into the oblivion of sleep where she didn't have to face consequences or regrets. But she couldn't afford to rouse Nan's suspicions any more.

"All right. Let me wash my face."

With the bathroom door closed behind her and the water running, a pain splintered through her abdomen, making her clutch the sides of the basin.

She'd been prepared for the nausea, but these pains the past several days were something else.

The nausea had started almost immediately. Otherwise she might not have suspected for quite a while. Like a lot of athletes, her periods were more erratic than cyclical. She wouldn't have thought anything of missing a period, if it hadn't been for being nauseated so much.

The day she should have started and didn't, she'd taken a bus to the next town over from where the ski team had been staying. It had taken two tries to find a pharmacy that had one of those home pregnancy tests. It had a layer of dust on it and instructions in six languages, but that's all she found.

Locked in the bathroom, with Nan off being Nan, she'd carefully followed the directions. There it was, big as life, exactly the way the pamphlet said it should look for someone who was pregnant.

She'd sat on the cold tile floor for hours.

Finally, she'd placed a trans-Atlantic call to her old family doctor. He said to tell the team doctor. She'd refused. He pointed out that if she were selected for the drug tests at the Olympics, which she surely would be if she medaled as everyone said she would, they could easily find out anyway. But she'd figured they would be looking for steroids or other banned substances, not pregnancy.

Besides, the tests were done after the races. And after the final race, Rob Zemlak would have no right to know. And she wouldn't have to see his face when he found out.

So the old family doctor, too wise to suggest telling her parents, had sighed deeply, told her the tests weren't one hundred percent accurate but to use common sense. She was perfectly healthy and chances were her pregnancy would be perfectly normal. Call if she had any questions.

She hadn't called back when the pain started. Maybe this was normal. And if it weren't, he'd just argue more about her telling the team doctors.

Who would tell Rob Zemlak.

The doctor had also told her that vigorous exercise would do absolutely no harm, with the mother accustomed to expending that level of energy.

And that she was. For fifteen years. Day after day, week after week. All to get here. All for a shot at the bit of medal that Rob had said she could have bought with her allowance as an eight-year-old. But that she could only earn now, as a twenty-three-year-old. All for this.

The pain subsided enough for her to straighten and splash the tepid water on her face.

"Hurry up!" Nan ordered from the room. "And while you're at it, put on some makeup. You've been looking all washed out lately."

✧ ✧ ✧ ✧

MIKEY SWEET CLAIMED Amy at the door.

"I've been telling the guys what a pinball wizard you are, kid. And I've bet the Italian goalie you can beat him, so – God, I hope you haven't lost your touch, have you?"

"Of course, not." Amy's haughtiness would have done a snooty matron proud. "I'll need a game to get the feel of the machine."

"All right! C'mon, Rikki. This ought to be something to see."

But Rikki had already seen something. In the dim light beyond the group of hockey players clustered around the pinball machines, one figure sat alone before a video game, maneuvering the control with complete concentration.

"Thanks, but I see some friends over there. You guys have fun." She caught Mikey's arm a second and said quietly, "I may not stay long. Keep an eye on her and get her back at a decent hour." He nodded, and she headed toward some French cross-country skiers she'd met. They were on the opposite side of the room from the intense, solitary figure by the video game.

Half an hour later, after dancing with a Finnish speed skater and talking to a Canadian ski jumper, she found herself near the video games. Amy still reigned at the pinball machines, but Lanny Kaminski was nowhere to be seen, not even in the shadowed corner he'd occupied earlier.

Curious, she sat at the game he'd been playing, and dropped in a token. After one game she didn't know much more than that it had something to do with guiding a Viking ship through fjords and past other dangers.

She put in a second token.

Her second ship was sinking – she'd gotten too close to the fjord wall – when she heard a low voice behind her.

"That's pitiful. Sinking already, and you didn't even get out to open sea to run into a real iceberg."

Not bothering to turn around, she dropped in another token.

"So how far did you get, Kaminski?"

"A lot farther than you're getting. Do you even know the object of the game?"

"Loot ancient Britain?"

"I bet you didn't even read the instructions."

"Nope."

"Why don't you –"

"It's just a game, Kaminski. I don't need a consultant to draw diagrams on napkins for me."

He lapsed into silence, but he didn't move. She heard his occasional sounds of disapproval at her haphazard play, and she could feel his presence behind her.

The more he restrained himself, the worse she felt for her churlishness. She'd sunk another ship and another token before she spoke, though.

"Good game this afternoon, Kaminski. Nice to get that first win."

"Yeah." He hesitated long enough to make her wonder if that was all. "I saw you there." He sounded puzzled and not entirely happy.

She shrugged. "I thought it might be fun for a change. I don't usually go to hockey games."

"Was it?"

"Was it what?"

"Fun for a change."

Fun? Not quite the right word. "Let's say interesting." And a little unsettling.

"Yeah, it was an interesting game for me, too."

"I'll bet. Would you have stopped if the referee hadn't made you? Or would you have just gone on adding color to the ice?"

"I don't ever notice when I'm bleeding."

She nodded as if she understood him totally. "Not the noticing sort, huh?"

"I guess not. I don't ever notice people in the stands, either."

He said it so flatly it took her a moment. Then she looked up at him. His dark brows were drawn down in a frown and his eyes were intense. But not with the same emotion she'd seen in them this afternoon at the hockey rink.

The game beeped, waiting for her next move.

He leaned over her.

"If you hold it this way you can get better leverage."

Annoyance and amusement warring in her, she turned to give him a glare over her right shoulder. "I'll hold it however I want, Kaminski. I can . . ."

The words died under the burning light of intention in his eyes and the weight of realization that his mouth practically touched hers. She was drawing in breath when he kissed her, craving sense-restoring oxygen and instead drawing in his scent and leaving herself slightly light-headed.

It was a brief kiss, a shifting of lips against lips, a fleeting fluke of proximity. And it rocked her.

He lifted his head. Still half leaning over her, his one hand rested on her back, the other around her neck. She held on to that wrist, with her other hand caught between her shoulder and his chest.

They stared at each other, stunned and wary.

"Holy shit."

She wanted to be amused, but his profane mutter too aptly fit her own reaction.

His expelled breath across her dampened lips made her shiver. He saw it, and swooped down to kiss her again. No fluke, nothing fleeting. A smoldering fuse of a kiss that parted her lips and welcomed his tongue to light dynamite deep inside of her.

Ka-boom!

She shifted to free her hand. Slipped it around the back of his neck to explore the texture of his hair – softer than she would have expected – and pull him closer. He tightened his hold on her, drawing

She tried to shift back, and felt the abyss of the bed's edge under her backside.

"Bed's small. There's not much room."

"Don't need much." He put his hand on her back and brought her flush against him. He kissed her below her ear, then brushed her hair out of the way and started testing the skin of her neck with his teeth and lips.

"I, uh, guess you have a roommate, huh?"

"I said that. Before."

"Oh. Yeah. Another hockey player?"

"Tonetti."

"The whole team's in the same area in the Village?"

"Uh-huh."

She managed to insert enough room between them to pull the sheet up over her breasts. "I guess you've been traveling with them for a while."

"Uh-huh."

"So, how do you feel about playing in the Olympics?"

That got his attention. "You're asking me how I feel about playing in the Olympics?"

Defiant in the face of his disbelief, she repeated, "Yeah, How do you feel about playing in the Olympics?"

Even in the shadows, his eyes were uncomfortably intense. "I feel great about it," he said slowly, watching her.

"Have you always wanted –"

He cut her off. "Let me save you some time here. You want the rundown? Fine. I've always wanted to play hockey. I've always dreamed of playing in the Olympics, ever since I was a red-blooded American boy whistling 'Yankee Doodle Dandy' a few streets over from Paul Revere's ride.

"My father's the manager of a service department for a big Buick dealership – been there twenty-nine years – and my mother works in a department store. Selling perfume right now. I have a younger sister who's married with two kids and a younger brother who's a fireman. I'm from Boston and –"

"I knew that from the accent." Her only shot in a losing battle.

"– I'm on a first-name basis with the nurses for the top two sports rehabilitation experts in the state of Massachusetts. I'd been in the minors most of twelve years when I got the call for the Olympics. I got about three courses left on a degree that wouldn't get me a job at McDonald's. I'm not married. Not involved. Disease free. No major debts. No assets, major or otherwise. Anything else you want to know?"

"You seem awfully at ease with this situation considering you don't do things like this." She resented the hell out of his ease.

"I made a decision and I don't regret it. Do you?"

"No!" Surprise loosened her hold on the sheet. Maybe she'd thought she should, but she didn't regret making love with Lanny Kaminski. "No."

"Good."

He kissed her in earnest then, slow and deep. Exploring with his tongue, stroking her mouth, setting the first beats of an unmistakable rhythm.

His lips touched her brow again, then dropped to her chin on the way to a thorough examination of her collarbone.

"Lanny?"

"Hmm?"

"After I said we should come here and you pulled me back in that corner?"

"More questions, huh?"

"Yes." She didn't apologize. If he was so intolerant, so unwilling to –

"Okay, what about when I pulled you into that corner?" He cupped a palm over her breast as he had in that corner, but now with no clothing to restrict his circling, stroking movements. The friction against her nipple triggered circuits of pleasure throughout her body.

"What was that all about?"

"Wanted to give you a chance to reconsider. A little more time to think about it, see?"

She laughed. The movement pressed her breast into his hand, and with training and everything . . ."

He leaned closer, his mouth near enough to her ear that no one else could hear the words.

"I hope you're not feeling shy after our private post-party." She tried hard not to let anything show, but he must have seen something, because his tone shifted. "I know I'd been partying more than my share that night, and if there weren't the skyrockets and pinwheels you'd been hoping for . . . Well, just remember, everybody should get a second run."

"Brad . . ."

He looked at her and she forced herself to meet his eyes.

She saw acceptance come into his, and she thought that perhaps Brad Lorrence was smarter than he was usually given credit for.

He sighed deeply, but she thought more for effect than emotion.

"Ah well, sometimes even I get disqualified on the first run. There's still no reason to avoid me. Who knows, maybe I'll change your mind. In the meantime, we can be friends – as long as you don't brag about how you broke my heart."

Nan popped up on Brad's other side like a wished-for genie. "What heart?" she scoffed.

"Hey, what are you doing – eavesdropping?"

"You bet. Who wouldn't for a scoop like that? People magazine could probably do a double-page spread on the newsflash that Brad Lorrence, America's Casanova of the slopes, actually has a heart."

Brad's arm slipped away from Kyle as he turned to do verbal battle with Nan. Bless her.

Free of Brad's hold, she planned to make her escape. She'd made an appearance, said some hellos. Surely no one would notice if she left now. Unfortunately, Brad and Nan blocked the most direct route. She'd have to go further into the room in order to find a way out.

Before she took a second step, a solid form of wool, denim and determination blocked her way. She looked up into the cool, disapproving gray eyes of Rob Zemlak, and wondered if Nan had been the only one watching her exchange with Brad.

"Kyle."

His voice was as dispassionate as his eyes. No residue of his earlier laughter lingered. Nor of his biting words from this afternoon. Looked like they were going to be civil tonight. She lifted her chin. "Hello, Rob."

"You look like crap."

A ribbon of anger snaked through her listlessness.

"How nice to see you, too. Did you have a nice talk with that nice reporter this afternoon? How nice. Yes, I am having a good time this evening. Thank you for asking. And you? Of course, you must be enjoying yourself now that you're once more surrounded by – what shall I call them? – admirers?"

He ignored her sarcasm, continuing to look at her as if weighing her value, the way he would survey a pair of skis. On second thought, he'd show more pleasure and excitement over skis.

"You look tired. And those training runs this afternoon showed it. Especially that last one."

"It was as good as the session before last year's World Cup here."

"It should have been better. You should be improving, not leveling off."

"Oh, excuse me! We're not all the great Rob Zemlak."

"No. But you're not going to be the great Kyle Armstrong, either, if you don't shape up."

They stared at each other. Her anger had to be visible; he merely looked implacable.

"Go home and get some sleep."

He was good. He was very good. He'd almost succeeded in giving that order as if he cared about her.

"How come you never tell Nan to go home? She's got to hit even more parties than you do."

"We both know she doesn't need more time to think herself into a knot. But from the looks of it – on the hill and off – you need time to rest."

"It's not curfew yet. You can't tell me to leave."

He held her look a moment after that challenge, then turned slowly away, and gazed off to the side. In one of those brief lulls that slip into a party's din, she could hear Nan and Brad still tossing verbal bombs. Then noise surged again.

In a neutral tone, Rob said, "Training on the official downhill course for the combined starts early tomorrow."

"I'll be there."

He took a step, starting past her, but stopped and turned his head only, so they stood side to side, her shoulder pressed into his arm by the crowd around them, looking directly at each other.

"See that you are. And see that you're worth a damn in the morning."

He moved away before she could respond and left her unable to do the two things she most wanted to do.

She wanted to leave; she couldn't. She'd sentenced herself to another forty minutes penance, since her declaration of independence rested on remaining until curfew.

She wanted to cry; she wouldn't. She'd also closed the door on that release, because now she and Nan would return to the apartment at the same time, and tears would only raise questions she didn't intend to answer.

Oh, but to let the tears slide from her eyes and down her face. To curl into a cocoon – the cocoon of Rob's body. To be held the way he'd held her once. She remembered how it felt, the sensation of being desired, cherished. She remembered –

And remembering, she changed her mind.

The mistake she'd made four weeks ago hadn't been the worst of her life, but the second-worst. The worst had come fifteen months ago. Last winter, when she fell in love with Rob Zemlak.

TESS SAT AMID the coaches, listening to things she'd heard a dozen times before. She'd made certain to take the solitary chair left in the second row. And she intended to slip out the side door she'd already spotted before the man propped against the back wall with his arms crossed on his broad chest had a chance to intercept her.

Until then she just had to ignore the sensation raised on the back of her neck by his unwavering stare.

IN HABITUAL REACTION to the cold wind trying to lick the back of his neck, Rob Zemlak hunched his shoulders to raise the collar of his jacket. He slid his hands into his front jeans pockets and propped his shoulders against the corner of the building.

From his shadowed post he could see the entrance to the apartment building that housed two members of the U.S. women's ski team without being spotted himself.

Damn fool. What are you waiting out here for?

He didn't move.

Not much light, but he wouldn't need much. He'd know Kyle by the way she moved if all he could see was a shadow in the dark.

The way she moved . . . That was the first thing he'd noticed. The way she came down a mountain with joy flowing in every line, excitement in every twist. They shared that. She loved it, too. She craved it, too. Not as a means to the bottom, not as a means to glory. But as an end in itself. As a necessity of living and breathing.

He'd seen that in her almost immediately after joining the phalanx of coaches assigned to the U.S. women's team. It had made him look at her as a person, as an individual, and not simply another of his charges. That broke his first rule.

He'd also seen that she was attracted to him.

She made no open advances; she didn't need to. He could feel her interest, sense her watching him, hear the slight difference in her voice when they talked. And he'd let himself revel in the knowledge. That broke a second rule.

But it hadn't gone any further, because he'd seen something more.

In her eyes he saw her vision of him. Not an accurate reflection of him, but of some outsized, glorified cardboard cutout of the image his exploits, that the media and time had constructed around him.

He'd gone through one marriage with a woman in love with another man she happened to think he was. Even if he'd been fool enough to pretend it was otherwise with Kyle, she'd said it. She'd come right out and told him how seeing him in the Olympics had inspired her to ski seriously. A well-to-do-girl from the East, determined to fight her way into the tight, competitive, supportively cutthroat world of international skiing. Because of some elusive image she'd built up of Rob Zemlak.

He'd accepted that. He'd been the object of crushes before, often enough to handle them with automatically gentle distance. He could be her coach and her friend, he told himself. But no more. Kyle Armstrong had the ability and the desire. He had the experience. He'd vowed to teach her the way to that medal she craved.

Glimpses of the way she moved, of the joy and life of the woman revealed in that movement, tormented him, but he'd gotten by. For months, they'd been no closer, no further apart than any of the other team members.

Until that night a year ago November.

It started simply enough. A ski area donated lodge space and use of its runs for a week for the team when snow started the season early. The coaches snapped up the opportunity for intensive training with all the prospects, even though it meant coordinating myriad schedules at the last moment.

He'd fought his way through a snowstorm to get there at the assigned time, only to discover that Kyle, a trainer and one junior men's skier were the only others to make it. They waited all that afternoon as the sky opened its pillowcase and dumped out white, wet feathers. They played Monopoly. They played cards. They ate sandwiches. And they waited.

At seven, the junior skier went to bed with a cold. At eight, the trainer went to bed with a mystery novel.

At eleven, Rob Zemlak went to bed with Kyle Armstrong.

He'd fought it. Hadn't he?

Not enough. Because in the end, he'd leaned across the slice of couch cushion that separated them and he'd let his mouth touch hers. She'd kissed him back without hesitation or caution. From that moment he hadn't even tried to stop himself. Some things that you did in life were things you shouldn't have done but couldn't regret, and you just lived with the aftermath.

God, more than a year later and he could still taste her. Because she tasted the way she moved. Joy. Excitement. Craving. Giving. Caring.

He had taken much from the mountains, the exultation of the most perfect downhill runs, but the mountains never gave. Kyle Armstrong gave. For that night, having her in his bed, holding her, making love with her, he had felt himself – not the image, but himself – reflected in her.

She had touched him, and he had felt the potential for what he could be, what he might yet achieve and become, not just what he had already done.

He'd taken it all.

The reckoning for what he had received had started almost immediately.

He'd been her friend and her coach. He'd forfeited the friendship the minute he'd taken advantage of her attraction to the image he'd carried for so long. If he let this play out, eventually she'd see her mistake. But if he did that, he wouldn't be able to remain her coach. And he couldn't forfeit that. He'd had too many good coaches he needed to repay. He'd had too many bad coaches he didn't want to replay.

He'd known what he had to do.

He'd started that morning by being out of the room before she awoke. He'd been lucky –*lucky*! The plows broke through early, and before she was up and dressed, they were insulated by other members of the team.

He'd cloaked himself in his responsibilities and tried to pretend he didn't see her looks, first shy, then questioning, then puzzled, then hurt. He'd been almost grateful when he finally saw anger.

By the end of that first day, they'd set the pattern for the months that followed. He'd told himself that eventually they'd be at ease with each other. But that never happened. He'd never been able to look at her without wanting, and that had to be fought at any expense.

Most often at the expense of courtesy, he thought with a grimace. He knew other team members – especially Nan – wondered at the animosity between them, but that couldn't be helped.

Just as it couldn't be helped that team members speculated about the relationship between Kyle and Brad. He'd battled his own speculations, late at night, alone, in his bed. For a long time he'd thought Kyle would be the first to withstand Brad's blandishments. Now . . . He told himself it couldn't matter to him.

Not unless it affected their skiing.

A frown tightened facial muscles that had gotten more and more used to this position over the past year.

But it *did* affect the skiing now.

Not Brad's – it would take a nuclear bomb to affect his skiing – but Kyle's. She really hadn't looked well tonight. And that last session . . . What was wrong with her?

He stiffened. Two figures had moved into his peripheral vision. Kyle and someone else. The tightness in his shoulders eased. Nan.

The two figures came into sharper focus as they reached the light over the main entrance. He could hear one voice, animated. Then the door closed behind them.

Nan had a level head – off the hill – and a good heart. If something was wrong with Kyle, he couldn't leave her in better hands.

He pushed himself away from the building with a sigh, hunched his shoulders tighter and headed for his room.

DAY 3 – MONDAY

6:19 A.M.

"SHIT."

Lanny Kaminski raised his torso off the bed, and glared at the alarm clock Rikki had just turned off.

"Six-twenty? Shit."

Eyes closed, he dropped back to the bed by simply unlocking his elbows.

Was his disgust for the early hour or for finding himself in her bed? Rikki waited two full minutes, breathing softly, but he didn't move.

He might be one of those people only an earthquake – or, in this case, a loud alarm clock at ear level – woke up. Or he might not. She eased to the edge of the bed, looking for her robe.

It was in the closet. The only clothes she could reach without leaving the security of the covers were her bra and the silky camisole she'd worn last night. Great, two layers for the top, none for the bottom.

Though this modest concern about his seeing her without clothes was rather late. Not only were they lying next to each other naked right this minute, but they'd done a lot more than look at each other last night.

Unconsciously she licked her lips; she could taste him, his mouth, his skin.

She slowly got out of bed with as little movement as she could manage.

Usually she showered, dressed and got on her way in twenty minutes. That way she could sleep as long as possible. But this being quiet took a lot more time, she decided as she bundled last night's clothes in one pile, then stealthily drew open a drawer to start gathering today's. If she knew he was a heavy sleeper, she could bang and crash to her heart's desire. . . .

Another of the myriad reasons Rochelle Lodge didn't do this sort of thing. You ended up the next morning not knowing what kind of sleeper you had in your room, not to mention whether he regretted waking up in your bed.

Last night he'd said no regrets. But regrets weren't necessarily nocturnal creatures; they blossomed in the morning light.

Six-twenty-nine. There went the shower. She slipped into the bathroom to brush her teeth and wash her face and as much else as a washcloth could cover in record time. She had on the pants of her training suit when she realized she'd forgotten a bra.

Holding her thermal top to her chest, she opened the door and met Lanny Kaminski's look head-on.

He sat up against the pillows, the covers low, his eyes slumberous but alert. The alertness seemed to increase when he saw her state.

He didn't say anything as his eyes followed her to the dresser, watched her extract a jogbra, then tracked her back to the bathroom. She began to close the door behind her, but he started talking, and to hear him she had to leave it part way open.

"You practice at this hour?"

"Warm-up jog. Then test some skis."

"God, in hockey only the runts get stuck with ice time this early. Or if the coach is pissed." She had her bra fastened in record time, faster even than in high school when her mother had nearly caught her petting with Jimmy Stevenson. His next sentence reached her rather muffled because she was pulling on a top. "What did you do wrong?"

"Maybe got in a sport nobody's heard of."

She had to return to the bedroom for her brush and the clip she used to hold her hair back for training.

"They've heard of it in Europe. Biathlon's big in Scandinavia, Russia, Germany, places like that isn't it?"

She shot him a look of surprise, but his face was bland, as if everyone knew the top biathlon powers.

"Yes. How did you know that?"

"You hear things around." Only if you asked. The thought warmed her. "So why are you practicing so early?"

"We're competing in the morning, so it makes sense to get used to being up and ready to go."

He nodded. "Okay. I might as well get up, too. Got a practice at one."

"But that'll give you hours. You could get more sleep." She gathered up sock liners, socks and the shoes she would wear for the jog before getting into her training gear at the course.

He slanted her another look. "You didn't get any more rest that I did." She couldn't believe it, but she felt heat in her cheeks. "Besides, I want to go over some tapes."

"Tapes?" That sounded like the coaches' duty to her.

"Yesterday's game, and a scouting tape on Germany."

Fully dressed now, she looked at him, sitting in her bed, the dark hair on his chest an arrow pointing to where the covers swept around his hips.

"You take this very seriously, don't you?"

He looked up, surprised, then a little defensive.

"Yeah. I take it seriously." He bent over to retrieve his pants from the floor. "And it's going to be a long day. I don't know when I'll get free to see you, so –"

"Oh, sure. I understand. That's fine." He straightened and glared at her. She turned away, dropping the cords holding her various ID passes over her head, gathering up her gloves. "Please try to be quiet leaving. Right across the hall is a young girl I'd just as soon not shock. I'll see you around, Kaminski."

Before she could reach her jacket, he was there in front of her, naked and scowling.

"I told you I don't do this, Rikki. I don't just jump into bed with somebody, and I sure as hell don't do one-night stands. So don't try to

Thank God. "It was a hitch."

His arms dropped away from her.

She stood slowly, not pushing too hard for fear the pain waited just beyond. He rose behind her. Not touching, but too close to let her fall if she'd wavered. She didn't.

"Rob."

It was a young woman, one of the media liaison people. Toni, was that her name?

"The reporters are asking what's wrong. A couple of them saw Kyle go down and want to know if she's hurt. Can she talk to them?"

"No." Another time Kyle would have argued with him for not giving her the option, would have insisted on going just because he'd said no. Not now. "I'll be there in a minute."

Toni left and Rob turned assessing eyes on her.

"What are you going to tell them?" she demanded.

"What do you want me to tell them?"

That surprised her, but she rallied. "I've had some nausea, some weakness." The truth. "It might be the flu."

Silently he tested her. But she'd had a lifetime of training at keeping her emotions to herself, with a graduate course the past fifteen months thanks to him.

"Okay," he said, begrudging the concession. "But I intend to know what's going on, Kyle. We'll talk about this tomorrow. Before the morning warm-up. No more bullshit about flu or nothing being wrong. You're going to tell me what's wrong with you."

The hell I will.

She gave that answer only with her eyes.

"And no damn partying tonight. Get to bed early and go to sleep." She didn't miss his emphasis on the last three words, as if he thought she might have had plans to do something else in bed. "You look like someone dug you out after eight days in a blizzard."

"Thank you, as always, for your kind words and concern, Coach Zemlak." She bit off her words with the precision of an alligator. "And go to hell."

DAY 3 – MONDAY

7 P.M.

"LOOKING FOR SOMEONE?"

Rikki's focus shifted from the entrance to Nan Monahan sitting next to her in the Ice Hall's stands.

She hadn't even been aware of watching the streams of people coming in. The subconscious was stronger than she gave it credit for. It had certainly won out when it came to leaving a note tacked to the apartment door. She'd felt like an infatuated idiot, especially since she hadn't heard a word from Lanny Kaminski between six-forty this morning and six-fifty tonight, when they'd left to watch the pairs figure skating short program.

Still, she'd left a note telling him where they'd gone. In case he wanted to join them.

"I guess I am. Stupid, huh."

Nan shook her head emphatically, though dimples flashed into evidence. "Un-unh. Not stupid at all."

"It's not like me . . . Especially at a big competition. I mean, my God, this is the Olympics. That's all I should be thinking about."

"That thinking can get you in trouble," Nan said with a grimace. "Take it from an expert in over-thinking. And the way I look at it, it's just about inevitable you'll find romance at the Olympics. I mean, look at the situation. You start off with all these healthy young bodies –"

"Or not-so-young," Rikki interpolated.

"Young," Nan insisted. "Young and healthy. With all this adrenaline swirling around, not to mention certain other potent hormones. Plus, these are people who've been so busy training they hardly see anyone outside their sport, which gets pretty boring from a romantic angle, not to mention starting to seem almost incestuous after a while. Then – boom! – you throw them into the Olympics with a bunch of fresh, young bodies they haven't met before. And to top it off, you pack them into close quarters in the Athletes' Villages for a couple weeks and basically shut them off from the world. I don't see how anybody can resist."

She grinned, obviously pleased with her summation. "Besides, I'd say this one you're waiting for is definitely worth waiting for. At least if it's the same one you were talking to at the rec center the other night and that I saw in the hall outside your room this morning."

"This morning –?"

Nan shook her head at Rikki's quick glance in Amy's direction. "She wasn't around, and he was quiet. I just happened to be up." She accompanied the end of her sentence with a fleeting frown toward Kyle, sitting in the row in front of them with Tess and Amy. "Kyle didn't feel well and I went to the kitchen to get her a glass for some water."

Genuine concern reinforced Rikki's desire to turn the subject. "Is Kyle all right?"

Nan shook her head, the frown entrenched. "I don't know." As if worry drew the words out of her, she rushed on. "I heard she had a bad spill at the end of a run today and that's not like her at all, but she wouldn't tell me much about it. Maybe it's a bug of some kind making her weak. But all she says is she's fine and –"

"That's because I am fine." Kyle turned around and spoke with emphatic patience. "I felt a little woozy on the run today, but I am fine now – better than fine. You worry too much, Monahan. I feel great."

Rikki could believe that Kyle Armstrong felt great. She looked better than she had since they'd met the day before the Opening Ceremonies. The fact that she'd come along to this event indicated a change for the better. And Nan's easing expression reflected that.

"And you'll feel even better after you see some of these pairs," said

Amy. She and Tess had been talking, so they caught only the end of Kyle's statement. "I watched them at practice, and it made me wonder what it would be like to be a pairs skater. I'm not too old to switch. Of course, I'd have to find a partner at my level, not just on the ice, but who thought like me, you know?"

Tess groaned. "I don't think I could handle coaching two of you."

Amy smiled and patted her coach on the leg. "I know, that's why I'm staying in singles."

The devilment in her eyes gave way to a different glow as she looked around at the rest of them. "But wait until you see what these people can do on ice. Especially Vladimir Metroveli. Wow."

With Amy seemingly lost in contemplation of the marvel of Vladimir Metroveli, Rikki turned to Tess and asked for a run-down of the top pairs. She'd pointed out several as the skaters warmed up before the first routine, with explanations of their styles and strengths, when Amy came to life again.

"I didn't know Andrei had been a pairs skater, Tess. I thought from what he'd said about you guys competing in the same Olympics that he skated singles."

"He was in pairs."

Tess's voice became very careful, but Amy went on.

"And somebody said Andrei might even have reached Vladimir Metroveli's class if he'd kept skating –"

"Better."

The single word stopped Amy and drew every eye to Tess. Totally intent on her own words, she appeared unaware of her audience's reaction.

"He was already better than Vladimir Metroveli is, and if he'd kept skating nobody would have had any doubt that he was the greatest pairs skater ever."

Rikki followed the direction of Tess's look and spotted the man she'd seen at the rec center the other night. The tall, blond-haired man who had watched Tess so single-mindedly. Inexplicably, her own heartbeat sped up.

Now the man – he had to be this Andrei that Amy and Tess talked about – stood with the other coaches, greeting the pairs as they came off the ice from warm-ups. He consulted with the favorites, the skaters Amy and Tess had pointed out as Vladimir Metroveli and Radja Rastnikova.

What was this man to Tess Rutledge? A link existed, she was certain of that. But what? What had –

"Rikki."

The voice and the hand on her shoulder stopped her heart, then jumped it into double time.

"I told you I'd find you."

She looked up and Lanny's dark eyes, bright and penetrating, filled her consciousness. This must be the way he looks on the ice. As if nothing is going to keep him from his goal. As if he sees only one reality, the reality of getting what he's after. She controlled an urge to shiver.

"Got room for me?"

"Sure." Nan scooted down the row, tugging at Rikki to follow her, and Lanny sat in the outside seat.

Rikki roused enough to start the introductions, but the specifics of the conversation went over her head, until Lanny turned his dark eyes back on her.

A grin lingered from something Amy had said as he asked her, "Have I missed anything?"

Had he? The talk with Nan about Kyle, Tess's words about this blond man Amy called Andrei – Rikki wasn't sure if those constituted "anything" or if her imagination worked overtime.

Just as her imagination had produced that reaction to Lanny a second ago.

"It's just getting started. You're right on time."

TESS SMILED AS she thanked the guard again. But she waited until he had disappeared back into the dark before she pushed off onto the hockey rink's ice, getting acquainted with the texture and pace of this particular ice with long, smooth strokes over its surface.

Something caught her eye in the black beyond a safety light at the far end of the rink. It could have been a movement. Had the guard come back? No, nothing. Her imagination at work in strange surroundings.

Not wanting to push the tolerance of the officials at the figure skating rink, even if they were inclined to indulge a gold medalist, tonight she'd decided to see if she could charm her way onto the deserted hockey ice.

She stroked more firmly along the ice, feeding into a simple spiral, her arms raised against the air, letting the drag pull them back into position, then holding the line.

The hockey rink guard had grumbled a little, but an extra smile had gotten him to admit that they'd be grooming the ice again before the first morning game, so as long as she didn't dig any divots, she couldn't do much harm.

She'd dug her share of divots in the five years she'd been with Will Stenner, but they'd all been on the golf course, when he'd tried to teach her the game that was his life and his livelihood.

She'd never defined her reaction to different rinks until she'd known Will and learned about golf. If grass could have different textures, different reactions, almost different moods from course to course or even from day to day on the same course, why couldn't ice? She thought it did. And what she'd once done on instinct, she'd learned during her years with Will to do consciously. To assess a new piece of ice, to gauge it and "play" it the way Will did a hole at Augusta.

Skating ahead, she stepped into an easy upright spin. It felt good, the childlike joy of twirling never quite forgotten. She flowed out of it, going for more speed as she went into a camel spin. "The Hood Ornament" Will had teased. She smiled now, even as she felt the stretch in her legs.

Those five years with him had been good; Will was fun, caring, attractive and as attentive as she could have expected from someone who traveled more than forty weeks a year playing on the pro golf tour. From the minute they'd met at the hospital benefit in Cincinnati, it had been nonstop his-and-hers schedule-juggling. Even when she wound down her performing career, the demands of coaching kept her on the run – to regionals and nationals, exhibitions and junior worlds.

But what had really ended the relationship had been her desire to make their lives even more complicated by having children. At least that's the way Will saw it. She'd seen it differently. They'd split about as amicably as two people could; she heard from him every couple of months, always at Christmas and her birthday, and she certainly wished him well. They only argued when he reminded her that here she was, four and a half years later, traveling even more and with Amy the closest thing she had to a child.

He didn't need to remind her.

As she entered an easy single axel a flicker in the shadows caught her eye, but it disappeared in the movement of the jump. She didn't like the jump, and tried another. That satisfied her, but she did a third to be sure.

Maybe that vulnerability had made it so hard two years ago, when the televised World Championships coverage had picked up on the story of a surprising new coach for the latest dynamic Russian figure skating pair – Andrei Chersakov.

Each mention of his name, each glimpse of his face struck like a blow against her ribs – from the inside or outside? Bruising either way. The mentions had become more frequent, her outward calm more secure as Rastnikova and Metroveli had climbed. She'd braced herself to cross paths with Andrei – someday.

Someday came long before she'd expected, long before she'd had time to prepare, when Amy stunned the skating world a month ago by finishing third in the U.S. Nationals and grabbing the final Olympic team berth when she outperformed two far more experienced skaters.

Seeing Andrei again shouldn't have been any different really from seeing an old flame at a high school reunion. It had been eighteen years, after all. And she had gone on and lived her life. Won championships, traveled the world, earned money, spent good years with a good man and found a satisfying second career in coaching.

But each time she saw him there came a shock of reaction, as if those eighteen years had collapsed like an opera hat into a thin wafer. Not nearly enough insulation to protect her from remembering what it felt like to fly on top of the world. To be so in love, so certain that he would agree to defect, to spend his life with her. To be so certain he loved her, and then to find out he didn't.

She'd learned it in the most brutally casual of ways. Already troubled that Andrei had not yet arrived for the World Championships a month after the Olympics, she was waiting her turn to practice when two skaters on the bench behind her started talking. She didn't even remember who they were, but she could hear their voices.

Did you hear about Andrei Chersakov and Tatiana Serginova.

No. What about them?

They're not coming.

You're kidding! How'd you hear that? Why aren't they coming?

I heard it from a German skater who'd talked to an East German who knows the Soviet team real well, and the word is they got married right after they got back from the Olympics.

Tatiana and ANDREI?

Yeah. I know. I would have thought he had more brains. Of course, you know the rumor was all over the Olympics that he'd fallen for somebody in a big way. But who would have thought it was Tatiana the Cat, huh?

Yes, who would have thought it. Certainly not naive little Tess Rutledge.

After that, the grapevine dried up on the subject of Andrei Chersakov. Not a word. Rumbles reached them that Tatiana might try a new partner, but if so they never competed outside the Soviet Union. And it hadn't made sense anyhow that after marrying they would find other partners. It was as if Chersakov and Serginova never had existed, never had skated, never had been touted as the next great Soviet pair.

But Tess Rutledge skated on. She moved up the hierarchy of international skating. After a finish out of the top fifteen at that first, devastating Worlds, she progressed steadily, advancing in exhibitions and smaller competitions. Then second in Nationals, fifth at Worlds. Two years running as U.S. champion with a third, then a first at

Worlds. Finally, the Olympic gold and stardom.

Odd, she barely remembered the Olympics when she took the gold. Over the years she must have had a thousand people tell her their memories of her skating that year. She'd seen the tapes. Yet it remained a blur. What she remembered was four years earlier, when she'd been a nobody, who skated out her heart because she had fallen in love with Andrei Chersakov.

✧ ✧ ✧ ✧

SOMETHING WAS WRONG. Terribly wrong.

From the edge of the bed, Kyle started to walk toward the bathroom, eight, maybe nine feet away. She could hear Nan's voice out in the living room through the open bedroom door. Who was she talking to? That suddenly seemed very important. More important even than putting each foot in front of the other despite the clench ripping at her insides.

She reached the bathroom door and leaned against the frame.

"Nan . . ." The wooden frame felt slick against her forehead. The feel of her own sweat. She'd felt so good earlier. As if the pain had never happened. Had it been saving up, recruiting its resources for this moment.

She needed help. Now.

"Nan!"

The pain split her, a driving spike ripping her even as she felt the floor coming up to her. A shout tore from her throat. "Nan!"

She must have passed out, but briefly. Nan's voice came to her, swimming through nausea and pain.

"Kyle. Oh my God, oh my God! Kyle!"

Then she could see Nan and another figure behind her, and hear Nan's voice more clearly.

"Amy, call the ambulance. That emergency list by the phone."

"No! No ambulance."

"Kyle, we have –"

"No ambulance. It would be all over. TV. Newspapers."

"This isn't the time to worry about that shit."

"No ambulance."

I'm sorry it's you, Amy. Better if it had been Tess or Rikki. Or if she'd been alone. It was over, she knew that.

Nan breathed out, two quick, panting breaths like she did before the start of a race.

"Okay. Okay. Amy, there's a number on that list for Rob Zemlak. Call him. He's our coach. Tell him –"

"No! No, you can't call him –"

"Kyle, damn it, hold still. Amy, go make that call. Now!"

"No, please." She knew she was crying, and she hated it. "Please, don't call Rob, please."

"Kyle, we've got to have help. Dear God, you're bleeding. You could be hemorrhaging. I'm sorry, but we've got to have help. Oh, Kyle, Kyle what have you done to yourself?"

The pain won again, or maybe despair. Time slid away. Or maybe she did. She knew only the jumbled impression of voices and movement around her.

But she knew Rob's voice said, "Where is the God damned ambulance?"

"No ambulance," she said. "No ambulance."

They ignored her. Nan said, "Amy called, right after she called you and they said they'd be right here, but –"

Rob Zemlak let loose a river of swearing. She tried to smile. What would that do to Mr. All-American's reputation? But the smile never made it.

Without slowing his cursing, Rob put one arm under her knees and the other around her back and scooped her up. Pain rose up in her body like a scream.

"I'm sorry, baby. But we've got to get you to somebody who'll help you. Nan, get a blanket, a couple blankets to cover her. We'll go to the clinic. It's closer. We're going to the clinic, Kyle. I'm going to get you help. It'll be okay. Do you understand? Can you hear me?"

She heard him. She understood. But it seemed so far away, so unimportant. It was all over. She tried to tell him all that, but only one word escaped before the pain enveloped her.

"Rob . . ."

"TESS!"

Andrei's voice calling her. Had she conjured his voice out of her memory?

"Tess!"

No, that was reality. As real as the dark form emerging from the shadows at the end of the rink. What was he doing here?

Tempting as it might be, it would be foolish to pretend she hadn't heard or seen him. She started slowly skating toward him, hands at her waist. Then a second figure took shape out of the darkness and she picked up speed.

"Amy?" What was Amy doing with Andrei?

"Oh, Tess," Amy's words caught and Tess's other questions disappeared. "I've looked all over for you. I thought you'd be at our rink and when you weren't I didn't know what to do. Then I thought maybe here, but – Oh, Tess, you've got to come quick."

Before Tess could leave the ice, Amy lunged into her arms, almost knocking her off balance. Andrei's arm went around her waist, a solid bar holding them both upright.

"What is it?"

"Nan sent me to get you. She said they need you, but I think –"

"Nan? Something's wrong with Nan?"

"No. It's Kyle."

"Kyle? What –"

Andrei cut in. "Let her tell it. It will come faster."

Amy shot him a look, blended of gratitude and curiosity. "I don't know what's wrong. But Nan said to go get you. I think she wanted to keep me from seeing the blood." She was pale, her eyes huge. "Kyle was on the bathroom floor and . . . and there was blood."

"Blood . . ." Tess had guessed something had been bothering Kyle Armstrong, but she'd never tried to find out what. She'd been so caught up in her own problems. Blood . . . Oh, God . . .

Andrei asked the practical, "Where is Kyle now?"

"The clinic. Kyle didn't want us to call anybody, but Nan told me
to. I called the hospital right after Nan had me call Rob somebody-or-
other – their coach. They said they'd send an ambulance, but it didn't
come and Rob just picked her up and started carrying her to the
Village clinic because it's closer. Rikki and Lanny got there just then
and Lanny helped. That's when Nan sent me to look for you."

"The clinic . . ."

"Come." Andrei took quiet control. "I know where it is. First, your
shoes."

As soon as Tess had traded her skates for shoes, Amy took hold of
the skates and Andrei took hold of Tess's hand. She didn't argue either
move.

Andrei's hold on her hand remained firm, during the taxi ride to
the Village and the walk across a snowy lawn to the clinic. He found
the directions for where they should go, and led her and Amy down
the short corridors to a tiny waiting room with four people nearly
filling it.

Andrei only released her hand in order for her to hold her arms out
to Nan.

"Tess." Saying that single word and the arms that came around her
seemed to break Nan's composure. "I'm sorry. I'm sorry." She sobbed,
apologized, and sobbed more.

Tess looked at the other people in the room. In Nan's eyes she'd
seen fear. Now, in Lanny's and Rikki's she saw shock and concern.
The fourth person in the room, the man around her own age, with
blood marking his jeans and his USA jacket must be Rob Zemlak. In
Rob Zemlak's eyes she saw torment.

"Have they said how she is?"

"No." Rikki cleared her voice and tried again. "No. The nurse
came by and said the doctor was with her and would come talk to us
when he could. That was about twenty minutes ago."

Another forty-five minutes passed before the nurse returned. In
that time they exchanged perfunctory introductions. Lanny took orders

for coffee, recruiting Amy to help him bring the cups from the machine down the hall. Nan told Tess briefly about hearing Kyle scream, then finding her in the bathroom, with blood on the floor.

At least the nurse brought encouraging news.

"The doctor says to tell you all that Ms. Armstrong has stabilized."

"Why isn't he here?" Rob Zemlak demanded. "You said he'd tell us how she's doing. I want to talk to the doctor."

"He had to go with a patient to the city hospital for a surgery – an emergency appendectomy. A luger from Canada. I can only tell you that Ms. Armstrong has stabilized and does not appear to be in any danger. If there had been any question of that she would have been transported to the hospital."

"When can we see her?"

The nurse shook her head at Nan. "Not until the doctor checks her again. Even then I can't guarantee he'll let anybody in tonight, and certainly not all of you, so you might as well go home."

"We'll stay."

It came from several voices. The nurse shrugged and left.

But as Tess looked around at the drawn faces, she decided she didn't give up as easily as the nurse. "There's no reason for everyone to stay. We know she's all right, and that's all they're going to tell us for now. Rikki, you have training in the morning, don't you?"

Rikki nodded, and met Tess's eyes. She nodded again, in comprehension and agreement this time.

"And Lanny has a game tomorrow. I think you're right, Tess. It's hard, but I think it makes more sense for us to go. Lanny?" He nodded and they stood together. Rikki put a hand on Nan's shoulder and squeezed. Her voice sounded thick as she added. "How about you, Amy? Why don't you come with –"

"No. I'm staying."

"No you're not," contradicted Tess. "You're going back to the apartment with Rikki and you're going to go to sleep."

"But –"

"No buts."

Amy studied her for a moment, then seemed to recognize the

futility of arguing. Rikki slung an arm around the girl's slumped shoulders as they headed out, and Tess knew Amy would be fine.

She looked across the small room at Nan, who simply shook her head.

Rob Zemlak didn't even look up from where he sat with his elbows on his knees, his head bent in contemplation of his clasped hands. There would be no budging either of them.

That left Andrei.

He'd sat quietly by her side since they'd arrived. Not touching her, not saying anything. Simply there.

When she turned to him, he was looking at her.

"Now you think to order me as you do young Amy?"

"I would if I could," she admitted. And to her amazement, a glint of amusement lit his eyes.

"You cannot."

"Really, Andrei. There's no sense to your staying."

"And what of you?"

"I have some responsibility here. I'm not just Amy's coach, I accepted some official duties when I agreed to be a team leader, even if Kyle's not a skater. And I'm . . . I'm – " She didn't know how to explain this feeling that she should have looked out better for Kyle, should have known, should have helped her somehow. "– I'm the oldest one here."

He gave one of those imperturbable Russian shrugs she'd found frustrating eighteen years ago, too. "I'm older."

"I mean in the apartment. It's like I see them all a little bit like Amy. You should understand that. You're a coach. And that's the reason you should go. Your skaters are going to need you in the morning. The day between skates, with all the media and the interviews and the pictures, is harder than the competing. Especially when all the adrenaline starts to ebb away from tonight, but they can't relax yet because there's still the long program Wednesday. Radja and Vladimir are going to need you."

"You do not need me?" The amusement was gone.

"No. I don't."

She met his stare. Then he nodded, once, in acceptance and she let out a breath as he stood.

"But I do thank you, Andrei. Thank you for everything tonight."

He turned back from the door to look at her. His face and voice were expressionless, that public face she'd hated so long ago.

"You are welcome, Tess Rutledge."

TESS SHIFTED AGAINST the scratchy upholstery of the insufficiently padded chair and opened her eyes. Why could the world gather its most graceful, most skilled athletes every four years in an amazing festival of effort and achievement, but it couldn't produce a comfortable place to sit in a waiting room?

Across the room, Nan had finally fallen asleep. Curling into a corner of the couch, she'd drawn her knees to her chest and tucked her arms tight in humanity's instinctive position of self-comfort.

Tess must have dozed herself. She turned her stiffening neck slowly and saw that Rob had not changed position. Except that now his hands clenched into tight, painful fists.

She slid forward and put one hand over his right fist.

"She's all right, Rob."

"I should have done something."

Without looking up, the harsh, staccato words seemed to be torn from him, a man accustomed to holding his feelings inside.

"You weren't responsible."

"I knew something was wrong and I put it off. I didn't make her tell me. I didn't make her let me help."

"You're not alone. I thought something was bothering her and I didn't try to find out what it was or how I could help."

He didn't seem to hear. "She wasn't skiing right, she didn't look right. And when she started having that pain . . . I should have done something."

"Pain?"

"When she collapsed on the course today, I should have brought her to the doctor right then, no matter what she said."

A kind of relief welled in Tess. Kyle had had pain, she'd collapsed and that was horrible, but Tess still thanked God. Kyle hadn't tried to commit suicide.

Her mind had kept telling her that no one who'd looked as at ease as Kyle had at the skating this evening would go back to the room and try to take her life. But that hadn't erased the knot in her stomach.

"You can't make someone let you help them, Rob."

"I should have," he said doggedly. "I'm her coach and I – I'm her coach."

"And that makes you God? A coach can't know everything that's going on with an athlete. The coach can be there if the athlete needs something, but you can't live their life for them. You can't compete for them and you can't protect them from living. They have to go out and do it themselves."

He lifted his head, and the pain in his eyes startled Tess. "I should have protected her. I should have –"

A nurse appeared in the doorway. "Nan Monahan?"

Nan jolted awake. "Yes. Me. I'm Nan." She started to rise, half stumbled on numbed legs, and Rob stood to steady her. "Is she okay? Is Kyle –?"

"Doing much better," the nurse assured her quickly. "The doctor's seen her again, and said she could have visitors – but very briefly. Just for a few minutes. She needs to rest. She's asked to see Nan Monahan and Tess Rutledge, if she's here."

"Yes, I'm here."

"I want to see her."

"I'm sorry, Mr., uh . . ."

"Zemlak. Rob Zemlak, I'm her coach. I want to see her."

"I'm sorry, sir. She said only Nan Monahan and Tess Rutledge. It's important right now that she get her rest, not get stirred up."

Tess wasn't sure Rob would accept that. Not even when she and Nan followed the nurse out of the cramped waiting room, leaving him staring after them.

✧ ✧ ✧ ✧

"I WAS PREGNANT, and I miscarried."

Kyle had decided while she waited for Nan and Tess to get that out right away. They were only halfway across the room when she blurted out the words. It seemed strange to say the word pregnant out loud when she'd barely whispered it even in her mind.

"Aw, Kyle." Nan took the last step to reach the bed, took a hold of her hand, and didn't let go. Kyle felt the first layer of fear peel away.

After that, words poured out. Neither Tess nor Nan interrupted. She watched their faces, but neither showed anything other than concern, even when she told them this had started with one, stupid night with Brad Lorrence.

"What does the doctor say?" Tess asked when she'd finished.

"He said I was lucky –"

"Lucky!"

"– That it was so early, Nan. Only a month. And he said I'll feel weak for a while from loss of blood, but should be a hundred percent quickly. And he said he didn't think this would necessarily mean any problems for me in the future, I mean if I want children later."

Tess nodded. "Are you satisfied with this doctor or do you want us to see about getting someone else –"

"No. No, he seems fine. He talks to me, and answers my questions. He said there shouldn't be any complications but to go to my gynecologist later."

"God, Kyle, why didn't you tell me? I could have helped you. I could have –"

"What, Nan? What could you have done?" The question was gentle. Kyle eyed her friend, so pale she looked as if *she* could use a hospital bed.

"I could have made sure you didn't go through it all alone."

Tears welled up. The first tears she didn't try to stop. "Thank you, Nan."

"Don't thank me, just be damned sure you tell me if you ever have something like this happen again!"

"I don't intend to have something like this happen again," Kyle said dryly. "It wasn't like we didn't use protection. But the doctor said even a tiny hole will do, even when it's just once. The odds are against it, but it can happen. If the luck goes against you."

"You've got to tell Rob. No matter what you think, he'll –"

Rob. *I'm sorry, baby . . . I'm going to get you help. It'll be okay.*

She'd tried to block memory of his calming words, of his arms, of his face.

Nan was still talking. "– know you didn't want me to call him, but I had to, Kyle. We needed help and I didn't know what to do, or how to do it and you were bleeding. You'd passed out and – oh, God –"

"I know." The words were tiny, all her throat would let pass, but she tightened her grip on Nan's hand.

Nan wiped away her tears with her free hand. "I'm glad you're not mad that I went against what you said, but I'd do the same thing again even if you were," she said stoutly. "And even if you're mad at me for saying this, I'm going to say it again – Rob's got to know what happened. You've got to tell him."

"I . . .I can't." Kyle looked down at Nan's hand clasped with hers. "Couldn't you –?"

"No. I'm not telling him. I'm not going to be the one to break his heart."

Kyle saw Tess give Nan a quick look, but didn't try to decipher it. "His heart won't be broken. I can still ski."

"Ski! Are you crazy? How can you ski?"

"The doctor said I should bounce back quickly and –"

"He's crazy! All that blood –"

"I didn't lose that much, not really. He explained that. He said the pregnancy wasn't right from the start and it was my body's trying to deal with that that caused the pain and nausea. But once I get some rest I should be back to normal real soon. Not for the combined –"

"God, I should hope not. That's tomorrow! Today! In just a few hours."

"I know. But maybe the giant slalom. And for sure the slalom. That's ten days away. I talked to the doctor. "Well, Rob won't let you,"

Nan said flatly. "Not after this."

"He'll have to. I'll make him."

"You can't make him if you don't talk to him."

Her weakened muscles did their best to tighten at the thought of facing Rob. She let her eyelids drop and laid her head back against the pillow, suddenly too tired to hold it up. She let go of Nan's hand.

"I can't. Not yet. Please."

In the quiet of the room, Kyle heard Nan's restless movement. Agitated steps led to the window, then back to the bedside.

"I'd do anything to help you out, Kyle, you know that. But don't ask me to tell Rob. Please. He's a friend, too."

The tension in the room broke with the shushing sound of the door opening. The nurse stood there, silently informing them it was time to go.

"I'll tell him if you want me to." Tess's quiet voice was a blessing.

"Thank you."

It was all Kyle could say.

Nan gave her another hug and Tess laid her hand on Kyle's before they started out.

At the doorway, Tess stopped, turning back to face her.

"But you will have to talk to him sometime, Kyle. Sometime soon. That man isn't going to disappear from your life that easily. Rob Zemlak isn't going to go away."

THE HARDEST THINGS you do in life aren't necessarily cloaked in big, dramatic moments, Tess thought as she walked alongside Rob in the crackling cold of predawn.

She'd once stood on the ice, still as a statue in the spotlight, her image flickering on television sets across the world watched by millions of people. She'd waited for her music to begin, knowing that how she performed in the next four minutes would determine if she won an Olympic gold medal or not. Knowing that to most of that world out there watching on television the next four minutes would decide whether all her years of effort had really paid off. Knowing that the next four minutes – disastrous or glorious – would have an impact on her for the rest of her life.

That had been easier than walking into the waiting room where Rob Zemlak sat alone and saying, "Let's go for a walk."

"I want to see Kyle."

"Not tonight. She's resting. And I think you should hear what I have to say before you talk to her."

In silence they walked away from the clinic.

She took a deep breath and started speaking. Calmly and simply she told him what she knew about Kyle Armstrong's brief pregnancy and miscarriage.

In the dark, she couldn't see his reaction. His steady pace never faltered, and he never interrupted her.

When she finished, the only sound was the crunch of their boots on the packed snow as they walked off another block, and came within sight of Tess's building.

"Does she love him?"

She hadn't expected that. And yet it made sense.

"Brad Lorrence – does she love him?" He repeated the demand, impatient and harsh. Tess wondered if he knew how much he revealed.

"No. No, Kyle doesn't love him."

She expected him to ask why Kyle had slept with him, then. Again he surprised her.

"Is she going to tell him?"

She shook her head, but in amazement, not as an answer. Incredible, that none of them had ever said anything about telling Brad Lorrence. All the discussion had been about telling Rob. That had never occurred to her until Rob brought it up.

"I don't think so," she said carefully. "There doesn't really seem to be a reason to, but you'd have to talk to Kyle about that."

He made a harsh sound. "You think she's going to talk to me? Seems like she took care of that by sending you."

"No," Tess said calmly, "I don't think so. I think what happens next is up to the two of you."

DAY 4 – TUESDAY

ANDREI WALKED UP the steps toward the apartment as Tess came out the door.

"You are leaving? I had hoped to ask how Kyle does today."

"I'm going to see her right now."

"I will go with you."

"I don't think –"

"Not to go in to see her. She does not know me. But I will walk with you."

They walked in silence. Not touching. Unnoticed in the hubbub of the Athletes Village's early evening. The day's events were over, the night's not yet begun. Laughter, calls in a kaleidoscope of languages echoed. Streams of people, predominantly young and exquisitely healthy, flowed past them, caught in occasional eddies of conversation or interest snagged by heated discussion of a strategy or result. The real competition was behind them, or ahead of them. They had the moment, and they intended to use it.

It left an ache in Tess's throat that hadn't diminished when they reached the hallway to Kyle's hospital room.

"Thank you for the escort, Andrei." The unnecessariness of that escort left her voice a shade dry. "I don't know how long I'll be, so –"

"I will wait."

"No. It's not –"

"I will wait."

"And later on, I have a meeting with the USOC." She met his eyes. "There's no sense in your waiting, Andrei. Not tonight, and not for me to decide we have anything else to talk about."

"I will wait for that, as well." If the Rock of Gibraltar had a voice this would be what it sounded like.

She tried not to think about him, but Kyle was asleep when she went into the room, and sitting quietly in the upright hospital chair was too damn conducive to thinking.

Well, Andrei Chersakov could wait all he wanted.

She'd done her share of waiting. That month between the Olympics and the Worlds eighteen years ago when she'd waited giddy with anticipation. The dragging days at the Worlds when she'd waited with growing anxiety. The weeks that had followed, when she'd waited with dying hope for a word, a communication. A miracle.

He'd betrayed her. Nothing could change that. But from this point in her life, she saw how young they had been and she could put aside his betrayal enough to treat him with dignity, and she had done that. But if he thought he could re-enter her heart after all these years . . . No.

Maybe he didn't want that. Maybe he wanted only her forgiveness, as they went on with their separate lives.

She didn't know if she could give that.

She should forgive. In order to be the sort of person she'd always been taught she should be, to be the kind and generous person she'd always wanted to be, she had to be able to forgive.

Maybe that was why she didn't want to talk to Andrei Chersakov. Because she feared he would ask for her forgiveness and she would not be able to give it. And then she would have to face the lack in herself.

Kyle stirred, and Tess knew only relief. Even recounting the bare facts of her early morning conversation with Rob was preferable to the discomfort of her own thoughts.

When a small nurse with a heavy French accent came in with the hospital dinner, Tess left Kyle. Andrei waited, just as he'd said he would.

Talking of Kyle, of the pairs final coming up the next night, of Amy – of everything but themselves and the past – he walked her back to her apartment door and left her there, still waiting for her to be ready to truly talk to him.

KYLE HAD KNOWN this was coming. All day she had known.

Nan had slipped in before her training run – and before official visiting hours – dropping off clothes, toiletries and promising a longer visit in the evening.

Alone Kyle watched the closed-circuit television coverage of the downhill runs of the women's combined. Odd how detached she felt. She watched the skiers come down, those who were expert in the downhill but would falter in tomorrow's slalom, those who endured the downhill in order to get to the slalom and those who had skill at both but greatness at neither. Watching the technique, weighing who would be good enough in the next day's slalom to have a chance at the overall medal.

Knowing she could have been up there with the leaders.

She heard that she'd missed the event after being stricken with the flu during yesterday's training. She wondered if Rob had told the announcers that or if they'd extrapolated it.

Nan had made a point this morning of telling her that they hadn't run into anyone last night when Rob had carried her to the clinic. It had been late enough that the athletes' living quarters were quiet; most were asleep and any night owls were at the rec center, on the other side of the Village.

Kyle hadn't paid much attention, but now realized Nan was thinking about the public story.

Flu was as good a story as any other.

Rikki Lodge came in not long after lunchtime with fresh fruit and nuts, then sat companionably eating with her while they watched speed skiing and men's luge. After Rikki left to go to the United States' hockey game, Kyle switched the TV to watch that. She wouldn't ever tell Lanny Kaminski that she fell asleep in the third period. At least the United States was safely ahead by that time.

Tess sat by her bed when Kyle awoke in the early evening. After dinner, Nan came back.

And with each opening of the door – for visitors, the doctor, the nurses – she had braced to see Rob standing there.

Now he was.

Had he delayed until now, the final minutes of visiting hours, to drag out her waiting?

"Well, I'll see you tomorrow, Kyle."

"No, wait, Nan –"

But Nan had already vacated the chair next to the bed. She stopped next to Rob, who'd paused two feet inside the door. "Don't want my coach to catch me out past curfew you know," she said.

"It's two hours until curfew. If you turned in now, I'd fall over in a faint."

Nan answered that with a saucy grin. But she also patted Rob on the arm, almost as if in consolation or encouragement.

The door closing behind Nan left silence. Kyle forced the words out she knew needed to be said.

"Thank you for your help last night, Rob."

"I don't want thanks, Kyle."

She hardly heard him. "I'm grateful for everything you did for me last night. If I it hadn't been for you . . . Well, tha –"

"Don't thank me, damn it!"

His harshness sealed another silence. For an instant she thought he might turn around and leave.

Instead, when he moved, it was to stand by the side of her bed, and all the harshness was gone when he spoke.

"How do you feel?"

"I'm all right."

That seemed to be another end of the conversation. Only his eyes moving as they scanned her face. She dropped her gaze to her hands, resting in her lap on top of the plain hospital blanket.

His right hand started a movement toward hers, but stopped short. Then, with an awkwardness she never remember seeing from him, he rested his hand on the back of the nearby chair.

"I'm sorry, Kyle."

That brought her eyes back to his face. "Sorry?" Why would he be sorry?

"That you got hurt."

His words hung there for an immeasurable moment, waiting for one or the other of them to acknowledge that the hurt came from fifteen months ago.

She looked away. "The pain's past now." The lie said, she masked it under the pretense that they were talking about the miscarriage. "A little more rest and I'll be fine. I'm just a little weak and the doctor agrees that should pass very quickly. I should be all healed physically in a few days."

"How about emotionally?"

For the second time in this brief visit he'd surprised her.

"What do you mean?"

"You must have a lot of mixed feelings about all this."

She fought tears with every bit as much stubbornness as she'd ever fought for an extra breath of speed on a mountain. Of all the people in the world to recognize the stream of sorrow that wound through her today . . .

The doctors, the nurses all seemed to assume she would be relieved. Even Nan, Tess and the others skirted any mention of what might have been if she hadn't miscarried. She couldn't blame them. How she felt made no sense.

All those hours and days that her head had throbbed with *What am I going to do? What am I going to do?* That was all gone. What would she have done? She still didn't know, but she felt an elemental emptiness now that the decision had been taken away.

"The doctors say it was for the best. This is nature's way of dealing with it when a pregnancy wasn't right. And it happened so early –"

He put his hand over hers. She jumped slightly at the contact. He didn't let go.

"How do you feel, Kyle?"

She remembered the power of that low voice. She hadn't wanted to fight it fifteen months ago, she'd gladly followed it. She fought it now, yet it drew her.

"I don't know." She swallowed hard. "Mixed, like you said . . . I don't know. Maybe I'll never know."

She couldn't break down now. Not now, and not in front of him. She needed something to stop the sorrow and tears welling in her. Something to combat the weakness his low voice pulled out her.

"Why didn't you tell me?"

Just that easily, he gave her the weapon she'd relied on so often the past fifteen months – anger.

She pulled her hands away from his.

"Tell you!" Her laugh sounded harsh to her own ears, and not at all convincing. "Don't you realize you were the last person I wanted to have know? There was no way I would ever have told you."

"Why?" Something in the question broke through to her. Anguish? No, more likely irritation.

"Why?" she flung back. "Oh, yeah, I can just see that. I'd go waltz-ing in and tell you I'd managed to get pregnant barely a month before the biggest event of my life. I can just see how that would confirm your already sterling opinion of me."

"My opinion of you . . ."

"You've never made a secret of it. I'd have to be an idiot not to know you don't think much of me."

"I have always admired you."

"Admired? I don't doubt that. The way you admire a powerful car or a useful piece of machinery."

"I didn't –"

"Pushing and prodding and fine-tuning the way you would an engine. You could even overlook that you didn't care for the person, as long as the muscles stayed tuned, the tendons didn't snap, the –"

"God damn it, Kyle! Stop it!"

His roar echoed between them as they stared at each other.

This is what he'll look like when he's old. The irrelevant thought trickled into her mind. When sorrow and joy and experience erode the boyish good looks and leave the essence of the man. *Oh, God, I wish I could be there with him then.*

A nurse, the small French nurse who'd earlier bullied Kyle through dinner, bustled in purposefully, then stopped. Her eyes went from one to the other, before she started more slowly toward Rob.

"Monsieur Zemlak." She circled a calming hand around his elbow and escorted him slowly away. "You must leave now and let our patient to rest."

She opened the door, and started to draw him across the threshold.

"I'm coming back tomorrow." The nurse merely nodded at his belligerent declaration, but then she probably knew as well as Kyle did where the belligerence was directed. He turned back toward the bed. "And I'm going to take you back to your apartment and get you settled in. And then I'm going to check on you each and every day."

"I don't –"

"Too bad. That's the way it's going to be, Kyle."

"Enough. Enough now, the two of you. You, Monsieur will leave. And you, Ms. Armstrong will rest. That will be the very best thing for her." The nurse looked up at the man a foot taller than herself. "You can trust us to take best care of her. She will be quite all right."

Kyle watched the small nurse effectively evict Rob and wondered if she would ever see the humor in that memory. She also wondered if she would ever again be "quite all right."

They hadn't said a word about the downhill part of the combined run today or the medal that might have been hers.

DAY 5 – WEDNESDAY

"LOOK AT THAT," Amy ordered in a harsh whisper. Like the other skaters scheduled for time on the practice rink, she'd changed in the locker room, then had come here to lace on her skates. A group should have been on the ice but a problem with the Zamboni had backed up everyone, and clogged the warm-up area.

Obeying, Tess looked to the far corner Amy indicated.

She had no reason to expect Andrei. He had no cause to be at the practice rink now that his skaters had pocketed their gold medal, much less this early in the morning. And Amy had no cause to sound so disapproving of Andrei.

Still, she must have expected to see him, otherwise she wouldn't have been so surprised to see Xi Ling's entourage.

The Chinese skater, delicate even in the bulky practice tights, a plain skating dress and knit gloves, appeared dwarfed by the down-jacket inflated figures of the two women and three men with her. She kept her eyes lowered while two of the men took turns talking with occasional contributions from the third. One woman remained quiet and still, but the other made fidgeting adjustments to Ling's hair, dress, even bending to twist the tight at her knee.

"The Gang of Five really goes at it don't they, even for a practice."

"Gang of Five?"

Amy didn't take her disapproving gaze from the group in the corner. "Everybody's calling them that."

"Who's everybody and what are they saying about Xi Ling."

"Oh, you know . . . Everybody. In the locker room and, oh, other places. Everybody thinks it's shitty –"

"Amy –"

"– they pick on her so much. She looks miserable. And they won't ever let her talk to the rest of us. I mean, it's not like we're all best friends, and some are real bitchy, but a lot are nice. It just seems a shame."

Amy was too studiedly casual. Tess would have to dig out what was behind this.

But for now that mystery remained less important than Amy's erratic triple lutz. She needed to land that jump to get the scores she needed. Needed to start a reputation. To build a career. To head toward a championship.

"It's a shame if she's unhappy. But you can't know she's unhappy from looking from the outside. And, Amy Catherine, you will not – repeat, *will not* – do anything to interfere between a skater and her coach. Not only would it be poking that nose of yours where it doesn't belong, but it would be horribly unfair so close to the competition."

"I wouldn't butt in or anything. Just –"

"No *justs*. You will leave her alone, and you will concentrate on your skating. Now, let me hear you go through the short program points you're going to work on today."

✧ ✧ ✧ ✧

THE STRAIN OF not looking at Rob was worse than adjusting to the unfamiliar sponginess of her muscles. Not weak, precisely, Kyle decided, but as if they'd forgotten over the past day and a half the finer details of functioning.

"Are you okay?"

"I'm fine."

Why the hell had he insisted on coming to the clinic to take her back to the apartment? She didn't want him here, and he clearly didn't want to be here. It showed in every stiff, awkward parody of his usually lithe movements.

He'd arrived soon after the finish of the combined. He must have left the hill immediately after the last American's final run. The top American had placed tenth. Not bad, but not what the team could have hoped for with Kyle Armstrong skiing.

With more energy than she felt, she crammed the book Nan had brought her in the mistaken belief she might have sufficient concentration to read into a bag Tess had dropped off this morning. Next to it on the bed sat the basket with the remains of the fruit and nuts Rikki had brought, along with a palm-sized teddy bear that had arrived yesterday from Amy.

She reached for the handles, but Rob beat her to them.

"Ready?"

Even his voice sounded strange, as if he had cotton stuffed in one side of his mouth.

"Ready."

"It's a lot of red tape to get a car in the Village and I didn't think you'd want to make a big deal of this, but if you don't think you can walk –"

"It's three blocks. I can walk it." He'd walked it two days ago, carrying her all the way.

"There are benches, so we'll stop so you can rest."

"Like hell. It's three blocks." She walked past him, out of the room and out of the clinic.

With a block to go, he asked, "Are you okay?"

She didn't answer. She would have fallen face down in the snow before she'd told him she wanted to sit. By the time they reached the apartment door, she worried if her hand could guide the key into the lock.

The issue didn't come up. He moved ahead without a word and opened the door with a key from his pocket. She'd find out where that came from later. For now, she concentrated on covering the long narrow hallway to the bedroom without putting a steadying hand on the wall.

Easily overtaking her, he carried in the bag and basket, placing both on the dresser. If he remembered the last time they'd been alone in a bedroom, he hid his feelings about it. His face showed nothing.

He didn't glance anywhere near the bed, or her.

"Get some rest now."

"I'm not tired." She intended to stride past him, but first her knees wobbled like putty, then she caught her hip on the edge of the dresser.

"Are you okay?"

God, if he didn't quit asking that . . .

"Fine. It's just a bump."

Maybe, despite a day and a half of lying in bed, she was more tired than she'd thought. Because it almost looked as if he flinched.

"Look, I thought. . ." He expelled a harsh breath. "I have to turn in these forms, then I'm coming back here to finish up other paperwork, make a few calls. That way if you need anything a little later, you can give a shout. I won't be gone long."

She didn't want him here at all, but didn't have the energy to argue.

"Nan gave me a spare key so if you're asleep you won't have to get up." She'd discuss that with Nan. To him, she said nothing. "I'll be in the kitchen for a few minutes, so if you think of anything you need before I go, let me know."

She said nothing.

"Okay, Kyle?" From his coachlike tone, she knew he'd remain at the door until she acknowledged him.

"Okay."

He left. She could go after him, apologize for her ungraciousness.

What was she thinking? His behavior surely was a temporary aberration. He'd been kind to her before, and look how long that had lasted.

She sat on the edge of the bed, considering whether she had the strength to reach down to remove her shoes.

Besides, he'd been the one so vehement about not being thanked.

RIKKI HAD STOOD outside the locker room exit long enough to wonder if Lanny had found another way out.

The door opened, but none of the three players who emerged and trudged past her was Lanny Kaminski.

She and Lanny had agreed to meet here to go to dinner together before attending the figure skating pairs finals tonight. But that was before she and Amy had watched Team USA absorb its first loss.

Maybe she should have gone with Amy back to the apartment. Maybe he wouldn't show.

The arena door opened again and Lanny emerged, dark brows lowered forbiddingly, in urgent conversation with a player she thought was called Swanson. That was the player whose unwise penalty gave Norway a two-man advantage and the opportunity to score the winning goal in a 3-2 game. But out of uniform she wasn't sure of his identity.

With a half step left before Lanny passed completely without looking at her, she spoke.

"Lanny?"

He finished the step before his head came up and he looked around. For an instant he didn't seem to recognize her.

"Oh. Rikki."

He paused. Swanson took advantage to break into a jog and catch up with the other three players.

"Swanson!" The other player didn't look back. "Shit. I wasn't done with him."

"Maybe you should give the teeth marks a chance to heal?" she suggested.

"What?"

"You know, from you chewing on his butt."

She chuckled, but it dried up under his silence. Rikki surveyed his dour face and wondered if, now that he had shown up, she would wish he hadn't.

"Give the guy a break," she added.

"He doesn't deserve a break. He screwed up. That cost us the game."

She blinked. He's raw from the loss, she excused.

"You're still in good shape to make the medal round."

"That's not the point. We lost when we could have won. We

should have beaten Norway. We had them. We let them go. We should be 3 and 0 in the standings, not 2 and 1."

"You weren't even expected to come close in this game. You should be hap –"

A slashing move of his hand negated the words she hadn't even spoken yet.

"We could have won if we'd played all-out, but people were being cautious, holding something back, already looking to the medal round. They can't do that any more." Amazing. He sounded almost satisfied.

"Swanson played all-out and you're angry at him."

"All-out stupid."

"A penalty doesn't –"

"Not just the penalty. He didn't clear screens, he didn't pass worth shit. He didn't do anything. Why the hell Coach doesn't . . ." He turned his back on her, and she waited a full minute before he faced her way again – not looking at her, but at least they were both headed the same direction. "Well, we're two and one. Swanson and some of the others better straighten up. No more screwups or we'll be out on our asses."

He lapsed into a grim silence that lasted through the first half of their meal in the cafeteria. They had the table to themselves. Anyone considering joining them steered clear once they caught sight of Lanny's face.

And she had plenty of time to think.

Maybe this was the difference between a team sport and a primarily individual sport like biathlon. Sure, biathlon had a team relay, but your relay leg belonged to you alone. You didn't rely on anyone else to clear the course or set your rifle. Besides, she didn't compete in the relay much.

Thank heavens she shook off the effects of not winning a hell of a lot more quickly than Lanny did, or she'd spend a lot of time miserable, since she'd never won a World Cup race. She gauged her performance by other standards – improved time, better placement or a personal best – while Lanny saw only the white or black of win or lose.

Still, when he abruptly started a lecture on the coach's error in strategy against faster-skating teams, a measure of admiration for his ability to focus mixed in to her reaction. When he grabbed a napkin and started diagramming, she almost smiled, though she didn't really follow what he said or drew.

He blindly reached for another napkin, catching her nearly full soft drink with his elbow on the return trip. He uprighted the glass almost immediately, but not in time.

She scraped her chair away, automatically piling napkins on the edge of the table to stop the waterfall. Too late. Soda spread on her white pants in a dusky stain.

Lanny tossed the remaining napkins on the mess, went to the service center in the middle of the cafeteria and returned with a new stack. He handed her dry ones as he sopped up the table.

"Spilled drinks and wet napkins do seem a recurring theme for us, don't they?"

He looked at her, but she could tell plays and defenses still filled his mind.

Then he blinked, his eyes changed and his mouth eased. Not quite a smile, but not the same grim line.

"Like the day we met?" she prompted.

"Not quite," he murmured. He moved her hands away from where she'd nearly finished blotting her pants. Deliberately, he took a fresh napkin and pressed it to the damp material, curving his hand around her thigh in the process. "That day we met I just thought about touching you. I didn't get to really do it."

He dropped the used napkin on the pile on the table and took another dry one. This, too, he pressed to her leg, but considerably higher than where the liquid had landed.

"More like the second day, huh?"

She let out a slow breath when he squeezed, then took oxygen back in as a quick hiss when he stretched his fingers to briefly tantalize.

"Like the second day," he repeated.

"The second day . . . We . . ."

"Your room."

She nodded.

Once inside the apartment, Lanny's hands at her waist urged her forward. But she stopped to read a note from Tess taped to her door, saying she and Amy had left for the pairs finals, and would look for them there later.

"Yeah, later," Lanny muttered, reading over her shoulder. He dropped his mouth to the juncture of her neck and shoulder, mouthing a bite as his hands slid from her waist to her buttocks.

But before she could get the door to her room open, the lock on the main door clicked open, and Nan Monahan came into the hall, her mouth and brows drawn down in concern.

"Oh, good," she said, seeing them. Some of her worry seemed to lift. "Have you guys seen Rob? Is he here?"

"No. Nobody's here except Kyle." Rikki nodded toward the closed door of Kyle and Nan's room. They'd automatically spoken quietly to avoid disturbing Kyle if she was sleeping. "Tess and Amy are at the skating, and we're going to follow them. We just got here ourselves." Nan's frown returned. "What's the matter?" Rikki asked her.

"I hoped Rob had come back here. I wanted to talk to him." She looked from Rikki to Lanny, and seemed to come to a decision. "I ran into a couple skiers who said Rob asked them where Brad Lorrence has been hanging out in town. They said Rob was acting real abrupt, not like himself."

"Went to clean the guy's clock." Lanny sounded more cheerful at that prospect than he had since the game.

"That's what I'm afraid of. I'd hoped to find him here and talk some sense into him. Would you guys mind coming with me to see what's going on?"

"Of course not," Rikki said. "Let me get changed."

"Thanks. I'll go check on Kyle." She turned back. "I, uh, think it would be better if Kyle didn't know. You know, if we didn't mention it. No sense upsetting her."

"No, no sense. You're right."

"I don't know why we can't leave the guy alone," Lanny objected, following Rikki into her room. "I'd rather spend the time in bed with you."

She turned and smiled at him, but then got busy.

"Me, too. But for one thing, if word gets out that Rob Zemlak and Brad Lorrence are feuding there'd be coverage. And if reporters start digging, looking for something on the ski team, how long do you think Kyle's private life will stay private? Not to mention it can't do Rob's coaching career good."

"Rob's not going to thank us."

"Maybe not now, but –"

"Probably not ever. Sometimes you've got to do something, no matter what it costs. It gets like that on the ice some games. But you know that from competing, don't you."

He didn't make it a question, and that was good. Because Rikki wasn't sure if she did know.

HOW HAD IT come to this? How had he let it go so wrong?

Rob had asked himself those questions for days, and found no answers. Maybe he should ask himself how he came to be here, outside the club whose second-story dance floor had become the court for the reigning deities of Alpine skiing. It might be the second or third place he'd tried. He couldn't really remember.

He barely remembered leaving Kyle's apartment the second time. The only thing he remembered clearly was Kyle's face, delicate and pale even against white, white sheets.

After leaving the apartment the first time to drop off the forms, he'd let himself back in with Nan's key. The absolute silence that greeted him cut across his nerves. Opening Kyle's door, seeing for himself that she was all right, simply sleeping, had made sense. Standing by the side of the bed watching her breathe made less sense. Returning to her bedside a second time, then a third between unproductive bouts of paper shuffling made no sense at all.

Once before he'd watched her sleep. But that night she'd been flush with health and satisfaction. She hadn't endured the fear, pain and loss she'd had in one short month of being pregnant.

Pregnant.

He shouldn't have pushed her so hard in training. He should have protected her. He should have . . . done something.

That was the thought that had pushed him out of the apartment the second time and started this manhunt.

Upstairs, he spotted Brad Lorrence immediately. Brad stood with four other skiers. Two Austrians, another American and an Italian. Girls eddied around them like bubbles; if the skiers tired of the general display, they simply scooped one out and examined it more closely.

With no more thought than Brad had given to sleeping with Kyle Armstrong.

Rob barreled through the froth, ignoring the glares at his lack of finesse, and gripped hard around Brad's arm.

"Hey, Coach!"

"I want to talk to you."

Oblivious as always, Brad's grin didn't fade, and his voice showed no puzzlement. "Sure."

A nearby door led to a balcony screened from inside by a row of large potted evergreens. "Outside."

"Sure thing."

Even when Rob gave him enough of an extra shove as they came through the door to cause a slight stumble, Brad simply righted himself with innate grace.

"What's up, Coach?"

Rob pushed tauntingly against Brad's chest. A frown replaced the grin; finally, Brad appeared to realize the other man's anger.

"Hey! What's the matter with you?"

"What's the matter with me? What's the matter with *you*, Lorrence? What's always been the matter with you?" Another shove. Brad backed up a step. "You come down the mountain in one piece because God gave you the body for it. To compensate for having the fucking brain of a jackass." Shove. Retreat. "The fucking morals of an alley cat." Shove. Retreat. "And the fucking conscience of a fucking sewer rat."

Rob shoved again. This time, Brad stood firm.

"I don't know what's the matter with you, Zemlak, but I'm not taking much more of this shit, coach or no coach."

"Good. You don't have to take any more of this shit. You can take this —"

The insults had done their job, they'd prepared Brad for the punch. He tried to stop it, but Rob's fist slid past his block with ease and connected on the side of his jaw.

Brad swung back. He landed a couple blows. One clipped the side of Rob's jaw, snapping his head back. Rob felt only the satisfying jolt each time his fist landed against Brad Lorrence's flesh and bone.

There weren't nearly enough blows to assuage his anger before Nan Monahan and two other people tumbled out onto the balcony. A second later strong arms grabbed him from behind, and Nan stepped between him and Brad, shoving the skier back.

"Stop it. Both of you."

"Me!" Brad grumbled. "I hadn't done a damn thing, Nan, and he starts coming at me like a fucking crazy man —"

Denied his prey, Rob's focus widened enough to recognize another of Kyle's apartment-mates, Rikki Lodge, from the other night. That meant the grip locked around his upper arms probably belonged to that hockey player, Lanny Kaminski.

"Shut up, Brad," Nan ordered.

Rob tried to shake off Kaminski's hold, but now Rikki had also stepped between the two fighters.

"This doesn't do Kyle any good, you know." Her quiet, calm words were worse than any of Lorrence's punches.

He knew that, dammit. If it would have done Kyle any good he would have done a lot more. And a lot sooner.

Maybe Rikki saw that in his eyes, because she nodded to the man behind him, who released him. Rob flexed his arms, working off the tightness of Kaminski's hold.

He didn't look at where Nan was talking to Brad, giving no thought to how she might explain this and barely registering as he walked through the room flanked by Rikki Lodge and Lanny Kaminski, that the party had gone on unabated, the revelers unaware of the scuffle on the balcony.

Pummeling Brad hadn't been for Kyle. Rob didn't deceive himself about that.

This had been for himself.

TESS AND AMY saw the figure skating pairs' final programs from the start. Rikki and Lanny arrived halfway through with a vague explanation of something coming up. They all stayed to the end, watching the medal ceremony with Radja Rastnikova and Vladimir Metroveli receiving the gold as expected.

While they stood on the podium at mid-ice, flanked to their right by the top American pair who had skated to a well-deserved silver and to their left by the graceful Czechs, listening to the anthem and watching their flag raise, Tess couldn't keep her eyes from Andrei.

What was going through his mind? Was he thinking how much things had changed since he'd skated under the Soviet anthem and flag years ago?

She could see only his back and an unrevealing slice of his face, and yet she felt such a river of emotion, of regret and pride, satisfaction and bitterness, sorrow and peace, almost as if they flowed into her from him. Or from her imagination.

DAY 6 – THURSDAY

"SHOOT!"

A corner of Lanny's lip curled as he taunted his opponent. "Go ahead and shoot. You won't get it past me."

Bent slightly at the waist, he lunged with his stick on a raid, just missing his object as his stockinged feet slid on the smooth floor.

"Shut up, Kaminski."

Rikki scooted backwards, the wad of paper subbing for a puck protectively hidden behind her "hockey stick" broom.

"C'mon, shoot!"

This is what she got for asking him at lunch to finish explaining his objection to the coach's strategy from the day before. There went more napkins. But the world could afford to sacrifice a few more napkins for him to cover with hieroglyphics if that would lift this mood. But sacrificing napkins hadn't satisfied him; he meant to sacrifice her.

He'd dragged her back to his room, deprived her of her shoes, outfitted her with a broom – *How come he got to use a real stick?* – found this uncarpeted hallway and demonstrated his point with her taking the role of every member of the opposition, while he filled his position and occasionally one other.

She had understood his point better from the exercise, but now he'd segued into shooting drills, and she hadn't asked a single question that this could be answering.

"Go for broke!"

"I've spent the morning training, while you sat around and

watched film –" Which had succeeded in making him angrier about the previous day's loss. "– and I've got to go back to test skis again this afternoon."

"And I've got a game tonight."

"All the more reason to take it easy this afternoon."

He ignored that. "C'mon, Lodge, shoot."

She gave the paper wad a half-hearted swipe. He returned it in a blink.

"C'mon, you can do better. Go all out. Go for –"

"Broke. I know!"

She faked to one side – deked, he called it – then the other, hooked the escaping wad with her broom and tried to scoot it beyond him. No go.

He stood upright, a considering look in his dark eyes. She didn't care for it. "Lodge, you've got to really want it. Down to your bones. C'mon!"

Of her next six tries, she got two past him.

"Enough! That's enough."

"You giving up?"

"It's your game, not mine. I'd like to see you on the biathlon course. You can't go hell-bent for leather out there. You have to pace yourself or you won't shoot worth a damn."

"I bet I could do it." Just a flick against his competitiveness and he fired up.

"No way. You'd ski yourself dead the first loop and then come in to the range about as steady as an Aspen in a tornado. And any miss means time lost on the course."

"What do you mean?"

"For each miss at the shooting target you have to take one lap on the penalty loop before you get back on the main course – that's in the seven-point-five kilometer race. In the fifteen K, they add a minute to your finish time for each missed target. You shoot four times – prone, standing, prone, standing – five targets each time, so if you can't shoot straight you have twenty minutes to make up. No matter how hell-bent for leather you ski, that's a helluva handicap. So, Mr. Go-For-Broke

Kaminski, biathletes have to pace themselves."

"That's why you like it."

"Because of the balance? Sure. You have to have endurance and strength, and then you have to turn around and have rock-steady concentration. I do like that."

His dark brown eyes seemed to probe right inside her. "So you don't go all out."

"I'd like to see you ski fifteen kilometers, and tell me that's not going all out. By the end your nose drips, your eyes water, your lungs burn and working your legs is like lifting a boulder with spaghetti."

He shook his head. "But not until the very end. Before that, all the time you're balancing it with the need to be steady to shoot. You can't push yourself until you have nothing left. Not until the very end, the last leg."

"That last leg's plenty, thank you," she said with a laugh.

"Hey, Kam! Hi, Rikki."

Mikey Sweet strode down the hall. The person with him peeled off and turned into a cross corridor. Rikki thought it was Swanson; she didn't blame him.

"Hi, Mikey. How are you?"

"Doing great. Went to the bobsled this morning. God, that's weird, all these guys piling into this little capsule, all crammed together, and they call it bobsleigh. But they go fast as hell, I wouldn't mind trying that."

"How about getting faster with your stick, Sweet?"

Tonetti, Swanson, Sweet – if she'd been one of the players Lanny laid into, she would tell him where to shove it. But Mikey gave an abashed smile and said, "I know." Then he added to Lanny, "Bus'll be here in a few minutes to watch the early game – you coming?"

"Yeah."

Mikey looked at her questioningly. "Not me, I've got to get back to the course." She checked her watch. "About now."

"Here, give me that." Lanny took the broom. "I'll get our stuff."

Rikki watched Lanny stride down the hall, purposeful even in such a mundane act.

"Is he always this easy-going?" she asked Mikey, who'd taken the stick from Lanny and stood over it as if lining up a golf putt.

"Naw. He's usually a lot more wound up about a tournament. You've been a good influence on him." He was serious. She gawked, Mikey remained oblivious. "I'm kind of surprised, what with it being the Olympics. But, then I haven't known him to get involved with anybody like this before. So I figure you're the difference."

"He's always like this?"

He looked up, surprised. "Sure. Oh, wait. You mean yesterday and today. Oh, that's because we lost. He hates losing." That seemed to satisfy him and he went back to waggling the stick.

"You don't think he's overreacted? I mean, let's be honest, you guys weren't given much of a chance coming into the tournament of getting out of round-robin play and into the medal round. And you weren't expected to keep up with that team yesterday at all."

"That's experts talking. What do they know? We thought we'd have a chance against them. And we can make the medal round. That's what Lanny's looking at. See, if we win our round-robin group, we play the No. 4 team in Group B. If we finish second, we have to play the No. 3 from Group B. And the top three teams are real tough. Lanny's thinking ahead to that."

"But don't guys get irked with him telling them what to do? I mean, he's not the coach."

"Even when it's the coach you get pissed, but that's usually more at yourself. You just take it out on them because they're the ones telling you. Besides, that's Kam, everybody knows that. And he's usually right. If you wanna get better, you listen. Coach doesn't always like it, but he won't take on Lanny directly. I've heard rumors about the association talking to Kam about being a coach when all this is over. Makes sense."

✧　✧　✧　✧

"WHAT THE HELL do you think you're doing?"

The door into the apartment opening to reveal Rob, startled Kyle, but she recovered sufficiently to drawl, "Well, I'll go out on a limb here – I'm taking dirty dishes to the kitchen."

"You're not supposed to be out of bed."

"Wrong, Dr. Zemlak. I'm supposed to be taking it easy."

He slammed the door, strode toward her, dropped his bag on the floor and tried to take the dishes. He got the cereal bowl, but she held on to the glass.

"Get back to bed, Kyle."

He started for the kitchen, clearly expecting her to obey. She followed him and clanked the glass into the sink.

"I'm not dead! I'm not even an invalid. If I'd gotten injured skiing, you'd be chewing my ass to keep as close to training as I could. When Nan had that last knee surgery you were all over her in rehabilitation like a son of a bitch."

"That's diff –"

"I miscarried, Zemlak. It happens. It's not going to kill me. It's not even going to keep me from training hard and racing. The doctor said I'll have discomfort, but it'll pass. And the sooner I get up and around, the sooner it'll pass."

She watched the struggle in his face, and braced for the next onslaught.

"Discomfort?" he repeated. "You were hurting like hell that night, Kyle. I've seen you in pain. But never like that."

It robbed her of balance, like someone yanking open a door she'd been pushing against.

"It's passed. Getting back on my feet isn't going to hurt me now. The doctor says –"

"Screw the doctor! He didn't see you on the floor that night. He didn't –" He bit it off, pivoted away and turned the faucet on with enough force to splash water out of the sink. He slammed it off, muttering curses as he mopped water off the counter with a towel.

She took a deep breath.

For one evening fifteen months ago she'd seen a relaxed Rob Zemlak, stripped of responsibilities and duties, loving. Since then she'd learned to deal with a cool, distant, demanding Rob Zemlak. This was neither.

"I'm not going to shatter, Rob. I'm tougher than that." *Look at the way I've survived you.* "I'm going to return to training, I'm going to return to racing, as fast as I can. I won't do anything stupid, but I'm not going to sit back and wait."

He turned to look at her. Even with water spatter-marks across the chest of his sweater, he was formidable. The cool gray of his eyes gave away little, but his face seemed drawn tighter, his thirty-four years apparent.

"I decide when you return to racing. And to training, for that matter."

"Don't make me go over your head, Zemlak."

"Don't try it."

Abruptly, he relaxed against the counter, hands cupped around the edges at either side of his hips, his head slightly dropped.

"Look, Kyle, I won't risk you getting hurt. Pushing to come back too fast has ended more careers than I can count."

"I know that. I said I won't do anything stupid."

"There's no chance in hell we'd agree on what's stupid," he said grimly, then held up a hand to stop her rejoinder. "But right now, how about doing me a favor and going back to bed and rest awhile."

"I'm not going to spend all day in bed. There's no reason –"

"There is a reason. I said as a favor, or were you too busy being autocratic Ms. Armstrong to hear that? That's better," he said of her tightly pressed lips. "The reason is somebody's coming in fifteen minutes to deliver a TV for this poor incapacitated skier who's about to climb the walls from boredom. And I'd hate to have the guy see what a liar I am. I played a full violin section about how disappointed she is to miss racing and how sad it is she can't even see her friends compete because there's no TV in her room."

She'd need time to fully absorb this gesture, but for now she started to the door, turning back to say, "Well, at least the part about climbing the walls from boredom was true."

And he almost smiled at her.

DAY 7 – FRIDAY

"C'MON, AMY, THE shuttle's here. If we're going to see ski jumping, we've got to catch this shuttle."

With her first competition the next day, Rikki had no official training scheduled today. She'd done her jog and stretch, plus a run through the course and equipment check. Lanny, too, had a light day. After games three days in a row, the coach held a light morning practice then gave the team the rest of the day off. Although Rikki had caught a mumble from Lanny about looking at tapes later.

In the meantime, Amy had talked them into a trip to the team ski jumping competition.

"I've gotta get something good out of getting up before the sun because some jerk scheduled us for the practice rink at the crack of dawn," she'd told them. "And I figure having most of the rest of the day free is it."

But when they reached the shuttle stop at the communications center, she disappeared inside. With the shuttle in view, Rikki started after her. They nearly collided at the door.

"Hurry up, Rikki, we'll miss the shuttle!" With the advantage of heading in the right direction, Amy sprinted ahead.

Rikki opened her mouth to respond, then gave it up, satisfying herself with poking Lanny, who laughed as they got on the shuttle.

"I can only stay an hour or so," Amy announced once they were settled. "I have to get back to the Ice Hall and, uh, meet somebody later. But you guys don't have to come."

"Okay. Where'd you disappear to, Amy?"

"I checked my e-mail, you know, on the special system here for the Games."

"Great messages, huh?" Lanny speculated deadpan.

Amy gave him a sidelong look and smiled slightly. "One's from, uh, a friend. Well, someone I admire, really, who I sent a message to, and now he sent one back and we're going to talk."

Amy didn't seem to notice she'd let a telltale pronoun slip. It sounded innocent enough – and Rikki thanked God that Tess had the responsibility of keeping track of Amy.

"And the other one?"

"My parents. What time they get in Monday, flight times, the hotel phone number and all that."

"You don't sound very excited."

"Oh, it'll be good to see them, but it's not a surprise like the other message. I knew they were coming. They always come to competitions."

"You're lucky," Rikki said, then wondered why. It wasn't as if she felt deprived, and pointing out their parents' virtues to fifteen-year-olds wasn't her style.

"Aren't your parents coming?"

"No. Dad died three years ago and Mom didn't expect me to make the team so she didn't want to gamble on early cheap package fares. She's never been that interested in my competition, anyhow."

Amy's eyes widened. "Didn't she come to your races and cheer for you?"

Rikki laughed, trying to imagine Arnette Lodge hollering at a biathlon meet. "Mom's never liked me racing. Her idea of a pep-talk is telling me not to get my hopes up too high. She says she hates to see me disappointed. She and Dad used to say they didn't come to watch us kids in school sports or plays or things because they didn't want us to think they had unreasonable expectations for us."

"That's awful," Amy breathed.

It had never seemed as awful to Rikki as it did at this moment, seeing compassion in a fifteen-year-old's eyes. Embarrassment flashed across her.

"I mean – uh, I didn't . . . I shouldn't have said –" Amy's fumbling made it worse.

"No problem, Amy. Don't –

"Hell, Rikki, the only kind of expectations my parents had for me were unreasonable." Lanny overrode both voices. "First time I picked up a hockey stick my father started talking about the National Hockey League's next Bobby Hull. Since I'm not playing for the Stanley Cup, I'll be lucky if he's bothering to watch the games on TV. But I hear Mikey Sweet's family's arrived this morning."

Nodding, Amy took the opening gratefully. "They're taking me to dinner with them tonight to a restaurant that's a couple hundred years old."

They reached the ski jump hill with no more mention of family or parents or expectations.

✧ ✧ ✧ ✧

KYLE WAITED TWENTY minutes after Rikki and Lanny left with Amy, emptying the apartment. Nan had gone first thing for training and Tess had a television interview at the media center. Training would fully occupy Rob.

So why did she keep looking for his familiar walk as she slipped out the building's side door?

She'd thought this through, selecting a loose sweatsuit of unremarkable gray, a face-shading billed hat large enough to stuff her hair into and bland sunglasses. All anonymous, none of it tagging her as a member of the U.S. team. She'd assessed the effect in the mirror. Her own mother wouldn't be able to pick her out of a crowd.

How reassuring is that, Armstrong? Your mother probably wouldn't be able to pick you out of a crowd in your regular clothing.

The first breath of cold air bit into her lungs. It felt good, familiar.

She pulled in another deep breath and took the first, cautious step. Then a second. Longer, more forceful. A twinge squeezed her pelvis, and her muscles clamped in defense. She took the third step anyhow. A fourth brought her to slow jogging speed. A fifth, a sixth. After that she stopped counting the steps.

"TESS."

Andrei's hand on her arm stopped her. The rest of the group flowed past, though Ron Sheffield darted an interested look back at them.

"I startled you."

"I didn't expect to see you here."

His eyebrows rose. "Where would I be?"

"With the pairs competition over, I thought you and your skaters might have headed to Russia by now."

Leaving without a goodbye – again.

The unspoken reminder hung between them. His face remained impassive, but she saw the recognition in his eyes. She waited for him to assure her he wouldn't leave without a goodbye and braced to repudiate the assurance.

"No, we remain here. First, they rest – kick back, Vladimir tells me. He is proud of his American slang. Then to the Worlds in four weeks. We have arranged for them to train in the area for the weeks before the competition. After the Worlds?" He gave a fatalistic movement of his shoulders. "That is why we remain here now."

She hadn't wanted his reassurance, but this cool imperturbability grated.

"Of course. It's an ideal place to feel out the offers for turning pro, isn't it?"

"Yes."

"Perhaps start talking about a TV deal, or hook up with other gold medalists for a special tour. I –"

"Tess."

"– hear that's worked quite well for some of the recent champions and it's certainly lucrative, so –"

"Tess." This time his low voice stopped her. "You are angry at me."

"Angry? No, of course not. Why should I be angry at you for helping your skaters capitalize on their success?"

"Capitalize, yes. To earn, to have money. Isn't that what is done in
America? The American Dream? As you did after you won your gold
medal."

"Oh, I see." Under the calm, her voice rustled with the brittleness
of the past. "So, that's why you passed up the opportunity to come to
the West before, a moral disdain for capitalism?"

"I did not –"

She sailed on. "You must have a difficult time seeing your country
turn toward capitalism. I hadn't realized you lived on a higher plane
than the rest of us. You must have spent years thanking your lucky
stars you escaped the clutches of this money-grubber. I can't imagine
how you stood it those two weeks when –"

He grated something in Russian that stopped her. He stood without moving, but she could feel the effort that cost him as if it were her
muscles clamped tight. His face wore that expressionless public mask.
No, not completely. His eyes went dark with emotions, some unreadable, some clear, like the frustration.

"Tess? Oh, good. Tess, you have to do something!"

Jerked from the intensity of Andrei's eyes, Tess tried to take in the
abrupt appearance of an out-of-breath Amy. More, that Amy had a
tearful Xi Ling in tow and that the party was completed by Denny
Kittrick, half of the United States' No. 2 ice dancing team.

"What on earth –"

"You've got to do something, Tess. That whole pack of people is
after Xi Ling and –"

"Amy, I told you –"

"Please," Xi Ling whispered, trying to back away from the group.
But Amy put an arm around the older girl protectively and drew her
forward.

"I didn't butt in, honest, Tess. But Denny and I heard her crying,
and we couldn't just leave here there."

"Leave her where?"

"Behind the curtain in that little closed-off corner by the Kiss and

Cry area. She was sobbing."

"And what were you doing in that closed-off corner?"

"Uh . . ."

"We really couldn't leave her." Denny gallantly took up the tale, though not, Tess noted, where it left off. "She was crying like crazy and huddled in the corner."

Xi Ling was a sorrowful sight. Her mouth drooped, her cheeks bore the tracks of tears even as more slipped from her swollen eyes. "Please," she whispered again, then added, barely audibly, "Sorry."

"What had happened?"

"We don't know – exactly. But you've seen how they're after her all the time. Anna – you know Anna, the tall ice dancer from England – well, she knows Chinese because her family spent years in Hong Kong, and she says those vultures hanging around her are always telling Xi Ling how she has to do better, that she has to be perfect or she'll bring dishonor on her family and her country."

"Amy, you can't –"

"They're not all even coaches. They're just hangers-on hassling her all the time."

"They're ghouls," Denny Kittrick added.

"Here." Andrei accompanied his first contribution to the conversation with action. He took Xi Ling by the shoulder, gently guided her and the other two skaters toward the men's locker room door. Then he gave Denny a firmer push. "Check. Inside, see if –"

"The coast's clear? Sure." The last word came back to them after he'd slipped inside.

"Andrei, you can't This is –"

He ignored her. Everyone ignored her.

Denny returned to the door, holding it wide and drawing in both Xing Li and Amy.

Tess objected automatically. "Amy –"

"Chaperone!" she responded gaily, and pulled the door closed behind them.

Tess took a step, but Andrei's hand on her wrist kept her at his side. She started to protest, but he wasn't looking at her, and when she saw where he was looking, she subsided.

He drew her around to face him as if in easy conversation, her back to the approaching group. He didn't release her.

She hoped they'd pass by, and she wouldn't have to make any difficult decisions.

Her peripheral vision caught them slowing, considering the multilingual legend on the door that in English read "Men's Locker Room," then turning toward Andrei and her.

"Excuse me."

The speaker's outfit and tag identified her as a member of the local organizing committee. She looked so flurried, Tess felt sorry for her, but looking beyond her to the Chinese officials – now numbering seven – her sympathy shifted more strongly to Xi Ling.

"Have you seen, em, that is, a skater has perhaps become confused in the corridors and lost her way. Have you seen a skater who appeared perhaps, em, confused?"

"No."

Smoothing over the sharp edge of Tess's answer, Andrei said, "A girl? Yes I saw a girl there, at the door."

He gestured down the hall beyond where the group had entered. In the distance, an exterior door let in a square of light. Even before the official translated, heads turned in that direction, and a muttered squabble in Chinese followed. Dissension had definitely hit the ranks.

"Toward the door?" the official asked in English, looking increasingly unhappy.

Andrei nodded. "I wondered. She wore no coat."

The squabble picked up volume and three of the group started toward the door. But one of those remaining made a demand of the translator, and jabbed a finger in Tess's direction, then Andrei's.

"He would like to know how long ago this happened, please." Tess would bet the original included no "please."

"Time? Ah, perhaps five minutes ago. Perhaps a little longer. I was occupied." Andrei offered the answer deadpan, but the translator's eyes slid from him to Tess and back. Her face reflected her conclusion.

As the official translated his answer, Tess tried to ease away, but

Andrei's grip on her wrist remained.

The three who'd gone ahead stopped and called to the others. Three more started slowly in that direction. But the same one spoke sharply to the translator, again pointing emphatically from Tess to Andrei.

"He asks why you saw this girl leaving, when the woman saw nothing."

Andrei's face relaxed into a slight, mocking smile. "That is obvious. To anyone. I face that way. The lady does not look to the door."

The man frowned fiercely at the translation, pivoted and marched after his colleagues. The local official, looking miserable, gave them a hurried thanks, and followed.

Tess watched Andrei's eyes as he followed their progress. Faintly she caught the sound of a door opening, then the voices ceased as the closed door cut them off.

Andrei released her wrist. "They are gone."

Neither of them moved.

"You . . . you never hesitated."

He gave her a look. Enigmatic, unrevealing, and yet she understood in that view of his eyes more of the pressure he must have felt being constantly watched and monitored by Soviet officials than she ever had in those long-ago weeks when she had watched him dodge and escape them to be with her.

She turned her head, aimlessly tracing seams of the hallway's concrete block with her eyes. Yet she knew when he cut across the hall to knock on the locker room door.

A Canadian singles skater opened it a slit.

"Whaddya want?"

"It is safe now."

"What do you mean?" he asked suspiciously.

"Tell Amy Yost that Andrei says it is safe."

"Yeah?" The skater's expression shifted as Andrei remained silent. "Okay." The door closed.

"Oh, for heaven's sake." Tess started toward the door, crossing near Andrei. He put out a hand that stopped her without touching her.

"Let them have their drama. There is no harm in them."

"No harm? How about a nice little international incident?"

"You were not so afraid of risking international incidents at one time, Tess."

When she finally broke the look, she pivoted and took two strides away from the door. Also away from Andrei.

Sounds announced the opening of the door, and Tess turned around, stopping cold.

Xi Ling wore a blonde Dolly Parton wig, overzealous mascara and an outsized white shirt as a tunic belted over her tights. With stiletto heals she might have been mistaken for a lady of the night in certain urban areas. But she wore three pairs of socks and a pair of battered athletic shoes. She clutched a Norway team jacket to her chest and looked timidly from Andrei to Tess.

"We improvised." Amy pointed out the details of the ensemble with pride. "We used Kevin's shirt. Gregorz gave us the belt. And Tomas's shoes, because he has the smallest feet, though we still needed the socks to keep them on. And Ian had his partner's stuff for their exhibition routine so that's how we got the wig. Isn't it great?"

"She's going to kill me," mumbled Ian.

"It's stunning," Tess said. Without thinking, she exchanged a look with Andrei. The humor in his eyes tempted, as always. She turned back to Xi Ling. Even at second glance the weight of blonde curls was startling against Xi Ling's complexion, dark eyes and brows. "But they're gone. A disguise isn't necessary."

"Sure it is. We're going to take her out for an afternoon. Xi Ling just wants some time to relax and have fun. So we all decided –" She gave a wave back to the locker room door where the disguise-contributors stood. "–we'd take her into the town, maybe to an event or two. She's psyched."

Since Tess had heard Xi Ling use two words in English – sorry and please – she suspected Amy of taking liberties with the translation. But for the first time the Chinese girl's eyes shimmered with something other than tears.

The group started to move off. "See you, Tess."

This was crazy. "Amy, you can't —"

Andrei took one step, and cut her off from Amy and Xi Ling, now joined by Denny Kittrick and four other male skaters from as many countries. Automatically, Tess looked up. Holding her look, he pitched his voice to the retreating group behind him. "Be cautious, Amy Yost."

"Sure."

"We'll make sure she gets back to her room by dinner," added Denny.

Amy's giggle came back as the skaters rounded the corner. "And without the disguise."

The two of them stood alone in the hallway now, the moment stretching as they faced each other, three inches from touching. Finally, Andrei stepped to one side, but kept his eyes on her face. "If there is an international incident, I will explain that you tried to stop them, and I prevented you."

She didn't like the light irony in his voice, but she deserved it. She had not been so cautious eighteen years ago. Not even when it had meant his safety. Had she been too sheltered and too naive to see that back then? Or had she realized it at some level, and ignored it in pursuit of her selfish ends?

"What you did – helping Xi Ling – was a . . . a very nice thing to do."

"I am not such an ogre in your eyes then, Tess Rutledge?"

She went stiff, a carving from a single piece of wood, a seamless shield. "I shouldn't have said those things to you, Andrei. I apologize. You are simply trying to do your best for your skaters and yourself. It was unforgivably rude to imply anything else. I apologize."

He gripped her arms; the stiffness worked against her, because it brought all of her into his hold, and her face under the beam of his eyes.

"No apology. I want no apology from you. I want —" His words hit a wall. "I want you, Tess . . ." She thought her heart stopped along with his words. His gaze dropped to her mouth, then returned to her eyes. ". . . I want you to talk to me. That is what I ask of you, Tess. Before these Olympic Games end, I hope you give that to me."

He released her and walked away without looking back.

KYLE WAS AWAKE before the knock on the front door, but felt no hurry to move. Before she could convince herself to get up, she heard the door open and Tess's voice.

The apartment had been empty when Kyle returned from her venture outside. It barely qualified as a jog, much less a run, but she'd been sweaty and eager for the warmth and cleansing of a shower. Afterward, she'd put on clean sweats and switched on the TV to catch up with early events. She remembered finishing an apple and cheese.

The TV was still on when she woke. She pushed herself to a sitting position and noticed the sky had darkened. Good Lord, had she been that wiped out?

That's when she heard the knock at the front door and Tess's voice from the hallway as she answered the door.

"Hello, Rob. Come in. How are you?"

"Fine. I, uh, wondered if Nan was around. I wanted to check something about the course today with her."

"I'm sorry, I don't think she's here. If Kyle's awake now, she might know when Nan'll be back."

"Yeah, she might. I'll look in on her."

The door opened wider, silhouetting Rob against the lighted hall. "You're awake."

She blinked and tried to look alert against the blue-gray strobing of the television screen. "Sure, I'm awake. I'm not an invalid. I don't spend all day sleeping."

"Tess said —"

"I must have drifted off for a few minutes."

"How are you feeling?"

"I'm fine." Her legs felt sore, her pelvis tender and her head fuzzy; it added an edge to her voice.

"Then you don't mind if I turn a light on." He flipped the switch before she could respond and she blinked hard. "Didn't your mother ever tell you about what watching TV in the dark could do to you?"

"No."

He didn't seem to hear that. He advanced into the room, his eyes on her. "You look pale."

"I haven't gotten much sun the past few days."

He ignored that, too. "Have you checked with the doctor –"

"There is no need to check with the doctor. I am recovering exactly on schedule – ahead of schedule." She spaced the words for emphasis. "Everything is all right."

He held her look long enough to make her aware of the facial muscles holding her expression in a glare, then turned to the TV, quietly chattering to itself.

"How's the TV working?"

"Fine." Social politeness was too deeply ingrained to withstand for more than an instant. "Thank you. It was considerate of you to arrange it for me."

"Don't thank me."

She was almost as tired of that refrain as of his asking how she felt. "I heard you asking Tess about Nan. I don't know where she is. Or when she might be back. Have no idea. It could be hours."

He barely seemed to hear. "Yeah? Okay." His attention remained on the screen. "Two-man bobsled. That's great stuff. I rode one once. Sort of like I'd imagine a space capsule. Haven't seen today's runs." He sat on Nan's bed, swung his long legs up and settled back. "Think I'll stick around a while and watch this."

No! She didn't want him here. Didn't want him comfortable and casual on the bed three feet away. Think of something to get him out of here. Something –

The thought snapped off the instant she became aware of his gray eyes fixed on her face.

"Unless you mind, of course," he added, the hint of a question not masking the challenge.

She shrugged, then wished she hadn't. "Why should I? It *is* your TV."

"Yeah." He crossed one ankle over the other and faced the screen. "It is."

DAY 8 – SATURDAY

ROB SAW THE head coach approaching, but finished making a notation on the sheet under his clipboard's waterproof cover. He'd have to remind both Jen Peters and Caryn Salenski about the tendency to take that gate too wide tonight when they went over video from these runs.

"Rob."

"Stephen."

"Missed you at last night's meeting."

"I was there."

"I should have said after the meeting. I had hoped we could go out for a beer afterwards."

Rob shifted his weight to his downhill ski, then back, evening his balance. Stephen Carlisle didn't socialize much with his assistants or athletes, even after a competition. During one was unheard of.

"In fact, I have been hoping to catch up with you the past few days." Stephen added with a dryness just short of suspicion, "You've been a hard guy to catch."

"Busy time. Should have e-mailed me. I check that regularly."

Stephen nodded. "I'll do that in the future."

They watched the next skier, a young Austrian, come down the hill in silence. But Rob knew Stephen hadn't finished.

"What's happening with Kyle Armstrong?"

"She's been ill."

"So you said when you told me she'd pulled from the combined with the flu." Rob looked at the older man. His weather-worn surface gave away nothing. "What I don't hear is how ill."

Silence.

"Do you know, Rob?"

"Yes."

Silence again. This time Stephen met Rob's eyes. "I see. Is it something I should know about?"

"I think, Stephen, that if she wanted you to know, you would." She sure as hell hadn't wanted Rob to know.

The head coach snorted. "What a skier wants me to know and what I *should* know can leave a lot of space between them, Rob. Answer my question."

"No, sir, it is nothing you should know about. Her skiing should be back in form in a week, maybe two after she returns to training."

"A week, maybe two? That's after the Games, even if she trains tomorrow. Do you plan to pull her from the slalom?"

For the first time Rob faltered. "I don't know. She wants to ski."

"What skier doesn't." Some of the stiffness left Stephen's posture, but not his voice. "I leave you a lot of latitude, Rob, because you've shown good sense. I hope you're not going to prove me wrong on this."

Stephen was out of earshot when Rob muttered, "I hope so, too."

RIKKI LUNGED ACROSS the finish line, each breath a harsh price paid to purchase precious oxygen. The Lithuanian racer she'd passed as they started the final hill came in behind her and collapsed into the snow, so close she almost toppled Rikki.

"Looks like top twenty, Rikki!" One of the coaches, Roy Welch, shouted from beyond the ropes. "Personal best."

A volunteer handed her a tissue to wipe her dripping nose and looped an arm around her waist, though Rikki was in no danger of falling.

"Congratulations," the volunteer said.

"Thank you." Rikki grinned, pulling in the air greedily and letting it out, scanning the spectators spread beyond the stands. There'd been people all long the course cut into the side of a mountain. Not bad, not bad at all. Biathlon competition often became an exercise in anonymity in the United States.

She slid into the finish chute, lined on either side by reporters. She recognized a woman from her hometown paper who'd interviewed her at Christmas, her only stop home since training started in earnest in October. The reporter waved her over. Before she got there another voice called.

"Rikki! AP here. How'd your race go?"

"Not bad. The shooting stayed straight, and with no penalty laps I did okay on the skiing."

She gave more details to the hometown reporter, pleased with her strong shooting at a target 50 meters away, talking about the vagaries of this course compared to World Cup events. A little about the altitude; the team had trained in comparable conditions. Then she was free. She skied to cool down, got out of her skis and unslung the rifle. By then she was glad to search out the warm clothes she'd left in the start area, where she'd been one of the earliest to go off.

A trainer draped a jacket around her shoulders as they stopped to cheer Jane North's sprint to the finish, her face tense with concentration and effort. She gave a last burst then crumpled just across the line, her back rising and falling with heaving breaths.

The trainer headed to Jane. Rikki turned to the stands, greeted by the parents, husbands and siblings of her teammates and competitors. Competition held so often in obscurity tended to form a tight-knit group.

"Rikki!"

She heard Amy's call and quickly spotted her in the stands with Lanny, Tess and Kyle. Rikki couldn't remember the last time she'd had her own cheering section.

"Congratulations, Rikki. We heard them say you had a personal best time. That's terrific." Tess smiled as she tugged Rikki down to sit between her and Lanny.

"We watched you shoot," added Amy, holding up a pair of field glasses. "That was awesome."

"Terrific," echoed Kyle. "I've done some cross-country, but to come in from the course and shoot." She shook her head.

"Thank you. And thanks for coming. But should you be out, Kyle?" The skier looked tired despite a tinge of color in her cheeks. Rikki wondered if Nan and Rob had known about this venture.

"Fresh air's good for me."

"It probably is," agreed Tess. "But you can have too much of a good thing too soon. I think I should get these two back. Let Kyle take a nap and maybe get this one –" She put her arm around Amy's shoulders. "– to rest before her ice time this afternoon."

"Aw, Tess. You're always trying to get me to rest."

"And seldom succeeding. C'mon, we better take the next shuttle."

Rikki got congratulations and a hug from each, then Tess, Amy and Kyle were gone, and Rikki realized Lanny hadn't said a word.

"You're quiet, Kaminski. Not exciting enough for you? I know it's not hockey, but . . . ."

"It was exciting."

"Then what is it?"

He turned his dark, intense eyes on her. "You could have done better."

"What?" Like an unexpected right to the jaw, surprise hit before pain.

"You could have done better."

Anger and a tinge of betrayal cut into her. "Since when did you become an expert in biathlon?"

"Biathlon, hockey, it doesn't matter. You held back and played it safe. You shot fine, but you could have skied a hell of a lot harder."

"You're full of shit, Kaminski. You can't do that in biathlon. If you go all-out on the course, you won't be able to shoot and that piles on penalty time. And then, no matter how hard you go at the finish, you can't make it up. You have to pace yourself."

"Pace yourself, yeah. But you have to push yourself, too. Right to the limit, right to the edge without going over. You were nowhere near."

He looked at her, and she suddenly remembered crossing the finish line standing up. Tired, yes, but not depleted of every ounce of energy like the Lithuanian skier behind her, like Jane North and others.

"You don't know what you're talking about." Falling at the end wasn't the hallmark of a good competitor or an all-out effort. Some people did, some didn't. "My coaches – the ones who know – are thrilled with my race. Where do you come off? You don't know anything about biathlon."

Wrapping his fingers around her chin, he made her meet his intense, demanding eyes. "I know you, Rikki. And I know you don't come anywhere near going all-out. In anything. You're too busy playing it safe."

She jerked free. "You don't know me. You don't know anything about me. A week, and you think you know me?"

His hand dropped to his side, the palm slapping his thigh with a sound that made her wince. He opened his mouth as if to say something, then closed it with a snap and walked away.

Rikki shivered in the cool air, then joined the team for the shuttle back to the Athletes Village, amid congratulations on her personal best.

✧   ✧   ✧   ✧

ARMS CURVED, AMY pivoted in grounded pantomime of a jump, took two steps and caught her right toe in the seam of the padded floor. "Damn!" She kicked at the floor.

Tess pushed off from the wall she'd leaned against for the half-hour of Amy's walk-throughs, but before she could take a step, the girl headed across the open floor. The warm-up room was a converted hallway, any wall space not interrupted by doors held mirrors. Six weight machines occupied one corner. In the space left open a woman skater from Italy continued her dry run, concentration untouched when Amy marched past and snatched a towel from near Tess.

"Three more run-throughs, Amy."

"I need a break."

Tess considered the girl's downcast face. "All right," she said slow-

ly. Off-ice work had never been Amy's strong point. Especially not
when she had to pit her concentration against the blare of music from
the ice, where ice dance couples held a final practice before the
evening's competition. "Take a break. Then the rest of the run-
throughs – fully focused."

Pulling on a warm-up jacket, Amy started away.

"Amy."

"All right." She didn't look back.

"She will be all right." Andrei put a hand on Tess's shoulder. She
jumped. "I did not mean to frighten you."

Tess's hand dropped from over her heart. "You didn't frighten me,
you startled me. I didn't see you come in."

"No." His gaze followed the direction Amy had gone. Through the
doorway they could see she had joined a clot of spectators watching
the practice. Amy's head turned, tracking one skater on the ice.

"She needs to follow through on her motion, each stroke, each
gesture. To finish, to draw out the movement as you did." Andrei
faced Tess. "But you know that, do you not?"

"Yes, I know it." In just a few times of seeing Amy skate, he'd hit
on the flaw that most concerned Tess. "I can't count how many times
I've told her to sustain a move."

"She is impatient. It cuts off her line, gives her skating a choppi-
ness the judges will not overlook."

His hand on her elbow eased her down next to him on the bench
of a nearby weight-lifting machine. She sighed.

"Amy has so much energy. I knew that, but this week, in close
quarters with her in the apartment, has really brought it home. Like on
the ice, when she barely finishes one thing before she's ready for the
next. It's so hard to get her to slow down. The year before last was
torture. She grew so fast, I wanted her to back off on skating rather
than risk damage when her bones were still changing. I practically had
to ban her from the rink.

"And on top of that, the extra height changed her center of gravity,
her balance, and she was so frustrated. It didn't fully come together for
her until early this fall. Her confidence hasn't been tested. I worry –"

That admission brought her up short. What was she doing babbling to Andrei about Amy? Revealing worries.

Being human. She hadn't talked like this about Amy to anyone.
Not to any of her assistants at the rink, not to the Yosts, and certainly
not to rival coaches. But Andrei wasn't a rival, yet he understood as
only a fellow coach could. Just look at the way his comments had
tapped into her concerns.

She turned toward him, and found him watching. No doubt he
learned more from his study of her than she did from his expression.

"I worry," she repeated deliberately, "about her program. If I'd
known in the fall that she had a shot at third at Nationals, of coming to
the Olympics, I would have gotten a choreographer." The words came
easier. "That's never been my strong point. I designed this program to
teach her, to make her stretch."

"It teaches her. I see that as she skates."

"But it doesn't mask her weaknesses, showcase her strengths the
way one by a top choreographer would have done. That's what
everyone else's program here will do. Like you did with Vladimir and
Radja. You were always good at that."

"How do you know I made their program?"

"It looked like you," she said simply.

He nodded, once. Accepting the compliment, the observation or
the memories?

"You are right. I did. For later, you are right about Amy. You are a
good choreographer. But your style, your strengths are not hers. You
know grace, she is energy. While you teach her grace, you can yet find
someone who can turn Amy's energy to an advantage with a program
designed for her."

"But not now."

He nodded again, agreeing. "There is no time."

"No." She sighed. "But I wish she could have more ice time to
work on the programs she has now. It's so limited here." She gestured
to the ice visible through the doorway. A new set of ice dancers had
taken over. "The top two American skaters aren't even in the Village.
Becca Stanelli left right after the Opening Ceremonies and Sherri

Rockford hasn't set foot here. They're both squirreled away somewhere with all the solitude and ice time they could want. But we didn't
have that luxury, so Amy's bouncing off the walls – no ice, no rest."

"I can do nothing for the rest, but I can give you ice."

"How?"

"Do not look so doubtful at me, Tessa. I would not make an offer
I could not make true. I rented time at a rink one half hour drive from
here for Radja and Vladimir. They practiced there before the competition. They go each day while we are here, talking as you said about 'the
deals.' But they do not need it so many hours each day. We can arrange
for Amy to go there." He lifted an eyebrow. "You object that she
might see Vladimir some times, perhaps stir that girl's crush?"

"No, I'm not worried about that." She nodded to where Amy
stood next to Denny Kittrick. "I wish I were."

"You are not relieved she no longer cares for Vladimir?"

"I don't know. In a way, having her mooning over Vladimir
Metroveli was safer. He was older, distant and he has a partner, so –"

"He has a fiancee, a woman who loves him."

She ignored his distinction. "And his event's over so he's not
around as much. But Denny's here and he's closer to her age, and he
seems to notice her back, God help me."

He smiled at her. So often only his eyes and an easing of muscles
in his face betrayed his amusement, but now he allowed himself a full
smile, widening his generous mouth, revealing his straight, white teeth.
She wanted to smile back. She didn't.

"I can't wait until her parents get here."

"When is that?"

"Monday."

"The stories some coaches have of parents are tales of horror. That
parents want to rule the skater and coach the coach. That worry," he
added dryly, "they never worried in the old Soviet system."

Eighteen years ago he'd said he hardly saw his parents. Had that
changed after he'd stopped skating? Was he close to them now? Were
they near retirement, looking forward to leisure? Or infirm, a source of
worry for him?

"Some parents are horrors," she said, talking fast enough to stop her questions from slipping out. "I've been lucky so far, and I've worked hard to be lucky. I make the lines clear on who's responsible for what, who rules what area of the skater's life – I have final word on anything that deals with the ice. My only real problem was one mother who wanted to turn her twelve-year-old into a burlesque queen. But the Yosts are great. Supportive, but not intrusive. Maybe because they have three more besides Amy, and they're just too busy."

He didn't join her laugh, but studied her with his expression unreadable.

"Why have you not had children?"

Stunned, she blurted, "I'm not married."

He didn't ask why she hadn't married. That would be the natural question. Instead he continued to study. Did he think she'd spent all this time mooning over him? Not marrying because of him?

"I was involved with someone for five years. We lived together." Andrei's focus slid from her to the doorway, leaving her his profile. "He's a wonderful man, and I still love him in many ways. We talked about marriage. It just didn't work out." She hadn't meant to bring up Will. Or maybe she had. She did want Andrei to know her life had gone on. "He didn't want children . . ."

The placid blue of Andrei's eyes refracted some emotion for too brief a second to read, and disappeared.

Now she knew why she'd backed away from asking questions about his parents. Such questions – and, even more, their answers – formed a bridge to the past. But the past was just that, and she didn't want it linked to the present. She wanted it left. To keep Andrei Chersakov filed there.

His gaze returned to her and she braced, but all Andrei said was, "So Amy's parents arrive on Monday."

"Yes. Monday."

"Good, then you will have time. We can do things. We can plan. First, when you bring Amy to skate at this place I have found."

"I don't know if this is a good idea –"

"You would deny young Amy the time to skate?"

"No, but –"

"Then that is settled."

"Andrei, I want to be clear about this. I don't want you to think –"

The smile returned full force, stopping her. "You think it is an accident we are in the same place, same time so often?

"You've followed me?"

He ignored the accusation in her voice. "I said I want you to talk to me, Tessa. I will make sure I am there when you are ready."

DAY 9 – SUNDAY

"AW, C'MON, TESS. Team USA is playing the earlier game. It'll be over by eight-thirty."

"No, Amy. You've been going full-tilt since the moment we got here, and you were out late last night with the Sweets. I don't want you to be a zombie when your parents arrive tomorrow. Besides, at this rate you won't be able to stand up on the ice by Wednesday, much less jump."

"It's four in the afternoon. I can't sleep now."

"I'm not saying to sleep right now. But you *do* have to slow down."

"I will. Later."

"You want to go to the ice dance finals tomorrow night, don't you?"

Pink sprinted into Amy's cheeks. "Of course. But Mikey's playing tonight."

"And he'll play again the day after tomorrow."

"But they can clinch a spot in the medal round —"

"The outcome will not hinge on whether you're there to cheer."

"But Rikki's going, aren't you, Rikki?"

Ever since Rikki had wandered into the kitchen a few minutes earlier, Tess had expected Amy to make that appeal. Tess had dealt with enough youngsters as a coach to know the "everybody's doing it" ploy. She hadn't expected Rikki's hesitation and the stiffening of her back as she bent for a bottled water from the fridge.

"Uh, no."

"You're not? Why not? You always go to Lanny's games." Amy

made it sound as if Rikki had personally called off Christmas.

"Not today. I decided to rest myself. Training's been tough and I've got another event coming up."

"But not for days and days. What –"

"Amy –" Tess caught her charge's eye, then went on smoothly. "Since we're all staying in this evening, why don't you see if Nan and Kyle are interested in making some popcorn and –"

"Watching the game on TV," Amy picked up. She flicked another look at Rikki, but didn't pursue that. "I've got to watch it on TV if you won't let me go."

"It's all right with me. But check with Kyle and Nan first. Rob got the TV for Kyle, not you."

"Okay."

Amy bounced out of the kitchen, leaving it very still.

"How about you?"

Rikki turned at Tess's quiet question. "How about me what?"

"Is watching the game all right with you?"

"Sure. That's fine. No problem for me. I'll even make the popcorn. I'm known as a pretty fair popcorn maker. It's all in the wrist. Shaking the pot."

She started opening doors in search of a pot. It would have been more convincing if she hadn't opened the narrow spice cabinet door and the silverware drawer.

"Rikki."

"We have popcorn and olive oil. You just need a splash at the bottom when you do it right."

Amy appeared at the door for that final speech. "Great. Everybody says fine and we're setting up seats in Kyle's room. So, bring on the popcorn."

"Ready in five," Rikki said to Amy's retreating back.

"You had a fight with Lanny, didn't you?" Tess's question stopped Rikki with a cabinet door halfway open. "I won't say anything more, but if you need someone to talk to . . . Well, I know with all the hubbub and pressure and living here away from your friends and teammates . . . So if you want to talk, even though I'm a virtual stranger –"

"You're not a stranger, Tess." She closed the cabinet door. "I don't think any of us are. Maybe we were before Kyle had the miscarriage, but we're definitely not now. Definitely not strangers, and I'd like to think we're at least on the way to being friends."

"Yes. That's why it's hard to see you hurting."

Rikki shook her head. "Not hurting – confused."

She pulled a pot out of a lower cabinet and put it on the stove, then stared at it with unfocused eyes. Tess went to the refrigerator for the popcorn Nan had bought, and put it on the counter.

She didn't necessarily buy Rikki's word substitution, but she would use it. "Confused?"

"I'm not used to this. It happened so quickly, this thing with Lanny." She gave an awkward laugh. "Listen to me, *this thing*. I never talk like that. But I don't know what to call it. Can you have a relationship with someone you've known a week – a real relationship? I don't know. I've never gotten involved with anyone so . . . so instantly, so intensely. From that first day we've hardly been apart except for training or competing."

Her voice faded on the last word, but picked up when she continued. "We probably both need breathing room. I know I do."

Rikki retrieved the oil, and set about making the popcorn with confident, decisive movements. Tess imagined she could see the other woman's attitude solidifying around her last words, convincing herself it was best if she and Lanny Kaminski went their separate ways.

Still, she felt the need to try.

"Don't dismiss your feelings simply because they came fast, Rikki," Tess said. "Sometimes the heart knows what it's doing before the head has any clue. I'm not saying the heart's always right when it falls fast. But it's not always wrong, either."

Rikki stopped, pot in one hand, the other holding the lid slightly ajar as steam drifted up to the ceiling.

"That smells great." Amy burst back into the room, releasing Rikki from her reverie.

"Slow down, girl," Rikki advised. *Thank you*, Tess thought. *Maybe it will sink in coming from someone else.* "Here's the first batch. I'll make a second now because this'll go fast, if I do compliment the chef myself."

"But the game's starting."

"Why don't you take that in, Amy. Rikki and I'll bring the second batch and some drinks."

"Okay." And she was gone.

Rikki started the next batch without turning around, but the single word she said was distinct. "Andrei."

"What?"

"I said *Andrei.* That's why you said my heart was smarter in falling for Lanny than my head's logic – because that's what happened with you and Andrei."

"I didn't say you should fall for Lanny. I said might – you *might* be having true feelings even if they came fast. That's what I said."

Rikki took her hand off the pot cover, which teetered as she shook the pot, then settled after she'd waved Tess's objection away.

"You fell for Andrei years ago, in the sixteen days of the Olympics. Your first Olympics, when you were eighteen and –"

"How do you know –"

Another wave silenced Tess and threatened the popcorn. "And now, being with him again, you're facing those feelings. You can't dismiss them as a kid's infatuation because you're feeling something now, too. Right? No, don't answer that. It's none of my business. I shouldn't be so nosy. I'm sorry. I really shouldn't –"

"Yes, I fell in love with Andrei Chersakov eighteen years ago."

My God, to say the words out loud. She closed her eyes against the rush of memories and emotions. Sorrow, joy, anger, peace.

"I've never told anyone . . ."

Rikki moved to put a comforting arm around her, but Tess held it off with a gesture. She had to hold together now.

"We met at a competition two months before my first Olympics. Met? No, we saw each other. In those days the Soviet Union kept their skaters closely watched. But we saw each other, and I knew – I *thought* – I saw in his eyes what I felt. We talked, oh, maybe five minutes in a hallway, with other skaters around us, jostling and congratulating him because he and his partner had won the pairs. Then a Soviet official came and I didn't see him again until the Olympics.

"It was easier there. With so much going on, he could slip away more often and we were together almost every day. I was so in love, so sure everything could work out. I was so certain he would defect at the Worlds the next month and we would be together."

"Together?"

Tess met Rikki's wise eyes. "Permanently, I mean. You're right, we'd already been together. He was my first lover."

How strange to be talking about all this after so long. Strange and . . . somehow it made those long-ago events more vivid and real than they had been for many years.

"When Andrei and his partner took the silver, I thought my heart would burst. They should have had gold, but skating was even more rigid then than now, and a more established pair won gold. I was a newcomer, not expected to do much, but because of what I felt for Andrei, I skated the best long program of my life . . . the best of my life."

Tess drew in a breath. She took a tray from atop a cabinet and began retrieving glasses to fill with ice.

"What happened, Tess?"

"He went back to Moscow after the Olympics, as we'd planned. But instead of coming back to . . . instead of coming to the Worlds and defecting, he married his partner. I didn't know about it until they didn't show up for the competition. News didn't come out of the Soviet Union in those days. All anybody knew was they'd stopped skating. And with no skating, they didn't get out of the country any more."

"You never found out why and you never saw him again until now?"

She shook her head. "I didn't hear from him. Not a word. And I didn't see him until here."

"Sounds like you have to decide now if you're going to forgive or forget."

"Don't you mean forgive *and* forget?"

"No. I figure if you can forget Andrei Chersakov, you don't have to bother to forgive him. But if you can't forget him, then you better find a way to forgive or you're going to drive yourself crazy."

"Forgiving isn't all that easy. You see, he didn't hurt only my pride or my heart. He hurt my skating. What I wanted to do most in the world. The talent I had to offer." She looked down at her hands, then met Rikki's clear eyes. "I never skated as well afterwards."

"But you won a gold medal, world championships."

Stubbornly, a little sadly, Tess said, "Yes, but I never skated as well as I did that night when I still believed in him."

The popcorn was long made, the drinks loaded on a tray, but neither moved toward the door.

"Because Andrei left you?"

"Yes."

"Aren't you looking at it backwards?"

"What do you mean?"

"Maybe all those other times it was your ability, your talent carrying you. But that one time you skated above your talent because Andrei loved you. Maybe he gave you that night, not took away something all the other nights."

ROB ARRIVED IN the second period.

He didn't even offer a lame excuse about needing to check something with Nan. He simply walked in and joined the group watching TV and eating popcorn. He took a seat on the floor, dropped a pillow behind his back and contributed a bit of commentary on the U.S. hockey game. Everyone accepted it as perfectly natural. Only Rikki seemed on edge, and Kyle figured her nervousness was because minute after minute ticked by without either hockey team scoring.

But Rob's easy-going behavior was an aberration of a few days' duration, weighed against fifteen months.

He joined the shouting when Dan Christopher knocked in a goal off an assist by Mikey Sweet, with barely two minutes left in the game. And he stayed as tense as the rest of them until the final seconds ticked off, and they all flopped back in relief and celebration.

"Medal round! They're in the medal round!" Amy shouted and pumped her arms in the air, and they all joined in the excited talk about how the team might fare against possible opponents in the next round.

All expect Rikki, Kyle noted. When the game ended in victory, her eyes teared up and she wore a can't-stop smile, but that didn't last. An hour after the interviews and postgame commentary, even when they'd made another batch of popcorn and the TV shifted to the day's other highlights, Rikki remained edgy. Jumping up whenever anyone needed anything, tapping her fingers on her thigh.

Kyle was relieved when Rikki finally stood up and mumbled, "Uh, I've got an errand to run."

She saw Tess and Rikki exchange a look as Rikki left, and hoped the look and the excuse meant what she thought they meant.

If someone looked at her the way Lanny Kaminski looked at Rikki Lodge, she'd be running errands, too.

Or maybe not. Not that kind of errand, not for a while yet, she thought with a tinge of humor.

She shifted against the bolster of pillows behind her, and felt a surge of satisfaction. No pain. Gradually, she was learning to trust her body again, to believe it wouldn't betray her any second.

In a lot of ways she felt better than she had in a long time. More rested, more at peace. More cared for.

She looked toward Rob. Mostly she saw the top of his head, the thick shining brown hair, wind-tousled as always. Only a slice of his face was visible, but she didn't need to see his expression; his posture told the story. He sat on the floor, his back propped against the side of the bed, one leg bent to support his elbow, the other stretched out.

Why couldn't she be that relaxed?

Because he had a lot to do with that 'cared for' feeling.

He'd been good to her these past six days. She admitted that. But she couldn't afford feelings other than polite gratitude. She couldn't rely on him. Worse, she couldn't risk falling for him again. He made that hard when he was being warm and generous. So much easier with the cold, distant Rob Zemlak.

Well, what she had to tell him tonight should take care of that.

THE TROUBLE WITH being a thirty-two-year-old on a team with a mean age of twenty-four and a mental age Lanny Kaminski often estimated at a decade behind that, was you felt damn old.

Not just the sore muscles, he thought as he let hot water beat on his head and sluice down his shoulders, onto his back, around his buttocks until it became a warm trickle down the backs of his thighs. He didn't like to take out the soreness in the locker room – no sense giving the coach any excuse to hold him out – so he saved these therapeutic showers for the privacy of his room in the Village.

The beat of something electronic, loud and devoid of melody reverberated from across the hall, through the walls of the bathroom and into the shower until the very water seemed to pulse with it. But the music didn't divide him from the rest of the team, either.

The Olympics did, what these eight games meant.

To these kids it was a beginning, a way to introduce themselves to the hockey world on the most dazzling of stages. A first step on a stairway they could only see carrying them to Stanley Cup trophies and National Hockey League most valuable player bonuses.

To him, it was not merely a last shot, but the only shot.

He wasn't going to make it to the NHL again, not even for the end-of-season stints he'd had a couple of times in his twenties. When these Games ended, so did his competitive career.

In a way, it was a miracle he'd held his aching, battered body together this long. That's what the team trainer called it, anyhow. At least in his complimentary moods. Other times he called it sheer stupidity.

Lanny called it making the most of what he had. Going for broke.

Bad luck, bad timing, bad injuries. He'd had them all. What he hadn't had was the success he knew in the burning center of his gut that he was capable of.

That's what pissed him off so badly about Rikki not using every ounce of the ability she had. Wasn't it?

Rikki. The thought, that's all it took, and his body, no matter how battered or old, tightened in response. In delight, in anticipation.

Shit.

Stepping out of the shower to a verse of curses, he wrapped a towel around his waist, as if that would deny his arousal.

He shouldn't have pushed. He knew about those times you needed to hang back and let a play develop instead of pushing it up the ice. But he'd sure as hell pushed with Rikki.

So what if she held back?

Opening the bathroom door, cool air poured in along with the recorded noise from across the hall. Tonetti must have left the hall door open, damn his irresponsible soul. Well, at least the cool air cut down the heat building in his groin.

He stopped dead on the threshold.

"Hi."

He hadn't realized he was afraid until he saw her standing in his room, shifting her weight from one foot to the other, within bolting distance of the door. God, Rikki . . . Shit, yes, he'd been afraid. Afraid when he walked away from her. Afraid when he wouldn't let himself go to her. Afraid when he didn't see her at the game.

Afraid because she was the type to be cautious, to hold back. And he didn't think he could be the same way, not with her.

His throat felt thick with a fear he hadn't admitted until this moment, when there was no more need for it, so he said nothing.

"Uh, Tonetti told me you were in his room – I mean, your room, both of yours room." From her coloring cheeks he figured Tonetti also said something about the number of nights this room had been a single. "He said, um, it would be all right to wait for you here."

She wore a sweater over a silky turtleneck that showed at throat and cuffs. The bulk of the sweater hid most of her curves. The turtleneck wouldn't. He knew that. As he knew how her hair would fall in a tangle after she pulled off the sweater – or he did. As he knew how her skin felt when the turtleneck, too, was gone.

"Is it?" she said.

"Is it what?"

"Okay to wait here."

"Guess that depends . . ."

He moved three feet to his left and gave the door a swat without looking at it. When it slammed closed, she flinched, but didn't retreat.

". . . On what you're waiting for."

He moved in front of her. Her breath, not quite regular, stirred the still damp hair on his chest. But he didn't touch her.

She took a deep breath. "Lanny, I . . ."

Her words held danger, he knew that from her tone of warning. He didn't want to hear it. "What are you waiting for, Rikki?"

"I —"

"What do you want, Rikki?" It came out harsher.

And miracle of miracles, those clear, clear eyes of hers came up and met his.

"You. I want you."

He took hold of the hem of her sweater, then paused.

Never taking her eyes from his, she slowly raised her arms. One quick move and the sweater was over her head and gone. Static electricity caught tendrils of hair, twisting them around each other, around his fingers when he curved a hand to the back of her head. It molded the turtleneck to her body. It crackled when he slid his hands underneath, too greedy for the feel of her skin to wait.

The touch didn't satisfy his greed. Pressing against her body, he nudged her toward the bed.

"Door — the door, Lanny."

"Tonetti won't be back." Not if he valued his life.

"Somebody could come."

"I'm counting on it."

He felt the laughter ripple through her as an echo in his own muscles and bones. She nipped at the side of his neck, then soothed the tingling spot with her tongue, and a different ripple went through him.

"Not in public," she said.

"Too uptight to make a public scene, huh?" Even as he asked the question, he took a step toward the door, keeping one arm tightly around her waist. The lock shot home, and he swung back to wrap her in both arms.

"Public, yes." She pulled his head down to hers. "But private . . ."

He swept the equipment bag, dirty clothes and papers that littered his bed to the floor with one arm, and guided her down with the other. His towel went next. Her clothes took longer, but not much. The packet of condoms in his jeans was too far away, but he knew Tonetti; he yanked open the drawer of the bedside table and grabbed.

He knew her body by now, he knew her reactions, how to please her. It was his own reactions he didn't recognize. From the first time he'd kissed her they'd seemed exaggerated, almost alien. Frightening and intoxicating to want a woman this badly. And powerful enough to soon obliterate anything like thought. Leaving only the need, the driving need.

He took the sounds of her pleasure, holding them in the intimacy where mouth joined mouth, at the same time his body drove her to cry out loud.

Later, after they'd made love a second time, in the spartan confines of the shower, he leaned back against the slick wall, eyes closed, and held her against him, letting the water pour over both of them.

"What?" she asked.

"What, what?"

"You made a sound just now. What did it mean?"

Without opening his eyes, he gave a wry grin. "It means I don't do things like this, Rochelle Lodge."

She chuckled, and he opened his eyes to discover her looking around at their surroundings as if seeing them for the first time.

"Me either, Kaminski."

"First time in a shower, huh?"

"As a matter of fact, yes. Just like you said, I definitely don't do things like this."

He slid his hands over her wet skin. They'd find other first-times together. But he hadn't meant sex. He'd meant needing someone.

✧ ✧ ✧ ✧

"BEFORE YOU GO, Rob . . ."

Kyle's opening caught everyone's attention.

Perhaps because Rob had shown no sign of leaving. But Tess had made a comment about Amy getting to bed, the group could break up any minute, and Kyle wanted the buffer of other people around. She wished she had a buffer from his searching look, too.

"What is it, Kyle?"

He had been good to her these past days. They'd even reached a kind of truce that wouldn't have seemed possible two weeks ago. But the cost of peace was too high. He had to stop feeling sorry for her soon. And she needed the mountain. Things had to go back the way they'd been.

"I'm returning to training tomorrow —"

"Kyle —"

She ignored Nan's worried whisper. She didn't take her eyes from Rob, though she was aware of everyone else frozen in place.

"And I intend to race Friday."

"You don't know what you're letting yourself in for."

The very flatness of his tone ignited her anger.

"I know better than anyone else. Even better than the all-knowing Zemlak." He got to his feet. For an instant, she thought he would walk out. Ignoring the rock that fell in her gut, she went on. "In fact, I'm the only one who can know, because I'm the one inside this body."

He glared at her, and she met it.

A mutter under his breath had the tenor of a curse. He jerked around and started off, but only to the window. He stood with his back to the room, hands jammed in pockets.

"It's crazy."

"It's not crazy, Zemlak, and you've got . . ." She let the immediate fire of her words cool off as she caught looks from Nan and Tess. Nan added a shake of her head and a palm-down gesture to cool it. Kyle took a deep breath and started again. "Rob, I feel fine. Really. I've been jogging the past three days —"

That spun him back to face her. "You've what!"

"And I haven't had any problem." A little pain yes, but no real problem. And less discomfort each day.

"The doctor said –"

"The doctor said I should take it at my own pace. That's what I'm doing. It's not like I'm demanding to go in the giant slalom Tuesday, because I know it would be pushing to race after two days back training. But with the slalom, I'll have four full days of hard training."

"That's not enough."

"It is enough. I was in great shape before . . . before. A couple days will get me back. I'll be ready."

"And the rest of it, will you be ready for that?"

"Rest of what?"

"Do you think you can disappear the day before the race you were a contender to medal in, then waltz back into the public eye a few days later and not face a barrage of questions? Are you ready for that? Are you ready for all the questions about the exact nature of your illness, Ms. Autocratic Armstrong? And the cameras and microphones shoved in your face, not to mention the looks and whispers?"

"It's none of their business where I was."

He tossed his hands up – in disgust, not acceptance. "You go and say that to those reporters, especially in that silver-spoon tone of yours and there won't be one that won't dig until their fingers bleed to find out all the details – and I do mean all. It doesn't matter that it's none of their business. How are you going to cope with that?"

Only the mutter of the TV announcer broke the silence.

She looked at Nan, then Tess, and saw in their faces the confirmation of what Rob said. She looked to Amy, who gave her a small, worried smile.

"I'm going to ski."

He turned away again, hands jammed once more in his pockets. She tried to explain to his back.

"If that's the price to ski, I'll pay it. And what difference does it make if it's now or a few weeks when I return to the World Cup? The questions will be the same, worse if I hide for the rest of the Olympics."

"It's not the same spotlight on the World Cup, you know that." He sounded remote, the austere Coach Zemlak. "There's not the same amount of coverage. You won't have the world's TV cameras on you like here."

"But, you know, that might work to her advantage." As she went on, Nan picked up speed. "If Kyle does a slew of interviews and tells everybody all about how she's had the flu, it won't be much of a story, because, let's face it, the flu isn't glamorous or exotic. And there're lots of stars here competing for reporters' interest. Besides, everybody will know exactly the same thing and have exactly the same tape. A passing human interest story maybe, but pretty boring, really."

"I think Nan has something there," added Tess.

"Thanks, both of you. You think I'll be so boring reporters won't want to have anything to do with me?" she said with light irony.

"Don't let your ego get in the way here, Kyle," Nan advised, a glint in her eyes. "The idea is to send the reporters on their way, not wow them."

Tess smiled. "I think Kyle will wow them no matter what. You know, I can't help thinking about Dan Jansen and Kurt Browning at the Albertville Olympics."

"American speed skater and Canadian figure skater, right? But I don't get the connection," Nan said.

"Both were expected to do very well and both were built up by the media, especially TV, and especially Dan Jansen because he'd had two terrible falls at Calgary four years before, after his sister had died."

"Oh, yeah," Nan said. "TV built it up that the '92 Olympics would mean some sort of redemption for him."

Kyle figured her friends were talking at least partly to cover the silence emanating from Rob.

"That's right. He didn't duck questions. He just kept saying with great patience and dignity that he didn't need to prove himself. When he didn't win at Albertville, he got more questions about how he felt about this horrible disappointment. He said, yes, he was disappointed, but it wasn't a tragedy. And Kurt, too, when he'd been built up as the big favorite, then had a disappointing finish, didn't hide. He talked about mistakes, acknowledged his disappointment, but said it wasn't the end of his world."

"Maybe I'm dense, but what's the connection to Kyle?"

"It seems to me that by responding with patience and dignity, these two athletes kept their situations from being blown out of proportion."

Rob turned around, but didn't look up or speak. He propped his hips against the windowsill, propped his forearms on his thighs and stared at his hands.

"I think I see," Kyle said. "If they'd hidden away or blown up or said it's none of your business, it would have been an even bigger deal. So they made the best of it."

"Right. And in the process they made a good impression on hundreds of thousands of people who watched."

"I think you're right, Tess, and I'll try my best." But she wouldn't like it. "So I guess I should call a news conference for tomorrow. Or should the coach do that?"

Nan cut a look to Rob's grim face. "Ask the media people to set it up. They'll know what to do. Say you want to take care of all those requests in one session."

"Right. So, everything's all set."

Everyone looked at Rob. He continued to look at his hands.

"Well, Amy. it's time you headed to bed." Tess efficiently herded her charge out, picking up a popcorn bowl and two glasses on her way. "And I better clean this up, and let you get some rest, Kyle."

"Let me help you with that," said Nan, quickly following with the rest of the dirty dishes, and leaving the room abruptly quiet.

So quiet that Rob's voice startled her.

"Look, Kyle, I'm not saying you wouldn't have had a chance of medaling in the slalom if you hadn't had this miscarriage, but the combined was your best shot –"

"And I blew that. I know. If I hadn't been so stupid . . . You don't have to remind me."

"I'm not –"

"So because I blew my best chance you're going to take away my one remaining chance? Does that make sense?"

"Why take the risk for something that was always a long shot? Kyle, I can't let you —"

"Yes, you can. And the reason you can is because it's my long shot to take. It's not just the shot at the medal, though a medal would be nice. Would have been nice," she corrected herself. "It's the race. It's the skiing."

"There'll be other races. You can —"

"I want this race." She needed this race, but how could she explain that without ruining their truce with harsh words from the past? "If you try to pull me from this race, I will raise such a stink, cause such a scene that my career will be over — nobody would touch me. And if there's one thing you can't stand, it's to see skiing talent wasted."

He knew she couldn't make good on her threat — no misbehavior short of a prison term would truly end her career, and they both knew it. But that last part, there she had him, and she pushed the advantage. To ski she'd do more than that.

"That's what claws at you about Brad. He coasts on his ability instead of pushing it, and you hate that. I'm amazed you haven't punched him before now." His head came up but stopped short of meeting her eyes. "Surprised I know? Everybody's been waiting for you two to trade punches, and nobody could keep quiet on a tidbit like that."

Rob pushed off from his windowsill seat and moved across the room before restlessly returning to the window.

At last, he faced her. It was the cool, detached look she would have expected two weeks ago. After the past few days, it chilled her.

"You can come to training tomorrow. We'll see how it goes. If I think you're in trouble, you're off the hill. No questions, no arguments. And I'm making no promises about the race. It'll be my decision. For the good of the team."

"I don't get to have a say in —?"

"No."

His expression, as much as the word and his tone, sliced off her response. He held her look for a long moment, gave one nod, then started toward the door.

Part way there, he turned, and to her amazement he grinned at her.

"You know, I think that's the first time you haven't interrupted me in the past half hour. For once, I got to interrupt the autocratic Ms. Armstrong." His voice dropped, but it didn't go soft. "See you in the morning, Kyle."

DAY 10 – MONDAY

"HOW ARE YOU feeling, Kyle?"

She shifted her legs under the cloth-covered table, grateful that none of the cameras focused on her had X-ray lenses to detect the soreness already burning her muscles. Rob had worked them hard, as always. She'd felt his sharp eyes on her often. Approval never softened those eyes, but at least he hadn't yanked her off the mountain.

She was also grateful the microphones littering the table weren't attached to lie detectors.

She pushed a smile and stuck as close to the truth as she could. "Better than I did a week ago!"

Gene, the U.S. media liaison, had described the turnout of about twenty as mediocre. She recognized two regulars from ski magazines in the front row and expected the rest would be strangers. Gene had explained rather apologetically that she would have gotten numbers the day of the combined. Since then, other stories had supplanted her withdrawal. At the Olympics the stories came too fast to linger over any that weren't blockbusters.

Kyle added that to her list of things to be grateful for – she wasn't a blockbuster.

"What was the matter with you?" The questioner was that reporter Nan had introduced her to last week. Benton something.

She gave him a wry smile. *Remember, no silver-spoon tone.* "How can I put this delicately? Let's say I spent more time, uh, examining my bathroom in the Olympic Village than I would have liked."

That drew a ripple of sympathetic chuckles for what they interpreted as part of the human condition – especially humanity that travels and is exposed to more bugs than flies.

"Will you race the GS tomorrow?"

"No. I wouldn't have sufficient training, and it wouldn't be fair to the team. The coaches re-set the lineup after I got ill, and those racers have been preparing hard. But I'll race Friday."

"How is this going to affect you in the slalom?"

"Clearly it's not ideal. I'm not going to say I wouldn't have been better off if it hadn't happened, but I was skiing strong before missing this time, and I think I'll be back close to that level very quickly."

"By Friday?"

She shrugged and gave a smile. "I wish I knew. All I can do is do my best in the next three days of training, then ski hard Friday. Today went well, so I'm optimistic."

This was working. It was really working. She'd been nervous as she headed to the news conference, wondering if she'd been crazy to volunteer to talk to the media. But now she could see what Nan and Tess had been talking about. She just had to remember to say what she wanted to say and not let herself become a reactor to the questions.

"We hear you're not housed with the ski team. Have you felt alienated from your teammates with being in another area and not seeing them these past days in training?"

"Not at all. I'm assigned to a pod with athletes from other sports, but my roommate's Nan Monahan, whom you all know is on the ski team. Nan kept me up to date. I had notes from team members. Also, the coaching staff –" Involuntarily, her eyes flicked to the second row from the back where she'd seen Rob take a seat. "– was supportive and kept me from feeling isolated." She produced another smile. "And I watched every minute of skiing that's been on TV – men's and women's."

A series of questions about the pod followed. Those were easy. Except the one time she almost faltered when, in responding to a question about potential friction among a group of strangers, she remembered how everyone had supported her – continued to support her. She swallowed down emotion while she kept her words light.

"You think it was flu or food poisoning? Some athletes have been complaining about food in the cafeteria. Could it have been that?"

"Not just the athletes," rumbled a reporter with an expanse of white cotton knit stretched across the slope above his belt. That drew general laughter.

Kyle recognized the expression of warning on Gene's face, but she didn't need it.

She shook her head when the room quieted. "I'm not going to speculate on that. It's past, and now what I need to do is focus on the future, including the slalom –"

"The combined's past, too," interrupted an overbearing voice. Not until he got to his feet did she catch sight of the bulbous nose, oiled hair and sneer. She'd only seen him for a moment, but he was the man Nan had pointed out, the one from the finish area last week, trying to get close enough to hear her argue with Rob. "That was your best chance for a medal, wasn't it? Probably America's best chance for an Alpine medal. And America was definitely watching, hoping you could win a race for them, but you weren't there. Don't you feel you let your country down?"

The room went still. She felt her face stiffen at the barely cloaked accusation. He had no business –

In the motionless, quiet room, a man stood. Rob. He waited until her eyes came to him. Held her look a full ten seconds, then moved deliberately into the aisle and to the back of the room.

She took a swallow of water, flicked a look at the man with the sneer, then deliberately addressed the others.

"I know a lot of people in America – and elsewhere – wished me well, and I know a lot of them shared some measure of my disappointment that I couldn't compete in the combined. I am grateful to them for that. I want to tell them all thank you. I hope they will extend me their good wishes in the slalom come Friday. I just wanted to let them know – through all of you – that I'm feeling much better now, and I appreciate the expressions of concern and support."

Three voices came at once.

"But, how do you –" from the sneering man.

"Thank you all for coming –" from the media liaison.

"What do you think of the mountain's condition?" From the same reporter who'd asked about how the lack of training time might affect her in the slalom.

She'd have to remember his thin, dark face; she owed him. His question allowed her to finish the news conference on her terms. So when she'd completed her answer, in more detail that she might have in other circumstances, and Gene succeeded in wrapping it up, there was no sense that Kyle Wetherington Armstrong was running away.

"Good job, Kyle. This way – we have a car waiting to take you back to the Village." Gene smiled as he held a door for her. "You handled it great."

"Thanks. They seemed really nice – mostly."

"Most of them are. Just like everything else, there's an exception or two."

"Who was he?" She wouldn't pretend they weren't both talking about the sneerer. "He sounded American."

"He is. Guess he started with some American papers, but he's been bouncing around Europe awhile. I hear he worked on some of the wilder London tabloids, then moved to their imitators on the continent." He shouldered open an outside door and gestured her through. "Ah, there's the car. We figured you'd be tired your first day back and wouldn't want to hoof it back to the Village."

"Thanks again. I am beat, but don't tell –"

Rob.

Who stood holding the back door of the compact car for her. Nothing in his face revealed if he'd heard her admission.

"Figured I'd grab a ride back with you, Kyle, if you don't mind. Since you rated limousine service."

"No problem." She thanked Gene, then got in the car, very aware of Rob's hand lightly guiding her, but ready to do more if she indicated she needed it. He slid in next to her.

"Sore?" he asked without looking at her.

"A little."

"Stretch it out when you get to the apartment."

"I will."

She couldn't gauge him. His manner was businesslike and to-the-point, but his tone didn't bite the way it had.

Trying to stretch her right leg in the confines of the back seat, her knee bumped his thigh. He looked at the spot they'd made contact, sent a lightning glance to her face then out the window.

She wasn't fast enough to intercept his look. Why was he so silent? At their most antagonistic he'd never hesitated to tell her what he thought.

"The news conference seemed to go well," she offered.

Nothing.

"Just like Nan and Tess said."

Still nothing.

"Didn't you think it went well?"

"Uh-huh." At least his gaze went from out the side window to straight ahead for those two syllables.

"I tried to remember what they said about Dan Jansen and Kurt Browning. I kept repeating the names in my head, to keep on track." She took a deep breath. "And I still almost blew it. When that jerk said – Well, you know what he said. I was just about to use my best – what did you call it? silver-spoon voice? – and then you stood up."

He flicked another look at her.

"Thank you," she added deliberately.

"No big deal." He turned toward his window again, but not before she'd seen something in his eyes she hadn't seen there in a long time – approval.

"**MONDAY. OUR SECOND** week here, can you believe it? Our last week."

Lanny glowered. "You anxious to leave?"

Since they were entangled in sheets and each other in her bed, that had a double edge to it.

"No, of course not."

Rikki kissed his collarbone, reveling in the taste and sensation of his skin. They'd come back here last night, to spend the short night in each other's arms without displacing Tonetti. The hockey team had an early practice, then a session with the tapes. She had training all morning and into the afternoon. She'd arrived back at the apartment with the short daylight departing and no one else around. Ordinarily she would have used the time for a nap or reading or some shopping in town. Nothing too strenuous, because she would want to conserve her energy for the coming competition. Instead, when Lanny arrived twenty minutes after her, she'd spent the time in definitely strenuous, energy-depleting – and highly satisfying – exercise.

Her lips curved as she kissed him again, lower this time, feeling the tickle of his chest hair. God, she'd be in the best shape of her life if this counted as training.

"I was just thinking how much has happened." Her fingers followed where her lips had touched, tracing the intricacies of his bone, muscle and flesh. "With us, with getting to know Tess and Amy and Kyle and Nan, and wondering what the future's going to bring. If we're going to stay friends. If we'll even stay in touch. I wonder how Amy's career will develop, and how Kyle'll bounce back, and if Nan's knees will hold out, and if Tess can forg – Uh, how things will work out for her. Don't you wonder about how things will change past these sixteen days?"

"No."

The terse word stopped her caressing fingers more effectively than an order.

She honestly hadn't been probing for his thoughts on what might happen with them after the Closing Ceremonies. She'd simply been ruminating in the mellow, philosophical twilight after being thoroughly loved.

They'd made no promises, explicit or implicit. She didn't know if she wanted promises. Still, his answer dropped a weight on her diaphragm – it wouldn't crush her, but, God, it did make each breath a labor.

"You don't think about what you'll do after the team disbands?"

"No."

She'd thought that would be safer ground, but his answer sounded no different. Here, however, she had no reluctance to probe.

"I heard you might have an opportunity to coach after the Olympics."

He said nothing, his dark eyes boring into the ceiling, his face tight.

"Hasn't the hockey association been talking to you?"

"Maybe, but I'm not talking to them."

"But why? I think you could be a great coach. You could use a little softening around those hard edges here and there –" He didn't ease at her teasing, didn't flicker at her touch on his chin. "–but I would think that's something you'd like to do after –"

"After! Quit talking about fucking goddamned after. It's not after for chrissakes. It's now, and that's what I'm thinking about, that's what I'm talking about."

"But if you don't let them know you're interested –"

"Tough shit." He rolled, one swift move that pinned her beneath him. "It's now I'm thinking about. Not a year from now, not a week from now. Just to tomorrow's game. And when that's over, I'll look at the next one. But until then, it's the Swedish team and their hot scorer Landragund and their goalie Andresson, who's real strong against low shots, but can be fooled by something high to the corners. That's what I'm thinking about. And that's all I'm thinking about."

He looked at her. She saw the shift of his mood in the heartbeat before he kissed her decisively.

"Nah, that's bullshit. What I'm thinking about right now is what it feels like to have you under me."

He rubbed his naked body along hers. Where a fold of sheet intruded, he levered his leg to catch it and yank it aside, so nothing separated them, and he could slide into the haven she created by opening her legs.

"That's what I'm thinking about," he repeated, kissing her again, longer and softer. Their bodies warmed, then burned, straining to mesh wherever they met. "What it feels like to be inside you. Thinking . . . to have you all around me . . . Until . . . can't think . . ."

✧ ✧ ✧ ✧

"HEY, KYLE, WHERE'D you go?" Nan motioned Kyle ahead of her in the cafeteria line. "I thought we were all going to eat together. First Tess says she might be along later. Then you disappear. One minute we're walking to the cafeteria and the next you're gone."

Kyle grinned. "You were so busy flirting with that Norwegian ski jumper, I figured you wouldn't notice I'd left until after you'd eaten and gone back to the room."

"It was at the door to the cafeteria," Nan said with great dignity. She grimaced, and added in a more natural tone, "His coach insisted he join the team. Something about a reception. So, where did you go to?"

"Went to make a phone call."

"We could have waited a couple minutes to leave the apartment. You could have called there."

"This worked out fine."

"Ah."

"Ah, what?"

"Ah, you're being the mysterious Kyle Armstrong, daughter of power and wealth."

Kyle stopped. "Nan –"

"Don't let it worry you, Kyle, I'm used to it." She accompanied the words with a grin that reassured and a friendly shove that got Kyle moving again.

"Nan, do you think I'm autocratic?" Rob had used that word. Along with the silver-spoon crack.

"Sure, but you don't scare me any." She emptied her tray and sat at the table. "Not any more."

"Did I?"

Nan seemed a little surprised at Kyle's serious response to her teasing.

"Sure," she said lightly. "You scared me. You also made me worry about becoming a jealous bitch. You were rich, beautiful, talented and had healthy knees – everything I'd always thought I wanted. But after we'd roomed together awhile, I saw the way you reacted to my family, as if they're some rare species –"

"They are."

"– And I realized I sure as hell didn't want your family, and since lives come as package deals instead of ala carte, I decided I'd let you keep yours and I'd keep mine, bad knees and all."

Kyle smiled very slightly. "Sometimes even the bad parts of our lives have their uses."

✧ ✧ ✧ ✧

ANDREI STEPPED OUT of a shadow, and it didn't even startle her. Which annoyed Tess. She was getting too damned used to him showing up.

"Hello, Tess."

"Andrei." She kept walking toward the cafeteria. He fell into step with her.

"You go to eat?"

"Yes." The Yosts had invited her to have dinner with them at their hotel, but Amy and her parents could use time alone.

"Do you object if I accompany you for the meal?"

Saying yes would be churlish. "No."

"Good, then you do not object –" He hooked a large gloved hand under her elbow. "– that we have the meal at a restaurant in the town."

"Andrei, I don't –"

"You can tell me you prefer the cafeteria to a restaurant? You like the cafeteria so much?"

"No, but –"

"I thought not."

The pressure on her elbow increased as he branched off onto a path away from the cafeteria. She could go along or she could try to yank her arm free. With a short sigh of irritation and acquiescence, she made the turn.

As placidly as ever, he kept talking. "The food is acceptable in the cafeteria, but always there is so much noise. This restaurant I have found is quiet, even with so many visitors. You will like it."

It was quiet and she did like it.

He ordered wine without asking if she wanted any. She didn't object. Living with athletes in training these past ten days hadn't been a hardship, but she'd missed certain pleasantries of life. Wine, for one. Ordering from a menu. Eating as a relaxed pleasure rather than a hurried stoking of calorie-depleted bodies.

They talked leisurely throughout the meal. Of events surrounding them. Of the report given out by the Chinese that Xi Ling had become separated from her coaches, tried to return to her room by herself and had gotten lost, only finding her way to the Athletes' Village hours later. Of their observations that the skater seemed livelier these past three days and the regiment of her coaches appeared somewhat diminished. They talked of a Swedish woman's compelling victory in cross-country skiing, of a surprising bronze by a young American in men's downhill, of the U.S. hockey team's prospects when the medal round started the next day. From there they circled closer. A discussion of figure skating scoring rules. Pros and cons of vocal music for competition. A shared view on the peculiarities of judges.

"Would you like to walk?" Andrei asked.

She stood outside the restaurant, pulling on gloves. The night was fairly warm. Perhaps not by the thermometer, but she had no need to huddle into her coat or rush out of the cold. By Winter Olympic standards that qualified as warm. The cloud cover that held in the day's warmth reflected the lights of twin churches in the distance into a glowing ceiling.

"Yes."

He made no move to touch her, to take her hand or her arm. He tipped his head to the right, and they started off that way. After several silent blocks, she realized they were headed away from the Athletes Village. She said nothing. She wasn't ready to go back.

"How is Kyle?" he asked. He seemed to have a destination in mind.

"She seems to be recovered. Physically. She went back to training today."

"Ah."

"Ah, what?"

"She is a very strong young lady."

"She had to be."

"Why does thinking of Kyle's situation make you angry?" He asked it in the same easy voice.

"She shouldn't have had to be so strong. She shouldn't have been so alone."

"No." The sound of their steps in the snow, not quite in time, came twice, then: "But there is something more, something you think of about yourself when you think of Kyle. What is that?"

She held the silence a moment, then wondered why. Why not say the words? "I could have been pregnant. Eighteen years ago. God knows we weren't sensible enough to use anything. I could easily have been pregnant."

"Yes."

"You thought of that?" She'd always told herself that if he'd thought of that he never would have left her alone as he had. On that count she'd excused him as young and thoughtless. Never thinking him heartless.

"After. Many times. I hoped . . ." Barely aware they'd stopped, she looked at his face, expecting remembered relief. He'd turned partly away, but even with that and the half-light, she recognized only one emotion in him: continued regret. "But there were reports of you and never any mention . . . So I knew you did not carry my child."

Stunned, she stared at him. "You knew I could have been pregnant and you still left me?" More than that, he'd *wanted* her to be pregnant. She repeated the final words, separating each into an accusation. "You left me."

So quickly that even her instinct froze, he spun on her and barked the words, harsh and quick. "I did not leave you." Then, softer, "I did not run away with you."

"How can you say that? You did leave me. Instead of defecting, you left me and you went back –"

"Yes. I went back. To my home. To the life I knew and to my family. Just as you did."

They stared at each other. She was beginning to see, and she didn't want to. Anger was familiar, comfortable. Understanding could be dangerous.

"You could have defected." She clung to that.

His smile was grim. "And you could have gone to live in Fiji. Defecting, living in the West had no more reality to me than living in Fiji had for you. Equally impossible." He drew off his gloves with deliberation, stowed them securely in a pocket, then slowly brought his head up to meet her eyes. "So neither of us ran away. I went back to my life. You went back to yours."

"And part of yours was marrying Tatiana."

"Ah, now we reach the pit at the center of the matter." He sounded . . . not cheerful, but relieved. The way she'd felt when the waiting ended and the time came to skate, to test her ability against the ice, her nerves and the judges' opinions. "Come. At the end of this street there is a park with benches. We will sit and we will talk."

Now he did take her arm, and started her walking.

A narrow triangle cut off by two intersecting roads and a stream formed the park. A stone wall separated it from one road and two benches sat at angles near the stream.

Just inside the park, Tess pulled back on his hold. "I don't want to sit."

For ten seconds, Andrei continued to look toward the benches, then he turned around, came back half a step so they stood face to face, and began.

"Do you think marrying Tatiana was my wish, my desire? I tell you now, it was not."

"You're saying they ordered you to marry Tatiana?" She made no effort to hide the skepticism. "How could they have made you do that? Even then?"

"She told them she was pregnant. She told them the baby was mine."

Tess's head snapped back as if from a blow. Almost immediately she stiffened, schooling her muscles into rigid, uncaring dignity.

"Ah, Tess . . ."

He had been very careful about touching her, ever since his fingertips on her arm had made her flinch outside the interview room eight days ago. But now he took her face between his palms, not hurting her but not allowing her to look anywhere but at him. She didn't try to pull away.

"I never made love with Tatiana. Not before those Olympics, not for the few, pitiful weeks of our marriage and God knows, not during those two weeks we were together, you and I. God, how could I even see another woman when my life was brilliant with you?"

She knew it was the truth. As surely, as deeply as she had known at the age of seven that gliding across the ice on blades of silver was the purest form of movement on earth.

"If you knew it wasn't your baby, how could you have married her?"

He dropped his hands. She felt the separation, the differentness.

"We were partners. They had made us partners, and over a decade we had sweated and cried together to skate out of the small, dark world we had come from. And we had succeeded. Together we had skated to the championships of Europe. To the Olympics."

She jerked off her gloves and jammed them in her pocket.

"She could have gotten another partner."

"No!" He slashed at the air with his hand. "That is what you don't understand, you Americans. Partners are not pieces to move here and there. Once two skaters are partners, truly partners, they are a unit. No longer two skaters, but one. They succeed as that one, they fail as that one. And they die as skaters as that one.

"Tatiana was my partner. We were as one. Pregnant, she faced disgrace. She asked that I help her." He looked at her then, seeking understanding but not really hoping for it. "She was my partner."

Her head spun with the shadows shifting over what she had believed for so long. Andrei had made love to her, then left her to marry his partner. A woman older, more sophisticated, more alluring than herself. But his words had changed that reality.

"But the father . . . The father of her baby . . ."

"When she admitted I was not the father, she said he was a married man, wanted nothing to do with the baby and was high in the government. High enough to make life uncomfortable for her. Life could be made most uncomfortable by the powerful in those times."

"So you dropped out of sight, stopped skating . . . But after she had the baby –"

"There was no baby."

"But –"

"There never was a baby. She lied. All lies. She was not pregnant. All lies to keep us skating together, to be sure I would not defect. Because she suspected. She knew me, and she saw me look at you, and she suspected."

"But you didn't – you didn't keep skating together. You disappeared. Nobody heard anything about you until a few years ago when you arrived at the European championships with Vladimir and Radja."

"No, we did not keep skating."

He sat on the low stone wall, hands on his thighs, and stared straight ahead.

She could see him on the ice, as he'd been at twenty. The power and the intensity. The lines made pure by a love for the movement.

She sat next to him and put her hand over his.

Very slowly his gaze came back from the distance and rested on her hand. Equally slowly, he turned his hand over, resting with hers, palm to palm, then closing his fingers around her hand with great deliberation. When his hand encircled hers, secure and warm, he started to talk.

"We married when we returned from the Olympics. At first, it seemed all would go on as it had. We practiced, we trained, we readied our costumes and prepared for the World Championships. The only difference was we shared an apartment. She had a much larger apartment, so I moved there – into an extra bedroom. There was no question of sharing a bed. She had not lied about that – her lover was a married man and in the government, though higher than she had said and very willing to give her anything she wanted.

"It was two days before our time to leave for the Worlds. I felt as if my heart would tear in two. I wanted to see you, so desperately to see you. But to tell you I had married Tatiana . . . She seemed to know my thoughts and it made her angry. She told me how stupid I was and that I had nearly ruined everything, but that she had saved it. She told me she wasn't pregnant. That she had tricked me to marrying her to prevent me from throwing away everything we had worked so hard for."

He didn't tighten his hold, yet Tess thought she could feel the vibration of his anger.

"I wanted to kill her."

So quiet, so chilling.

"She had betrayed me. She had tricked me. She had lied to me. I told her I would never skate with her. And she said if I did not skate with her, I would skate with no one because she would tell the authorities I planned to defect, that I had formed an alliance with an American. She would see to it that I never skated again. As I walked out, I told her to do her worst. I already knew that she would, and I no longer cared."

Tess put her other hand on top of his, resting her cheek against his shoulder.

No longer cared? Oh, yes, he had cared. He had been exiled from the sport he loved, from the world he had been destined to conquer. Sentenced by the very woman he had given his loyalty to.

"What did you do?"

"I survived." He brushed her hair from her forehead, stroking over the crown. "Tatiana had connections to see that I did not skate. But I could teach. She tried to prevent that, too, but our old coach stood strong and they sent me to one of the small centers to work with the young ones. Some did very well, and then I would send them on to the national center. My pupils, my old friends would tell me of what happened in skating. I knew of your rise. I heard when you became champion of the world."

He bent and kissed her forehead, a benediction of warmth on her skin.

"I was so proud of you, Tessa. And at the Olympics . . . A friend, a genius with machines, arranged so we received a television signal. We watched in secrecy, but I saw you win the gold medal. I knew you would. But to see you . . . To see you stand with the medal, and the tears . . . Ah, don't cry, Tessa."

He wiped at the moisture on her cheeks, but tears kept coming. She didn't try to stop them, she didn't try to move.

"You broke my heart, Andrei."

"I know, Tessa, I know."

DAY 11 – TUESDAY

KYLE BLINKED AWAKE, certain something was different.

Something was, she realized more clearly after a moment. Nan was up before her. Up, fully dressed and fidgeting. At the moment she fidgeted with her gloves, but she'd find a dozen things to fidget with before her race today.

Her race. Kyle sat up. Nan raced in the giant slalom today.

It had taken Kyle a while to realize Nan had no moment of utter peace at leaving all the world behind at the beginning of each run. Kyle didn't remember exactly when she'd first realized that Nan, outwardly easy-going and nonchalant, absorbed all the nervous chatter and tense muscles that most skiers experienced and carried them inside her all along the course. But the realization had been the true beginning of their friendship. Keeping up her own image of self-containment hadn't seemed quite as important, and Kyle had relaxed.

"Hey. Morning."

"Oh, you're up. Didn't mean to wake you. Sorry. I tried to be quiet."

"You must have been. I didn't even hear you in the shower."

Nan's hands stilled. "I didn't."

"What?"

"Oh, shit, I forgot to shower. Shit! How could I do that?"

Kyle treated the question as rhetorical. "Well, get in there now because I've got to shower, too."

"Yeah, yeah. Okay."

Nan disappeared into the bathroom, peeling off her clothes.

Kyle closed her eyes again, but didn't sleep. She seriously doubted that God kept track of such things as Olympic ski results, but she still said a prayer for Nan.

✧   ✧   ✧   ✧

RIKKI CARRIED AS much momentum from the downhill slide as she could into the flat. This section was tricky, with that turn coming right after. Too much speed and you risked a crash. Too little and you lost the "free" ride of the downhill – earned inch by painful inch of getting up its other side.

She'd have to point out to Nan and Kyle that they had the easy half of skiing – all downhill. Her mouth muscles twitched to a smile, then returned to a mask of effort.

Downhill. God, please don't let it be downhill for Lanny. With the quarterfinal tonight, she could feel his tension. Hard to believe he could get any more intense, but he did. She saw it, felt it. Not only in his words and looks, but in the way he moved. Even making love last night. Even when he slept, with his arms around her and their legs tangled, she'd seen it in the pulse at the base of his throat caught as a rhythmic movement in the faint light. She'd felt it in the tendons, sinew and muscle taut in preparation under her lightly stroking fingers.

He wanted this so much. He needed it. At least he thought he did. He believed that with the same intensity he did everything. It awed her. It frightened her.

"Hey, Rikki! Good time." An assistant coach called out a time that snagged her brows in a frown. She hadn't intended to push this interval that hard. "You're cooking!"

✧   ✧   ✧   ✧

NAN AND THE other three Americans who would ski the giant slalom took a couple warm-up runs with the rest of the team, then gathered with the coaches to head over to inspect the race course. While the rest of the team started to the top again to train in earnest, Kyle at the bottom lingered to see Nan off.

"Now, remember, rookie," Nan instructed a young skier named Marilynne Ramsey. "If they catch you going through a gate while we're inspecting the course, you're out of there. Curb your natural instincts and just crab along the hill like the rest of us."

It was like reminding a pro basketball player that the guy with the whistle is the referee. Marilynne was young, but she'd raced a long time and had been on the World Cup tour all season – she didn't need the directions, though from the tightness of her laugh, she could use the distraction.

Nan sounded perfectly at ease, but Kyle saw her finger tapping relentlessly at the goggles in her hand.

"Okay, let's go." Rob waved the group toward the van. "Armstrong, you should be up top for your next run."

"The mountain will still be there in five minutes." She turned her back on his frown, and faced Nan. "I probably won't make it until after your first run. But we'll meet between runs, okay? I'd tell you to break a leg, but you probably would." As she hugged Nan, she added in a whisper, "Just ski, don't think." She gave Nan a final squeeze, pulled back, said "Good luck" out loud, then headed for the lift without looking toward Rob.

By a trick of the cold air and gusting wind that ignored the fact they were walking in opposite directions, she heard Nan's voice distinctly.

"Honestly, how do you think she's doing, Rob? Do you think she's okay? Is she pushing herself too hard too fast?"

The air and wind didn't bring her Rob's answer.

AMY WENT UP. Perfect arm position, good height, tight rotation, aligned body. One turn. Two. And the extra half a rotation that separated an axel from other jumps.

Her blade reconnected with the ice, then seemed to hop. Her ankle bent, her knee followed and she pitched back to her butt, skidding from her momentum.

She scrambled up and skated hard to catch up with her music blaring from the loudspeaker at the rink Andrei had found. She didn't look back at where Tess stood.

Six attempted double axels today, four falls, one turned into a single and one landed with both feet.

Amy completed the rest of her short program without a hitch, including the difficult combination of a triple lutz directly to a double toe loop. Two jumps with barely time to draw breath, gain momentum or gauge balance. She also completed the rest of the program without her usual verve.

The music over, Amy skated slow, easy loops while she waited for the attendant to key it once more. At the opposite end of the arena from her coach.

Tess allowed herself a sigh.

"Bad practice?"

Tess didn't jump at Andrei's sudden appearance by her side. No question, she was used to it. She'd been a little surprised – perhaps more than a little relieved? – not to see him at the official practice earlier this morning at the Ice Hall or when they'd arrived at this rink.

Especially after last night.

She had left him with no words of understanding or forgiveness, refusing to talk any more after she'd already confessed much, too much. He'd accepted her silence. Then. But she knew that under his patience rode determination. Had he come for the words now?

Not now. She had too many other things on her mind. She had to concentrate on Amy – Amy's needs, Amy's chances. She couldn't afford to think of anything else. She owed that to Amy. Any energy left over belonged to Kyle and her situation, and whatever troubled Rikki beneath her calm surface, and . . . She wasn't ready.

"Not good. The official practice started all right – not great, but all right. But each run-through since has been worse. I've considered cutting the session short, but I keep hoping she can finish on an up, then we'll go catch the end of Nan's competition. And I've promised we'll go to the hockey quarterfinal. Maybe she's doing too much . . . But it does take her mind off skating and maybe today's practices won't stick with her."

Tess watched the figure moving almost listlessly on the ice, then added, "I don't know what's gotten into her."

"Perhaps nothing."

She shook her head, frowning. "This isn't like her. Not only the trouble with the axel, but the whole way she's moving. Maybe she's coming down with something."

"She appears healthy."

"Maybe it's a pull or a soreness she's not telling me about."

"She does not look to favor a leg. I think she is all right, Tess. Everyone has a day that is over."

She smiled for the first time. "An off day."

"What?"

"A day that is over," she quoted. "The expression is that you've had an off day, a day that's off. Not over."

"Ah."

She looked up at him, and caught the glint in his eyes. "Which you very well knew."

"Ah, well. Perhaps. It does not matter. You smiled."

He held her look, and she couldn't break it. Didn't want to. A memory burst open, vivid as *deja vu*, of looking at Andrei like this, that first time they'd seen each other, and thinking that she understood where the phrase eye contact came from. Because when Andrei looked at her she felt the imprint of a touch on her skin, on her heart.

She blinked, a slight shiver skimmed her nerves, and she turned back to the rink, just in time to see Amy glide into the perfect landing on her double axel.

Smiling again, Tess turned to Andrei. He was walking away.

AS SOON AS Kyle arrived at the giant slalom course, she headed for the lodge to look for Nan. Halfway there, she saw Scott Stanicek, a member of the men's team, coming toward her.

"Hey, Kyle, you're going the wrong way. Nan's about to go. I'm just heading out."

"You're kidding." But she pivoted and fell in step with him. "Why're they running so late?"

"Bunch of crashes. They've taken two off on stretchers, two more were hurt and another one just went off the course. Arnette Polaski. Probably saved her neck doing it." He looked over at her. "Polly's out."

"Oh, no." At twenty, Polly Tresser was upbeat and personable, and one of the U.S. team's top contenders in the giant slalom. "Was she hurt?"

"Yeah. She's one of the ones taken off on a stretcher."

"How bad?"

"She got a knock on the head, but she was conscious. It's her knees. They're not sure how bad. Won't know until they do tests down at the hospital. But with knees . . ."

"Shit." The racer's fear. It bound them together over divisions of language, nationality or rivalry.

Cowbells up the course announced the arrival of a skier. Kyle watched a speck dressed in green – so it wasn't Nan – come into sight, scalloping the snow, still high on the mountain.

"What the hell's causing all the crashes up there?" she asked Scott.

"Word is they've got the gates set so you carry a hell of a lot of speed into the turns. Too much. There've been protests from coaches, but they aren't going to stop it now. Looks like the key's to survive this first run, then make time when they reset the course for the second run."

Survive.

The word echoed in Kyle's mind as she and Scott found spots by the finish and watched the huge video screen that showed Nan in the start house, next skier up. The word echoed and echoed until it became an exhortation, a command.

Survive.

She repeated it as Nan flew from the start.

Survive, Nan Monahan. Survive, with your five knee operations and your too active mind and your good heart. Survive.

Nan caught air on one bump, seemed to wobble in mid-flight, then righted herself as her skis met snow. At a gate, she fought for control as her skis tried to go at right-angles to her body. She won.

Kyle sucked in a breath.

Survive.

Cowbells clamored closer, and Kyle deserted the video screen to focus on the speck hurtling along. *Don't lean back on your skis. Keep your arms forward. Survive!*

Nan did.

A rocky performance, but good enough to put Nan Monahan in seventh after one run.

Kyle waved goodbye to Scott and pushed toward the highest noise level around the finish area. That's where the Monahans would be, and that's where Nan would head.

✧   ✧   ✧   ✧

KYLE LEFT NAN with Rikki in the lodge.

Before inspecting the re-set course, Nan had dismissed her family so she could concentrate on the second run. But now, waiting out a timing system repair, she was too busy complaining about her boots to spare a thought for the run.

Other competitors sat scattered around on chairs and benches, eyes closed, individual music systems on, turned inside to prepare for the race. All except Nan, who described to Rikki in excruciating detail why she thought these boots weren't suited for this course, this weather, this time of day or this phase of the moon.

Rikki listened patiently, but Kyle couldn't take it any longer. Not only did Nan's babbling make her nervous, but she had something to do – and she needed to do it now to have any hope. "I'll be back."

Word had come that Polly Tresser had ligament damage – not torn, fortunately, but badly strained. She wouldn't ski the next day's Super-G. And while Kyle wished the racer hadn't been injured, the fact that she was had spawned an idea.

She found Rob outside, listening to another coach tell him by the newest electronic version of a walkie-talkie that the timing snafu was cleared and they were ready to go. He stayed quiet for the first sentence and a half of Kyle's argument.

". . .so with Polly out, I'm the logical repla –"

"No." The device in his hand squawked, and he turned down the volume.

"It makes sense –"

"You weren't ever going to race the Super-G. You were listed for the combined and slalom. The giant slalom wasn't even that sure a thing no matter what you think. Never the Super-G."

"But that was before Polly got hurt. You don't have to give them the start lists until tonight, so there's time." He shook his head, but she went on. "There's a spot now, and I want it, Rob. I know I can ski. I know I –"

"No." His eyes were as implacable as a winter sky that denied the sun entrance. "It's already set. Stephen and I talked. We agreed. Marilynne's going for Polly tomorrow."

"I'm a better racer than Marilynne."

"Yes, you are."

"Then how can you do this? I'm all right. I can –"

"This isn't about you, Kyle. This is about the team, and what's best for it. Not just for this race or this week, but for the years coming up, too. Maybe you could take this race physically, but I don't even have to wonder about that, because it's not a factor."

Her skeptical look didn't daunt him or slow his words.

"You're right, Marilynne isn't as strong a skier technically as you are. She doesn't have the poise or the finesse on the course you do. But she can become a very good Super-G racer – if we give her the experience and she makes good use of it. You're already as good as you're going to get in the Super-G, because it's not your race. I expect, with all other things being equal, you'd finish maybe top ten. Marilynne won't. But in a couple more years she might give the team shots at Super-G medals and you won't."

From his tone and his eyes she knew she'd lost, if she'd ever had any chance. But she wasn't sure she believed him on the why.

"Rob!" It was Nan, coming up behind her. "I've got to change these boots. I think they might have been tampered with or something and –"

Kyle barely heard her, all her focus on the man in front of her.

"Are you saying that if it were best for the team, you would put me in tomorrow's Super-G?"

"What!" Nan's screech came from over her right shoulder, but Kyle didn't take her eyes off Rob, and his return look didn't flicker.

"I'm the coach, Kyle. My decisions have to be based on what's best for the team. Most times whatever's going to help an individual skier get stronger, better, more experienced is also going to be best for the team. But not always, and when that happens, the team has to come first. For the coach, it has to be that way."

"What are you talking about? Tell me I'm not hearing what I think I'm hearing."

Rob held Kyle's look an extra beat, then turned to Nan, but ignored her questions. "Timing's fixed. They're ready to go." He nodded to Rikki and headed toward the finish area.

Nan pulled her around by her arm. "Kyle Armstrong, you tell me what the hell's going on right now or you're going to see a fine example of the Irish temper I'm usually too polite to show."

"I wanted to take Polly's place in the Super-G tomorrow. But Zemlak said they're putting in Marily –"

"You wanted to what? Are you crazy? You're –"

"Nan, it's not crazy. I'm all ri . . ." The words trailed off at a squeeze on her elbow that, even through parka and sweater, threatened to border on painful. She looked over her shoulder to meet Rikki's intense look. Rikki shook her head slightly. But even if Kyle had tried to keep talking, Nan would have prevailed.

"– Crazier than I already thought. Totally devoid of the upper crust good sense and restraint my mother's always telling me to imitate. If she only knew. Listen to me, Armstrong, you have been back at training two days. Two lousy days. And Super-G isn't even one of your events."

"I just thought –"

Nan waved her off. "No, you didn't think. Christ! The slalom's pushing it, anyhow. But at least you know which way to go on the slalom hill. You haven't done the Super-G in so long you probably would try to go up! God Almighty, now I've heard everything."

She shouldered past Kyle, who asked, "Where are you going?"

"I'm going to find Zemlak to make absolutely sure he's going to keep your butt out of the Super-G tomorrow."

Kyle turned to face Rikki. The biathlete's mouth twitched in something near a smile.

"What was that all about? Why'd you shut me up?"

"It occurred to me that Nan could use something else to fret about."

Kyle frowned. "But she should be thinking about her second run, not about me. Her concentration –"

"She didn't seem to be concentrating much before. Just fussing, right?"

Kyle nodded slowly. It was Nan's way.

"So, maybe a diversion will be good for her." Rikki grinned. "At least she's not obsessing about her boots anymore."

"HOLD YOUR LINE, Nan. Hold your line."

Kyle whispered the instructions to the figure on the video screen. Not a plea, not a prayer. Because Nan Monahan was going to do a lot more than survive this run of the Olympic giant slalom.

"There she is! I see her!"

At Amy's call everyone around her shifted focus from the screen to the mountain. Nan came barreling down, hardly seeming to deflect from a straight line, but still clicking through the gates. She passed the last gate and had only the final straightaway left.

She came across the line with enough speed that her turn in the finish area sprayed snow. She dragged off her goggles and looked over her shoulder at the electronic display of her time.

Then she stopped dead and gawked.

The board flashed her time for the run, her overall time and her overall place. Second. Nine one-hundredths of a second behind the leader.

"Yes! Yes!"

Kyle doubted if even Rikki, standing right next to her, could hear her amid the clamor of shouts, horns and bells. Nan Monahan clearly was popular, well beyond the knot of family, friends and Olympic roommates.

"But there are still six to go," Rikki protested when she could make herself heard. "And if they finished better in the first run . . ."

"That first run was all jumbled around because of the wild course. Some of those first-run leaders were fluky. And Nan has the best time of this run. By far."

Nan's older brother, Roger, added, "She blew 'em out of the water! The pipsqueak blew 'em the hell out of the fucking water!"

"Roger!" automatically protested Mrs. Monahan, while tears slipped over her soft cheeks.

"This is so good for her. So good. Her confidence, her belief in herself . . ."

Kyle's voice trailed off as Nan, still moving as if befuddled, neared the area where the coaches and competitors milled. She stopped, turned her head, finally gave a smile and stepped right into a bear hug from Rob. With the tape that marked off the finish area caught between them, he squeezed her tight, thumped her on the back twice, then tousled her hair, beaming all the while.

Kyle's breath hitched, but she couldn't take her eyes off them. Off Nan.

The video screen had switched to the next skier, pushing off from the start house, but no one around Kyle paid attention. Rob said something to Nan, who turned and looked in their direction. A thicket of hands went up in a wave, and she spotted them immediately, waving back, then giving an imitation of a boxer's hands-clenched, arms-raised victory salute.

But she stayed by Rob.

As the next skier came down the mountain and finished safely behind Nan's overall time, Kyle understood.

Right now Nan had a medal. But with five skiers still to race, it could evaporate. Her great run would always stand, and it would help her confidence. But at the moment that was hard to see beyond the potential glitter of an Olympic medal.

Another skier finished, and Nan's position stood. Four to go. Kyle stopped watching Nan. If someone could sense when they were being watched, they might be able to sense when they were being worried about, too. Kyle would keep her nerves and fears to herself.

"What about this one, Kyle? How good is this Russian?" Amy asked.

"She's good. But she's pretty new. She had the best run of her career to get third in the first run. If she can do that again . . ."

The youngster came nowhere near duplicating her first run, and finished well back.

"How about this one, Kyle?" Amy was bouncing on the balls of her feet with nerves.

"She's good. She's had an injury but I hear she's been training real well here. I don't know."

Kyle felt as if she held her breath as the skier's intermediate times flashed up – close, so close to Nan's. The Austrian finally crossed the line, and a visible puff of air went up in the cold air from Nan's relieved backers. The Austrian stood third. Nan remained second, with two one-hundredths of a second to spare.

"God, I don't know if my heart can take this," muttered Rikki.

"It gets worse," said Kyle, watching the woman on the screen, preparing for her start. "Isobelle Chernier is probably the most dangerous skier on the circuit. If she's on, she's practically unbeatable. And that first run looks as if she's on."

She was.

She finished in front of them with a hand-pumping flourish as the screen flashed her name into first place. The former leader dropped to second and Nan to third. With one racer to go.

Kyle risked a glance at Nan. She stared up the mountain, though nothing could be seen there. Rob had his arm around her, casual not comforting, and was talking and smiling. Totally at ease.

"I've never wished for a skier to fall in my life," muttered Mrs. Monahan, as if she'd just put temptation behind her.

"Oh God, oh God," mumbled Amy.

Rikki gave an involuntary jerk beside her and Kyle turned to the screen to see the final racer already started. Thank heavens nobody'd asked her about this final threat to Nan. The young German was one Kyle had had in mind when she'd mentioned fluky results in the first run. But that didn't mean the skier couldn't do it again. Couldn't do just well enough to knock Nan to fourth and out of a medal.

Kyle focused on the racer's technique, blocking out intermediate times, computations of possible placements. Looking at line and curves, balance and movement.

A little back on her skis there, that cost some time. Nice turn, tight, in the groove. Another nice one. Kyle blinked, trying to ease eyes that burned. Oh, her arms were back, that cut more speed. Then a little wide around a gate, not holding her line as well.

The finish.

Kyle closed her eyes. Not avoiding the moment, just soothing her eyes, just – Noise! Shouts. Amy and Rikki and Tess. Roger Monahan and his wife and two of Nan's sisters and her mother. Whooping and cheering.

Kyle opened her eyes to a scoreboard that gave Nan Monahan, USA, the Olympic bronze medal.

NERVES RIKKI HAD lived thirty-one years without knowing she possessed jangled a cacophony in her head until her temples pounded with it.

One more thing Rochelle Lodge never did, but now was doing under Lanny Kaminski's tutelage – getting toss-your-lunch nervous before an event.

Not even her own event for chrissakes. A biathlon she could face with the calm of experience, the knowledge that her performance depended on calm, and the certainty that her performance would not make or break her self-image. She wasn't so sure about Lanny.

American fans hooted and hollered around her, including Amy and Kyle. Even Tess cheered. But Rikki couldn't relax. Team USA led Sweden, 2-0, in the third period, but that didn't placate her tyrant nerves. Because, while the Americans were winning the game, they were losing the demolition derby taking place on the rink.

First, Tonetti went out with a first-period gash at the corner of his eye. He came back with a bandage covering the wound and a badly swollen face – and Rikki suspected at least a couple stitches.

Dan Christopher wasn't as lucky in the second period.

Rikki was watching Landragund, the player Lanny had mentioned as Sweden's hot scorer, so she didn't see it, but she heard it. The solid, sickening sound of a body blasted into the boards, then the crowd's groan. Dan lay awkwardly limp on the ice, not moving.

The athletes' section had come to its feet as one, watching in silent empathy.

He came to quickly, with the help of whatever the trainers held under his nose. But blood flowed from a cut at the side of his mouth and, more seriously, he looked disoriented. The crowd applauded him when he was helped off the ice, but nobody could mistake the wobble in his legs. Concussion, the whisper went through the athletes and beyond. He had not come back.

After that, there were several pushing and shoving exchanges on the ice, with penalties freely handed out. It didn't stop the roughness. A Swede left with blood flowing from a cut in his mouth. A third American went out limping after another tangle.

In the final minute of the second period, Mikey Sweet crashed to the ice after a check from a Swedish player and slid into the Swedish goalie, Andresson, taking him down like a bowling pin. A third Swedish player grabbed Sweet, throwing a punch while the American tried to get up.

"Hey!" Amy jumped up in futile protest. "That wasn't Mikey's fault. He didn't mean –"

Rikki stood just in time to see Lanny skate full-speed into the melee and bump the Swede wearing No. 11, knocking him down into the heap. Sweet extricated himself, and by the time the third Swedish player had gotten up and swung around with murder in his eyes, the officials had arrived to keep the combatants separate.

"Lanny's made an enemy," Kyle said.

"Yes."

"He was only sticking up for Mikey," objected Amy.

"It doesn't matter to No. 11," said Rikki. From then on, she kept track of that player.

His opportunity came late in the third period, just after the Americans turned away a Swedish shot. A whistle ended the play, everyone drifting while the officials sorted things out. Lanny had his left arm raised, shaking his glove into a better position – and leaving his side fully exposed. No. 11 moved so fast Rikki hardly saw him raise his stick waist high, held horizontally between his hands, skate fast toward Lanny and jam the stick into Lanny's exposed side.

"YOU'RE DONE ALREADY? With the X-ray and everything?"

Lanny's quick arrival surprised her. She'd been prepared to wait after Mikey, face swollen and bruised, had stopped outside the locker room door to tell her Lanny was being examined for suspected broken ribs. She'd hoped the wait would give her stomach a chance to settle down after watching him double over in pain.

Instead, he came out of the door not five minutes after Mikey, only a slight gingerliness apparent in his walk.

"No X-ray. It's bruised." He raised his arm to put it around her shoulders. A flash of pain whitened his face and he let the arm drop, instead taking her hand.

"You can't know that without an X-ray. It might be broken."

"Either way, they do the same thing. Tape it up and tell me to heal."

"You can't play with a broken rib."

He released her hand. "Like hell I can't. I have before and I don't care if the damned thing's splintered like glass, I'm playing, so get off my back, Rikki."

AS SOON AS Tess opened the door, she heard the slice of blades on ice against the night quiet of the rink.

She juggled the shoes she'd already traded for her skates and closed the door quietly behind her. Staying in the shadow of the open gate, she reached the edge of the ice.

Andrei had just started skating. She could tell by the way he moved. Not tentatively, but with respect, reserve. God, she hadn't seen him skate in eighteen years but everything about him on the ice was familiar, the power of his moves, the certainty of his balance, the simplicity of his grace.

She blinked.

But a blink didn't erase the past, or the years.

Neither did his explanation.

She could withdraw now, unseen. And he would accept that, too, as he had accepted last night, as he had this afternoon.

The message was clear. He'd demanded that she truly talk to him, truly listen. She had. He demanded no more. She could slip away now, and that would be the end of it.

But she wanted to skate with him.

She wanted that, and she deserved it. Beyond that? Beyond that, she wouldn't look.

She tugged off the skate guards, dropped them, shoes and parka in a jumble on a bench, and stepped through the opening onto the ice.

He turned from the far end of the rink. Instead of heading directly toward her, he set a diagonal course, skating easily, hands on hips, never taking his eyes off her. Reaching the boards, he turned for the next leg of his zig-zag route.

Intensely aware of his tacking approach, she concentrated her first, warming moves on the ice in one small area.

He wore a dark blue shirt and black pants. Without lurex, spandex

or sequins he was a compelling figure. He came to a stop in front of
her and she stopped, too.

"Tess. Will you skate with me again?"

I want to skate with you. I want to hold you on the ice, and kiss you. And
then, every time I skate, I will hold you again. In my heart.

But what if someone sees us. What if they tell —

It won't matter. I will have you in my heart.

"Yes."

They started off side by side without speaking. Not touching. Feeling first for a rhythm that bound them without touching. He took her
hand before she was ready, but kept his hold loose enough for her to
pull away if she wanted to. After covering another quarter of the rink,
she had the gauge of their unified motion. His grip firmed.

"You are more accustomed to a partner now," he said.

"All those years in ice shows and exhibitions."

He nodded and said no more. His arm went around her waist,
turning her so they skated face to face, so close each movement had to
be a mirror image of the other's or they would collide.

"This way." He guided her with the pressure of his hip, the movement of his thigh, the tightening of his arm.

She tried to laugh. It came out ragged. "You know what they said
about Ginger Rogers, don't you?"

"No."

"She had to do everything Fred Astaire did, only backwards and in
high heels."

"I do not make you wear high heels," he protested.

She laughed for real, and a smile touched his eyes.

No, he didn't make her wear high heels, but he did make her
dance, dance as she hadn't in a long time on the ice – with a partner.
With an equal.

He tightened his hold around her waist, drawing her around so
they were side by side once more.

"Spiral," he said, but she already knew. Into the move, she felt his
arm around her, felt his free arm and leg parallel hers as they glided,
synchronized without a note of music.

"I know, the death spiral now."

She didn't look back at him, just put out her right hand. He took it. Their grips locked as she arched her back, the momentum of the spin carrying her out. His hold counterbalanced that force, was her only support as she dropped lower and lower. Laid out almost parallel with the ice, still spinning, she let her head go back, knowing her hair brushed the ice, trusting Andrei's strength to pull her slowly, gracefully up from the spin until they skated easily side by side once more.

"Excellent."

His single word of praise heated her with pleasure.

"Pairs sit spin." His tone threaded a line between question and demand.

"Okay."

He brought her around to face him once more, his arms around her, hands locked at the back of her waist. Her arms held out in balancing grace. Slowly, they lowered into the spin. Each with one bent leg carrying the spin, the free leg extended, parallel. The movement put her right knee between his thighs, arched her back toward him, brought their faces close. Sweat beaded on his forehead, slipped down in a line that traced the strong bones of one cheek. She felt the strength and heat of his hands at her back, the power of his legs on either side of hers, the exertion of his breathing.

Their eyes locked, spinning in a world where everything was out of focus except each other.

Andrei must have brought them out of the spin. She knew only that her heartbeat had slowed little as they skated slowly to the opening where she'd left her things. They didn't discuss it; she figured they both knew they'd had enough.

He held out a thermos of water in one hand and a towel in the other. She took the water, swallowing greedily, hoping it would cool what pounded in her veins.

When she handed it back, he put it on the bench, then turned to her.

With the corner of the soft towel, he wiped her face. She stood absolutely still under his touch, not willing to meet it, afraid to shatter it. His eyes followed the deliberate motion of his hand. First one cheek, then the other. Across her forehead, then the temples, sweeping back to her hairline. Again, and again.

Then the towel was gone and his fingers slipped into her hair, pulling the pins that held it up, burying his hands into the strands so his palms molded to the shape of her skull. Restraint vibrated in his hold, but there was no restraint in his kiss.

When his lips first touched hers they were cool and slightly dry. So the heat must have come from inside her. He kissed her, changed the angle and kissed her again. And again. She held on to him, needing to feel his flesh and muscle under her fingers.

"Tess, give me your mouth."

She parted her lips and met his tongue, mingling a groan with his. Her breasts were crushed against him, her lower body reacting to the pressure of his, not as she had on the ice by retreating when he advanced, but by returning the pressure. No longer a mirror image, but two straining for the impossibility of meshing into one.

He released her mouth, but held her close enough that they felt each other's quick, panting breaths, his question in his touch and his eyes.

"Andrei . . . Andrei, I don't know."

"I want you, Tessa. In my bed. Do you want me?"

"I should go back to the apartment. If Amy wakes –"

"Tessa." She hadn't answered, but that was an answer. "Come."

In the handful of mundane minutes of trading skates for shoes, pulling on jackets, the brief walk to his small hotel, the climb up the stairs, she thought a hundred times that she would stop this. She would slip her hand from his and walk away, in one more second. She never did.

He closed the room door behind them, then took her skate bag and coat from her. When he turned from hanging both coats in the closet, she stood in the same spot, watching him. He started toward her.

She was a grown woman. A successful woman. A woman experienced and desirable. She felt, again, as untried as the eighteen-year-old who had first made love with Andrei Chersakov.

"Tess."

He made no move to kiss her or caress her or embrace her. He simply lifted her hand and placed it on his chest, high, so the tips of two fingers grazed the skin exposed by his open collar.

She wanted to see him, to touch him. She opened his shirt, and he let her, accepting her touches, not reciprocating, even when they sat on the edge of the soft bed and she pushed the shirt off his shoulders and down his arms, even when the movement brushed the silk-covered tip of her breast against his chest, even when he had to close his eyes and fist his hands as she trailed soft fingers over him.

It was a stranger's body, yet familiar. The structure the same, the texture of the skin known, as she traced the stark collarbone, but the shoulders heavier, the ribs more marked with muscle. She kissed a remembered scar just below his waist, a souvenir, he'd told her in that other lifetime, of a neophyte's botched attempt at a lift. A lesson taught by pain. More flesh here than the youthful Andrei had carried.

Would he find her body the same mixture of remembered and new? Would he be disappointed?

He opened her blouse and bra, but didn't remove them. Slipping his hand under the cloth to touch her, the way he had in those snatched moments of intimacy from their past. Parting the fabric so his mouth could fit over her hardened nipple and draw on her desire. When his other hand slid down her abdomen, and beneath the band of her leggings, then panties, she expected the urgency of the past.

But Andrei Chersakov had changed beyond the physical. Their joinings eighteen years ago had been hurried, stolen moments . . . only moments. Rushed by their circumstances and their untried hunger.

This was different. He had learned to linger.

She might have preferred it otherwise.

He made each touch a question, each moment a decision. She kept answering yes.

He stroked and kissed her skin alive, refusing her efforts to reciprocate, denying her any hurry.

The gathering started deep inside her, the drawing together in her womb of emotion and sensation. She tried to let him know. She wanted him there, too.

"Andrei!"

He lifted his head from her breast, but his touch deepened inside her.

"Now, Tessa."

Yes, now.

She held on to him as she fell, fast and spinning, tumbling through sensation, then landed so slowly and softly, she wasn't sure when she touched down.

Lifting her eyelids became a conscious act. But they stayed open of their own accord.

Andrei was above her, his face drawn tight, his eyes burning with satisfaction. She touched his cheek, then traced the line of a vein from his chest, to his shoulder and down his arm to the inside of his elbow. Stretching to place a kiss at that spot.

He muttered something in Russian that had the tenor of a curse. She didn't mind, not even when he jerked away from her as if stung. Because he efficiently stripped off the rest of his clothes, then turned to her and as relentlessly removed hers.

Laying her back on the bed, he kissed her waist, the under curve of her breast and her abdomen, then knelt between her legs.

He took her hands in his and drew her to a sitting position, guiding her hands to wrap around his shaft, then he followed her back to the mattress, his hands still over hers. She opened to him and, hands guiding hands, they merged. He stilled deep inside her, a long unmeasured moment, then slowly began to withdraw.

She tried to hold him. Internal muscles, hands on his buttocks, legs wrapped tight, all to drew him deep again.

But he pulled back, until one more breath would separate them. She stopped trying to hold him. She stopped breathing.

"Tessa."

Pain sounded in his voice, but he wouldn't let her soothe it.

Then he came back into her, deep and slow.

Almost before she could realize the satisfaction of it, he started the withdrawal again.

"Andrei –"

The appeal, the efforts to keep him deep inside, nothing could withstand his slow, inexorable withdrawal. Sweat beaded his upper lip, slicked the hair at his temples. Veins routed his straining arms, but still he paused, an interminable tick of some inner clock. This time she met his return.

She stroked his back and watched, not fighting, as he paid this penance – that's what it seemed to her – a third time.

He sank into her, and she lifted her hips, taking him deeper than ever before. This time he stayed.

With the drive to move thrumming through both of them, they laid still. Stroking his hair, the back of his neck, his shoulders, she accepted his weight on her, his presence in her.

He shuddered against her. Something in Russian, dark and low. He raised up to meet her eyes, and rocked his hips against hers. And she knew there would be no more stillness until no energy, no emotion remained to move either of them.

DAY 12 – WEDNESDAY

"AMY, ARE YOU ready?"

It wasn't like Amy not to be the first one at the door, ready to go to the rink.

Today of all days, Tess didn't want any variation in her student's usual patterns, because tonight the ladies singles figure skating competed in the short program. Eight required elements packed into less than three minutes yet still expected to be artistic, graceful, interesting and fit the music. Any error in any required elements lost precious points in the score that counted as one-third of the overall results.

Tonight was all Tess would allow into her thoughts. Not last night, not the predawn hour when she slipped away while Andrei slept, not eighteen years ago and not tomorrow.

Tess's question drew only a shuffling sound. She pushed the door to Amy's room open wider.

First, Tess noted with relief, that Amy was dressed, ready for the easy skate-through at Andrei's rink. She sat, cross-legged on the crumpled covers of her bed, slipping newspaper clippings into an envelope.

"What's that you've got, Amy?"

"Just some stuff my parents brought me. Is it time to leave already?" She bounced up from the bed, flipping the envelope into the flotsam atop her dresser. "I'm all set. Let's go."

In a blur, she grabbed her bag and jacket and passed Tess in the doorway. Tess moved slower, eyeing that envelope as she closed the door.

✧   ✧   ✧   ✧

"NAN, THE MEDIA folks are asking if you'll do a news conference after training today. Say about two?"

Kyle had seen Rob approaching where she and Nan waited before their first training runs. She tugged at her gloves, watching her fingers flex in them.

Nan emitted an exaggerated sigh. "God, I didn't realize this medal-winning took so much energy after the race."

"You want to give it away?" Kyle offered.

"No way, Armstrong. I've seen the way you look at it. No way am I letting you near it." Kyle grinned. "Okay, Rob. Tell them sure. Oh, no – wait. We're going to the U.S.-Finland hockey game. Tell them five-thirty. That should give me time."

"Okay." He turned and started off.

"Hey, Rob!" At Nan's call he stopped about four feet from them and looked back. "Do you think you could . . . I mean, would you mind being there, too?

"No, I wouldn't mind." His gaze flicked to Kyle for the first time, then back to Nan. "I'll be there, Monahan."

Kyle watched him ski slowly down the course, making a last check before letting his skiers try it, and wondered about that look.

✧   ✧   ✧   ✧

AFTER THE INJURIES from the quarterfinal victory, the U.S. hockey team was like a house missing several beams and foundation blocks. It could stay standing as long as a strong wind didn't blow.

The wind blew in the third period.

A goal by Tonetti, still bandaged and puffy-faced, and strong goal-tending had Team USA down by only 2-1 midway through the final period, even though Finland's team had twice as many shots on goal and had seemed to control the puck two-thirds of the time.

The referee's whistle blew signifying a penalty.

"What penalty? Who's it on? Us or them?" Rikki demanded. But none of the Americans sitting around her and her apartment-mates could answer.

The referee indicated a roughing penalty, against Team USA. The players milled angrily, the American supporters booed. Even the Finnish team seemed somewhat puzzled as the American went to the penalty box, leaving his team one player short for the two minutes of his sentence.

"Look, Lanny's really going after that official."

Kyle pointed, but Rikki was already watching Lanny jawing at the man in the black and white stripes.

"Don't make it worse, Kaminski," she whispered. "Don't blow up, don't blow."

The coach might have been thinking the same thing. He shouted, and Lanny finally backed away. Another shout from the coach, and he slowly skated to the bench.

"He's taking Lanny out. He won't make him sit out the rest of the game, will he?"

Lanny didn't say a word in response to the coach, but his stiff movements as he sat said volumes. When the coach sent out a player who'd just finished a long, tiring shift on the ice, Rikki clenched her hands. "God, I wish he'd left Lanny on to kill this penalty. He would have cooled down in a second."

Instead, the Finnish team heated up. They skated around, past and between the man-short Americans. The U.S. goalie stopped shots twice. Then a third time. But not the fourth. The score was 3-1.

Before Lanny got back on the ice after being held out an extra shift, it was 4-1, and all but over. Weakened by injury, Team USA was collapsing under the strong wind. For the first time in the tournament, an opponent scored a goal while Lanny Kaminski was on the ice, and it ended at 5-1.

At center ice, Finland's team celebrated the victory and the trip to the gold medal game.

Rikki stood silently among the other Americans, applauding and many shouting would-be consolation.

"Nobody thought they'd go this far, coming in," said Tess. "They should be proud of themselves."

"Don't tell Lanny that," Rikki advised, trying for humor. It didn't work. He'd wanted this so much.

She'd agreed to meet Lanny in a high corner of the stands. If Team USA had won, he would have wanted to stay to see the second semifinal and get a live look at the gold medal game opponent. Now, she wasn't sure.

Each of her apartment-mates touched her on the shoulder or arm as they left, as if offering consolation.

Some time later, when she caught sight of Lanny, grimly climbing the stairs toward her, she wished it were that simple. The crowd from the first game had cleared out and the stands had started to fill for the second game before he appeared. But empty seats still surrounded her distant spot. He glanced up once, spotted her, then dropped his gaze to his feet as he climbed.

He didn't meet her look when he dropped into the seat beside her.

"Hi." She put her hand on his.

He didn't acknowledge her greeting or her touch.

"Do you want to stay for this game? We've got some time, but remember, we're all going to watch Amy skate tonight. Give her a real rooting section for her first competition. I told you about that, didn't I?"

"Yeah."

"We thought we could all meet at the cafeteria for dinner beforehand. It would be nice to eat in town, but it could be late by the time the skating's done and I've got my competition tomorrow. Maybe we can have dinner in town tom –" No, that wouldn't work. Because he would now be playing for the bronze medal on Friday instead of having the day off and playing for the gold the following day. "So it makes more sense to just eat together in the cafeteria tonight and –"

"I'm not in the mood."

"Oh, come on, Lanny. This will do you good. You'll feel better –"

"Bullshit. Sitting around the cafeteria pretending with all your friends isn't going to me make feel better. You go if you want to."

"But the figure skating –"

"I'm not going. I've had my fill of skating today."

"Amy hasn't. She could use our support." More than her patience wearing thin, a kind of fear hit her that the Mr. Hyde before her had permanently replaced Dr. Jekyll. "So you didn't win this game, there's –"

"We lost. We didn't not win, we fucking lost."

"I know, but –"

"Lost, do you understand? It's the only thing left when you don't win."

"Lanny, for heaven's sake, your life isn't over. There's –"

"What the fuck do you know about it? I'm a hockey player, and that's all I've ever been. And I've got one God-damned game left. One game. One more chance to do something, be something. Not the best, because we blew that to hell today, but something. One more chance to take something away from this, from all the years."

"You will take something away from it no matter what, because you've put so much into it –"

"Horseshit."

She took a deep breath. "It might take a while, but you'll see that you've gotten a lot out of your years playing hockey –"

"Yeah, a bank account that couldn't buy me a ticket home and a body so messed up they should turn me into glue like they do horses."

"A tremendous knowledge of your sport and people. You could coach. You'd be a good coach. A great coach if you learned some patience for other people's frailties." Her pain at his bitterness had produced sharper words than she'd intended. She pushed it back and tried again. "I can understand how disappointed you are now, when you've worked so hard for this, and put everything in to trying to –"

"How can you understand when you've never put everything into anything in your life? You always play it safe, hold something back. Don't ever risk giving it all, that's you."

Her pain came first as heat, then turned cold. She thought her teeth would chatter with the cold, so she clenched her jaw.

"Lanny." She glanced around at the interested faces turned toward the corner where they sat. Many probably didn't understand all the words, but the emotions were universal. "This isn't the place –"

"Oh, the perfect Rochelle Lodge," he sneered. "How could I forget? Can't have a public scene."

The bitter hurt didn't leave, but its roiling slowed, settled by the cleansing burn of her rare anger. "I can't imagine how you could forget, since Lanny Kaminski never lets go of anything – including thoughts, opinions and decisions. He can't see there's a difference between giving up and going on."

He was too far gone to recognize the snarl under her words.

"Perfect Rochelle Lodge," he sneered, "who operates on some plane above all the rest of us. Never sullying herself with anything as coarse as competition or – God forbid – ambition. She never makes a mistake, because she never ventures that far out on a limb. She never fails, because she never puts herself on the line."

She stood, rigid with the determination to get away before she said – or heard – unbridgable words.

"Sure, walk away. Don't risk being part of anything as common as a scene. Don't –"

"Shut up! Just shut the fuck up!" Even at that moment, a layer of her mind understood that he pushed her away out of fear. But understanding didn't stop the pain from cracking her composure and letting the anger pour out. "You want a scene, Kaminski? Okay, here it is.

"Fail? Yeah, I sure as hell do fail. I've failed totally in making you see beyond your holy competition, to make you see how damn shallow wins and losses are. But that's the way you want it. It's not just all you know, it's all you *want* to know. You have no compassion for anyone else, no understanding that everyone isn't like you, everyone isn't going to pour their souls into a game. And you're so sure you're better than these other people. And I'm sick to death of it. I can't take another minute of it, because it makes you a pathetic excuse for a man. Mistakes? You want to hear about mistakes?"

The sound that should have been a laugh held no humor. Lanny half rose toward her, but said nothing.

"How about the mistake of a lifetime? How about my falling in love with you? You asshole."

She spun on the last two words and got out of there.

NAN HAD THEM eating out of her hand.

Rob had figured she wouldn't need him around, but she'd asked – unlike Kyle, who'd never asked his help in any way – and he was happy to lend whatever support he provided by holding up the wall at the back of the crowded room.

She answered the questions, she laughed, she was self-deprecating, skipped the cliches, gave them great quotes and ideal sound-bites. What more could a reporter ask?

"Ms. Monahan . . ." The voice raised the hair on the back of Rob's neck. Before he even leaned around the person in front of him to get a look at the speaker, he visualized the bulbous nose and sneer. "You're friends with Kyle Armstrong, aren't you?"

"Sure." Nan's face showed only puzzlement.

"What do you think of her missing the combined and now the giant slalom races?"

"I think it's a tremendous disappointment to her."

"And to all the people who had hoped for medals from her in those races."

"Are you trying to make a point?" Rob could see the temper rising in Nan. He pushed the man in front of him out of the way, trying to catch her eye, but Nan was riveted on the reporter.

"My point is that Kyle Armstrong didn't ski in the GS and her great friend – you – won a medal."

"So?"

"Would you have won that medal if Kyle Armstrong had been in that race?"

"How should I know? I might not have gotten the bronze if there'd been another kind of wax on my skis or if the temperature had been two degrees warmer or if the sun had gone behind a cloud just before my run or if my goggles had slipped a fraction or a thousand other ifs. The fact is I won the bronze."

"The fact also is that people have been expecting for the past two years that Kyle Armstrong would come into these Olympics as the savior of American women's Alpine skiing and so far she has skipped her two scheduled races –"

"The fact is people like you have made Kyle into that so-called savior of American skiing – as if we needed a savior in the first place. And for the past two years Kyle's had to ski with that load of crap on her back. Where have you been the past two years, Mister? I haven't seen you around. I haven't seen you at the weight room at eight in the morning, or out on the hill taking one more run after a day full of runs just to try to slice a hundredth of a second off a training time. I haven't seen you with knees that ached like hell or Technicolor bruises all up your arms from slapping against gates. And until I do see you out there for a couple years straight, I don't want to hear any more crap from you about expectations and disappointments."

She scanned the rest of the room with narrowed eyes. "Any more questions?"

Two beats of silence, then a voice slowly ventured. "Uh, Nan, what are you expecting from Friday's slalom?"

Rob held his breath until Nan's expression eased. Apparently she, too, had recognized one of the regulars from the World Cup circuit, and answered civilly.

When the news conference broke up, he collared one of the media liaison people to find out about the bulbous-nosed reporter. The answer didn't reassure him.

"Hey, champ," he greeted Nan when they met up to start back to the Athletes' Village. "That was a hell of a right to that guy's jaw."

"Who the hell is he? Do you know who he writes for?"

"Yeah. He freelances a lot. For the tabloids, mostly around Europe, some in South America. Apparently he's got accreditation through some rag in Brazil."

"The tabloids?" They'd both spent too much time in Europe not to have seen the gaudy sheets, and the blaring headlines that would feel right at home among the American grocery store gossip tabloids. "I didn't even know they sent anybody to the Olympics. I thought their coverage stuck to which minor royalty messed around with which starlet and who was seen how drunk at what nightspot."

"They've gone after some athletes. Couple tennis players especially got raked over the coals. Family, finances and love lives. That sort of thing."

They exchanged a look.

"That sucks," she said.

"Yeah, it does."

"Those questions about Kyle. Do you think . . ."

"I don't know."

✧   ✧   ✧   ✧

"RIKKI?"

In the dark living room, Tess could just make out the auburn hair of the figure huddled in the chair by the window. There was no answer. She moved closer, and slowly lowered herself into the chair across from Rikki's.

"Rikki, are you okay?"

"Fine." She stirred, but kept her knees pulled up to her chin and her arms wrapped around her legs. "Just thinking."

"We heard about the hockey game. It's a shame. They all worked so hard. I'm sorry."

For once Amy hadn't argued about not going to the game. With her short program tonight, she'd agreed to Tess's schedule of skate-throughs this morning, then the official practice before a light meal and the nap she was taking now. But when they'd heard the hockey score, she'd given Tess a stricken look, as if the Americans had lost only because Amy Yost hadn't been there.

"Yeah. It's a shame."

"Rikki, what is it? Is something wrong? With you and Lanny?"

"Not any more." She released her legs, dropping her knees to the side and folding her hands in her lap. She spoke without heat. "What was wrong was Lanny and me. But that's all over now."

"What are you saying? You broke up?"

"You can't call it breaking up when two people barely knew each other. More a case of lust, I suppose." She sounded rational and calm. "If I'd had more experience with that sort of thing, I probably would have recognized it for what it was. But I didn't, so I thought great sex meant we were more involved than we were. In reality, it was simply physical desire. Chemistry. Lust. Whatever you want to call it."

"Rikki, that's crazy. I've seen you and Lanny together, it's more than a couple people working off their libidos. You care about each other."

"The way we'd care about a pleasant seatmate on a long plane trip, perhaps, someone you get a glimpse inside but will never see again." Rikki shook her head. "My mistake was fooling myself into thinking it could be any more than that. I never should have tried to get involved with him. We're too different. He sees things so simplistically, so black and white. Win or lose. Give everything all the time or you're not trying. He doesn't understand there are times you have to hold back, balance, be cautious."

"Are you talking about competition or relationships, Rikki?"

"I don't think you're anybody to be giving advice here, Tess. When you straighten out your mess with Andrei, then you come back and tell me how to run my life and maybe I'll listen."

Tess stilled her instinct to recoil from the words, still spoken in the same rational tone.

Almost immediately Rikki leaned across the gap between their chairs, putting her hand on Tess's.

"Oh, God, I'm sorry, Tess. I shouldn't have said that." Rikki's false calm had finally broken, along with her voice. "I had no right –"

"But you're right. You're absolutely right. I'm not anybody to be giving advice." She stood.

"Tess, please –"

"It's all right, Rikki. It's about time I woke up Amy. Are you going to come tonight?"

"Yes, of course. But don't . . . don't tell Amy about this, okay? I mean Lanny and . . . Well, not tonight, anyhow, okay?"

"No, I won't. Not tonight. But she's very quick. She'll figure it out. Especially tomorrow at your race. If Lanny isn't –"

"He won't be there."

"Maybe, maybe not."

"He won't."

"But the rest of us will be, Rikki."

"Thanks, Tess."

Tess saw the sheen of tears in Rikki's eyes before she turned away.

RIKKI CALLED ROY Welch, the assistant coach who doubled as coordinator for the biathlon team, with her request while she waited for Kyle and Nan to leave for the figure skating.

"God, I don't know, Rikki. This late, I don't know if I can get you on a flight."

"Try, Roy, okay?"

"I'll try. When's your original flight out? You were going to stick around, weren't you?"

"Yeah. My flight was Monday. But with my last event tomorrow, I'd rather get out of here earlier. Friday if possible."

"Friday? Geez, I don't know. That doesn't give me much time."

"I know. Just try, okay?"

"Sure."

She hung up to find Kyle leaning against the doorjamb watching her.

"You're leaving Friday?"

"Trying," Rikki corrected. "He's not sure he can get me anything, but it's worth a try. It would give me a little break back home. Give me a chance to see my mother, that sort of thing."

Kyle nodded. "That's understandable. Although I wish you could stick around for the slalom Friday, watch Nan and me ski."

"Oh, my God. The slalom! How could I forget? I'm so sorry. I don't know what I was thinking –"

"Probably about getting out of here before the hockey team plays Friday night."

Kyle's tone was mild, but her eyes were sharp. Rikki opened her mouth, then shut it without making the denial.

"That's understandable, too, Rikki. Tess said you and Lanny had decided to go separate ways."

"Not quite that civilized, I'm afraid, but that's the general idea." Such a polite phrase for a screaming public fight.

"If you can't get an earlier flight –"

"I'll definitely be at the slalom finish Friday afternoon."

THE WARM-UP DID not go well.

For six minutes Tess stood behind the boards that separated her from the Olympic Ice Hall rink watching Amy share the ice with the five other skaters in her group. Random draw determined the order of skating, with a break after every five or six skaters to resurface the ice and allow the next set of skaters to warm up. Luck had placed Amy as the second skater in the second-to-last group, along with Xi Ling, the No. 2 American and a medal contender from Denmark.

It hadn't been good luck.

Being matched so directly with top skaters was definitely distracting and possibly intimidating. Amy kept watching the other skaters instead of focusing on her own work. What attention she had to spare went to the filled arena, shimmering with waving flags, and the cameras, still and television, that tracked the skaters' every breath. Her movements looked jerky and slow. The one time she went up for what should have been a triple lutz, she doubled it.

One by one, the skaters came through the gate, leaving the ice to Xi Ling, the first of their group to skate. Amy was the last one off.

"Did you see what she did?" she demanded of Tess.

"Who?"

"Xi Ling. She didn't even look at me when I said hi, after everything we did for her."

With no cameras and no audience, Tess might have taken Amy by the shoulders and given her a shake. But she didn't have that option.

"You tried to talk to her out there? You know better than that. She's concentrating on her skate. You should have been, too."

Amy looked sullen, but muttered only, "I was trying to be friendly."

The announcer's voice blared Xi Ling's introduction, and the skater headed for the center of the rink.

Tess led Amy into a back hallway, hoping Amy could concentrate there. The girl had been so calm at the nationals. With nothing to lose, she'd been focused and at-ease. Now her eyes darted from activity down the hall to the television monitor showing Xi Ling's powerful and graceful performance.

She's not ready.

The uncertainty of the past month, swirling disagreeably in Tess's stomach as Amy's practices had deteriorated the past few days, solidified into a rock. Amy wasn't ready for this level of pressure; she had too much experience to ignore it and not enough to cope with it.

Applause rumbled over them for the end of Xi Ling's program, and an official beckoned to Amy that she could get on the ice while Xi Ling awaited her scores. Mechanically, Amy handed her skate guards to Tess.

"Have fun," Tess forced herself to say.

Amy didn't even look up; she might not have heard the familiar words.

She did look up as Xi Ling's impressive scores were called off.

Don't look at the scores, Amy. Don't think about them. Don't think about anything but your program. Don't . . .

Wishes spoken against the wind. Tess had an irrational urge to run across the ice, snatch Amy back and hide her away. Away from all these eyes, away from all these cameras.

Too late. The music started, and Amy began.

It was as if her body took over the familiar task her mind had forgotten how to perform. The hours and hours of learning the program, perfecting it, performing it created a Pavlovian response; she heard the music and her muscles reacted.

But the spirit, the emotion, the sparkle, the fun were not there.

Amy performed the required step a and spiral sequence without a mistake, then built up speed for her first jump, a double axel, where the forward takeoff and backward landing would add an extra half a revolution. But she didn't have her usual momentum going in. Tess saw Amy bend her knee more than usual, trying to gain lift.

Get it straight before the landing.

Before the thought completed in Tess' mind, Amy had spun once, twice, and another half turn in the air, and was coming down. Her blade struck the ice solid, but her balance was off, her momentum driving her body toward the ground. Instinctively, she touched her other skate to the ice, forcing herself upright.

It wasn't pretty, despite the crowd's applause for her effort, and two-footing a landing would cost her, but not as much as falling would have.

Tess started to release a relieved breath, then sucked it in.

Amy still looked back at the spot on the ice where she'd almost fallen, instead of refocusing on the combination jump that came next – her most difficult maneuver and another required element.

From the moment Amy left the ice, Tess knew the triple lutz was trouble. Amy had tilted so far back that when she landed, gravity carried her down, her skate going out from under her. She landed hard, cushioning her hip with one arm. She scrambled up automatically, but the music had left her behind; she'd missed the second half of the combination, a double toe loop jump, and her score would tumble.

The crowd groaned in sympathy, but Amy didn't fold. If anything the trouble with the jumps seemed to shake her out of her lethargy. The rest of her program, while not her best, was crisp and clean. She landed a perfect double flip and drew applause with her flying jump spin that changed into a sit spin.

She held her finish pose for longer than normal, gave the bare minimum of curtsies to the audience, skated in and took the guards from Tess without looking at her.

But Tess had seen Amy's eyes – wide and slightly glazed, almost stricken. She wanted to fold the girl in her arms, but if Amy broke down now, she might never put herself back together. Tess did take Amy's hand, holding it tight as they settled on the bench for the scores, not entirely sure who gave and who received comfort from the touch.

Amy took the stems of flowers offered, one accompanied by a small American flag, and even managed a half smile for the little girl who delivered them.

It faded when she saw the scores.

✦ ✦ ✦ ✦

TESS PACED ALONG the side of the apartment building, the calm exterior giving way now.

It had served its purpose. With well-meaning people from Amy's parents to Mikey Sweet offering sympathy as if Amy had been the victim of a natural disaster, she'd needed someone to treat the whole thing as unfortunate, but undramatic.

When Mr. Yost called the judges brutal, Tess said they were tough, but not unfair. When Mrs. Yost questioned the quality of the ice, she said it was the same ice everyone else had skated. When Mikey awkwardly patted Amy's shoulder and mumbled something about tough luck, though, she said nothing.

Tough luck might not have felled Amy tonight, but luck had been a factor. The luck – and injuries to top contenders – that had allowed her to finish third in the Nationals and gain this trip to the Olympics so early in her career. And the luck that had given her a famous coach, and considerably more attention because of it.

Through all of it, Amy remained silent. Not crying, not complaining. Almost stunned, more withdrawn than Tess had ever seen her.

"Tess."

"Oh, Andrei." He arrived from the darkness, as he so often did. Perhaps as she'd known he would. "I can't see you. Not tonight. I just came out for some air because Rikki insisted. But Amy might need me. I have to go right back in. I can't see you."

"You are seeing me."

"I meant —"

"I know what you meant. Sex is not all I want of you, Tess Rutledge. That is not all I have to give."

"I didn't —"

He stopped her words by folding her into his arms, tight and warm and so comforting. "I know."

He held her, long enough for her shoulders to relax, her hands to unclench. Finally, she tunneled her hands inside his open jacket and slid them around his waist, returning the embrace.

"You can not hold all the pain away from her, Tess. It is a part of growing to a woman. Also of growing to a skater, a wonderful skater."

"I know. And when she's ready, I'll talk to her about this. But now, to see her feeling that she's failed, and so publicly, so horribly publicly — it hurts to watch. I love that girl, Andrei, and it hurts to watch her in pain."

His arms tightened around her and he kissed her hair, then her temple.

DAY 13 – THURSDAY

STARE LONG ENOUGH, especially in the hesitant light of an early morning in mid-winter, and the white of an anonymous ceiling became the white of snow, which soon took on the familiar pattern of the course she would ski in a few hours.

Rikki stared until she saw each dip, rise, curve and hollow of the course she'd traced daily. She negotiated them, remembering the feel of the track under her skis, the way they bit in this curve, the amount of pressure needed to nurse the most speed from that downhill. Her hands curled into position around poles, her shoulder felt the weight of the rifle.

In a few hours, she would do just what she'd planned. She'd worked too hard and too long to arrive at that start line to let anything or anyone intrude.

Lanny.

No. She wouldn't think of him. He wanted only victory. She wouldn't let him interfere with her finding victory within the effort. She wouldn't . . .

The white of the mental course imposed over the white of the ceiling wavered, slipping toward the bluer white of ice marked off by colored lines. No –

She closed her eyes and conjured up the safe image of the targets. Set. Sighted. Steadied. Shot.

✧ ✧ ✧ ✧

"AMY, ARE YOU nearly ready?"

"Practice isn't for three hours." Amy's words barely reached beyond the closed door.

Without waiting for an invitation or knocking and thus risking a rejection, Tess opened the door. Amy sat sideways on the tousled bed, her back against the wall, wearing the hip-length T-shirt she used as a night gown, a pair of knit leggings and oversized socks. She hadn't brushed her hair or washed her face.

"What's the matter?"

Tess's question drew a disdainful noise. "Nothing. Not a thing." The sarcasm slid away. "I just stunk up so badly last night I don't ever want to show my face again."

"There's not a skater alive who hasn't had a disastrous performance. What matters is where you go from here. How you react."

"I let everybody down."

"Everybody?"

"My parents. You –"

"Let's start with your parents. What did they say to you? What did they do?"

"They said they were proud of me. They hugged me," Amy mumbled mechanically.

"But you don't believe them?"

"Parents just say those things."

"So your parents are liars?"

"No!"

"Then you owe them the courtesy of believing them. Now, for me. I know I haven't said that you let me down, because I don't feel that way."

Amy gave her a look blended of disbelief and disgust. Tess wasn't sure how much of the disgust Amy meant for her and how much for herself. "You're a champion, a great skater. You must have expected me to do well or you wouldn't've wasted your time on me."

"Wasted my time? Is that what you think of me? How many classes of beginners do I teach most weeks, Amy? How many?"

"I dunno."

"Take a guess."

"Two?"

"Five. Three children's and two adults'. Do you think I'm teaching them to scout out future champions? If I am, I'm pretty damn stupid, since I doubt Mrs. Zolaski will see sixty again. But if that's what you think of me, you'd better go looking for another coach after this is all over. Someone who's not a mercenary."

Amy's eyes went wide with shock. Tess had to steel herself against the tears that filled their corners.

"I don't want another coach."

"Good, because I wouldn't want anyone else to get the credit when you become a champion."

Tears slipped free, clearly surprising Amy. "Oh, Tess, I'll never . . ."

She wrapped her arms around the girl. So often the woman she would become showed in Amy that everyone around her forgot about the child not yet left behind.

"You will be, Amy. You will be. It's going to take time, a lot more hard work and some changes. You might have programs that go even worse than last night's, but you *will* be a champion."

The first change, Tess had already decided, would be a choreographer. An image of Andrei flashed into her head. No. She'd find someone else to help mold Amy's programs into the showcases she needed while Tess strengthened her skills.

"Now, since we've eliminated your parents and me, tell me about this 'everyone' you've let down."

Amy lifted her head and wiped away tears with the tips of her fingers. Not like a child who rubs with her fist or palm, but like an adult. Tess swallowed down her own sudden tears.

Amy waved toward her dresser. "Everybody who was pulling for me."

Tess followed the direction of the wave and spotted the manila envelope. "What's in the envelope?"

"Newspaper stories Mom and Dad brought from home. All these stories about how a local girl was going to the Olympics. A bunch of letters and e-mails from people telling me they hope I do well, and I don't even know these people."

Tess let out a breath, then drew in another. She was going to have to have a long, quiet talk with Elizabeth and Greg Yost about the delicate balance of confidence skaters needed. They would talk after this was all over – and before the World Championships next month.

She took Amy's face between her palms.

"You listen to me now, Amy Yost, because this is very important. As well-intentioned as all those people probably are, you can't carry them on to the ice with you. No skater can. Those people aren't there all the hours you practice and practice and practice to get one move. They're not there when you're sore from a fall or you've pulled a muscle. They're not there when you have to skip a school party because you're getting up early the next morning for a competition. They're not there for all those hard times and you can't let them be there when the spotlight hits you and it's your turn to skate. They have no right to be there, but they don't really know that. You have to shut them out. That's your responsibility. Even your parents who are there for the hard times, even me. You have to skate from within yourself, for yourself.

"When you're on that ice, only you exist, but you exist in a way you can exist nowhere else on earth. But to do that, you have to leave everyone else behind and be alone out there. No one to help you, no one to hold you back. Just you. Do you understand?"

Amy's clear, young eyes looked at Tess.

"I don't know."

Tess released her and laughed, a little uneasy with her own vehemence. "Well, that's honest. And it's a good start."

She stood, picked up a pair of tights dangling from the dresser top and tossed them to Amy.

"For now, get dressed. We have ninety minutes at Andrei's rink, and if we don't leave soon, we'll be late." She looked back and saw Amy's relief that her return to the ice after last night's fiasco would not be in front of the avid spectators at the Olympic Ice Hall.

"Okay. Give me five minutes."

But at the door, Tess was stopped by Amy's voice.

matter. You didn't get a second shot, so the only thing to do was keep moving.

This time she looked back. She'd hit it! All five targets hit!

Relief sagged her shoulders, even as she kept moving. No penalty time. No real damage done – except to her nerves.

"Stick with it, Rikki. Still top ten. C'mon, ski!"

She set her rhythm, aware now of pacing herself.

"You're slipping back, Rikki!"

That refrain echoed through the next two and a half loops. From seventh to tenth, then thirteenth. The gap widening between her and the top skiers. From twenty seconds to forty-two, then a minute, two, almost three.

But she was shooting fine. Collected, concentrated. With three trips to the range done and one to go, she'd knocked off all but one target. Not bad for the fifteen kilometer race. Very few made it through that distance and that many targets without a miss. She just had to make sure not to miss more; she couldn't make it up on the course.

She skied methodically, not risking her steadiness at the range. She shot carefully, not risking penalty minutes.

Another skier passed her. She didn't try to identify the individual or the country. Just another jacket splashed with variations of red, white and blue. Amazing how many countries used those colors. A lot of them had passed her over the past half hour.

Biathlon, hockey, it doesn't matter. You didn't put everything in to it. You held back and played it safe.

Damn him! Why wouldn't Lanny stay out of her head?

"Rikki! Pick it up! Pick it up!"

Roy Welch leaned forward from the crowd to shout the words. She heard the frustration in the assistant coach's voice. Now only American coaches called her times, letting her know how she stood – how much she'd slipped.

It had started to snow. Fine flakes, almost invisible individually, but together they veiled the jacket of the skier who'd passed her just now.

I know you, Rikki. And I know you don't come anywhere near going all-out.

That jacket.

What country was it from? She had to know. She couldn't let it get away. She clung to the sight of it until her eyes burned. Each slide forward she made a little longer, a little stronger, trying to close the gap to that red, white and blue jacket. Like someone climbing a rope, hand over painful hand, with an abyss below, she skated her skies, planted her poles, dropped her head and drove herself another mite forward.

"C'mon, Rikki, you can do it! You're almost there. Go harder!"

Did that voice came from inside her head? It almost sounded like Lanny. It had to be a coach, a trainer, a teammate's relative who recognized her struggle. Looking to identify the shouter would take time. She didn't look.

The pattern on the jacket took form now, the snow no barrier. The edge between the splash of red and the blue was piped with a darker blue. What country was it from?

Passing took concentration. Keeping the rhythm, not impeding the other skier, easing around.

But she looked back as she settled in.

France. The jacket was from France.

Satisfaction propelled her, pumping a reserve of adrenaline when she'd thought she had none left.

She was nearing the range for her final five targets. She should slow her pace so she'd be steady, especially with that climbing approach to the range. But there was another jacket just visible ahead. Was that Italy or Germany. . .?

Italy.

But she didn't confirm it until the final hundred meters before the range. Her body still pulsing with the extra effort, she slid into position No. 3 and shot.

The first must have been a homing pigeon. No way the bullet she'd dispatched so willy-nilly should have made acquaintance with the target. But it did. She struggled not to grin. Deserved or not, she'd take it. A hit, by God, a hit!

The second was textbook, her breathing controlled, concentration firm.

The third felt the same. She stared at the target an extra second, waiting for the paddle to come up to acknowledge the hit. Nothing.

A miss. *A minute.* An infinity of burning thighs and laboring lungs. Those sixty seconds she'd made up on the French skier, bought and paid for in pain and effort. Gone.

She felt despair knot in her stomach, even as she drained it from her mind, sighted and squeezed. And again.

Automatically she headed onto the course. The last two had hit. But the damage had already been done. That miss left her with two. Two minutes penalty to add to her time.

She dug her poles in and shot down an incline.

Damn him, damn him to hell. Hope you're damn happy now, Kaminski. You had to keep pushing, didn't you?

You're too busy playing it safe.

Well, screw him. She hadn't played it safe and she'd missed a damn target. What the hell right did he have to say she played it safe when she sure as hell hadn't played it safe when it came to – An urge to smile wasn't strong enough to rearrange facial muscles rigid with effort. – well, screwing him?

Playing it safe. Safe? Getting involved with him? More like demented. Masochistic. Self-destructive. He was a crazy man. Driven and competitive and intense. That wasn't what she wanted. She didn't need –

"You're going great, Rikki. You're making up time this lap. Ninety-one seconds behind the leader, Rikki!"

That startled her so much she turned her head and tried to holler back. It came out a croak. "What?"

Roy Welch's face popped out of the crowd before she had to return her attention to where the course curved right. "Ninety-one seconds behind. One minute, thirty-one seconds!"

But her misses. Why did he sound so excited when they'd have to add two minutes to that?

"Penalties!" was all she had breath for.

But she'd already left Roy behind as the course turned. No – there he was, pushing his way to the edge of the course. He must have cut across the area open to spectators while the course took the less direct route.

"That includes penalties! That includes penalties!" he started shouting while she was still skiing toward his new position. "You can do it, Rikki. Give it all you got!"

The people around him must have picked up his urgency because they started clapping and urging her on in a chorus of languages. A tingle passed through her body, almost like electricity. Not painful but a little unnerving. She gave an extra surge, and the noise intensified.

She had no sense of time, only of her body's struggle. Once again coaches and trainers from other teams called out numbers to her, but she couldn't take it in.

Then she heard nothing except the roar inside her head as she started up the incline toward the finish. The course had become a mountain face she had to climb with legs as burning and slow-going as lava.

The finish loomed above, lined by photographers with cameras grown surrealistically large, ready to zoom in on her distress.

Just finish. Just finish.

Go for broke. Go for broke.

Her legs were cramping. With each extension they tightened into a ball of pain that fought her orders to straighten so she could start the next extension. She did it anyhow. Forcing her leg to extend, straighten, extend, straighten. Each step a triumph of determination.

"C'mon, Rikki! C'mon!"

The tide of shouts from the stands along the finish was buoying and heartening and she would have traded them all for a Kleenex to wipe her streaming nose and a second to use it.

But she couldn't afford a second. Not until she crossed the finish line.

The line.

An orange thread in the snow. She lunged for it, her skis sliding smoothly across, her knees buckling as she released her muscles from servitude to her will.

The ground wouldn't stay still, spinning and shifting with each heaving breath. Vaguely she was aware of hands spreading a blanket over her, and a strange voice asking if she was all right. But it didn't seem to expect an answer.

The cold against her cheek finally forced her to lift her head from the snow-packed earth; the rest of her body would have much preferred to stay put. A different volunteer helped her rise, kept a shoulder under her arm and pressed something into her hand – two tissues! What luxury.

The volunteer handed her over to Roy at the opening from the finish area. Coaches weren't supposed to be there, but nobody complained, least of all her as he wrapped her in a long-armed hug. He was breathing hard. He must have run from that last spot she'd seen him on the course. At least he'd had a direct path, wasn't carrying a ten-pound rifle on his back and hadn't already gone fourteen and a half kilometers.

"Personal best, Rikki?" shouted a reporter.

"Personal best?" Roy repeated. "That was a personal fucking great!"

"What place?" the reporter pursued.

"Don't know yet. Won't know for a while, but it looks real good for top ten."

"Top ten?" she whispered.

"Damn right." As he guided her along, he added so only she heard, "Ninth for sure, maybe eighth."

"Eighth?" She barely mouthed the word.

"Yeah, so now you won't be pissed at me for not getting that earlier flight – you'll want to stick around and celebrate."

"Rikki? Can I talk to you?" She identified the reporter from her hometown.

"She has to cool down." Roy kept her moving.

"I'll come back," she promised.

Roy also kept her moving as she received a stream of congratulations from teammates, officials, competitors, teammates' families, unknown spectators and, finally, her private cheering section, swelled by a troop of Monahans.

Satisfied she was sufficiently cooled down, Roy helped her remove her skis. He only left her side after giving Tess firm instructions about getting Rikki into dry, warm clothes.

"For Pete's sake, Roy, I can take care of myself."

He ignored her protest, handed a pile of clothing he'd had someone retrieve from the start area and headed off to take care of another skier who'd just finished.

"I can take care of this myself," Rikki repeated, reaching to take her clothes from Tess.

Tess backed up a step. "I'm sure you can, but I follow orders. We don't want you sick for our celebration later."

Rikki was smiling by the time she'd stripped off the wet outer layers and let Tess help her replace them with warm, dry clothes.

"Okay, now that Rikki's all set, we can go celebrate," declared Amy.

"Oh, no we can't. We can go back to the apartment, get our things and head for the rink for another run-through, young lady. I should have my head examined for letting you come out here at all."

"Aw, Tess . . ."

"Besides, you guys can't celebrate tonight, because Kyle and I have a race tomorrow, and no celebration's complete without me," Nan declared.

"She is the champion celebrator," agreed Kyle.

"See? So, we'll have one big celebration tomorrow night –"

"After Amy skates," interposed Tess.

"After Amy skates," agreed Nan. "And we'll show this town the true meaning of personal best!"

Pulling on gloves, Rikki let her smile grow.

That's when she saw Lanny.

He stood about thirty feet away, leaning against a temporary fence on the far side of a stream of spectators flowing both directions.

It *was* his voice she'd heard out on the course, the voice urging her to catch up with the French skier. Not just in her head, but for real.

He straightened away from the fence. He was going to come over here. They were going to talk. What would she say? That he'd been right? That she'd still cursed him on the trail? That anger at him had propelled her into the strong finish? That she missed him? That she wasn't sure she could ever love someone as driven as Lanny Kaminski? That she loved him anyhow?

She looked down at the gloves, pulling them until her short finger-nails dug deep into the lining.

When she looked up, he was gone.

Her throat stung with regret, but she also knew relief. Still, her eyes kept checking the flow of spectators.

Keeping her promise, she returned for an interview for her hometown paper. The results were official – she had eighth. Eighth! Word spread about the surprisingly strong showing for an American woman and several other reporters asked for comment.

She'd never received this much attention – biathletes were not at the top of many interview lists, even at the Olympics, and for the other three years, eleven months and two weeks the media seemed to think biathletes hibernated. It might be fun under other circumstances. But not when you looked for a certain dark-haired man with intense brown eyes. Especially not when you didn't find him.

WHEN THE KNOCK came at the apartment door, Kyle answered it because no one else was around. Rikki hadn't come back yet from a post-race meal with her teammates and coaches, Tess and Amy had gone for a run-through at that rink Andrei had rented and Nan had gone off to shop with her sisters and sister-in-law. They'd invited Kyle, but she opted to rest.

Rob stood in the doorway.

He hadn't been to the apartment in four days, since the night she'd told him she was going back into training. Now he stood at her door. Hands jammed in his jeans pockets, holding back the side flaps of his open parka, his mouth grim, his eyes slate gray.

She felt as if she'd just gone off a rise she hadn't expected, that breath-caught suspension, wondering where you'll land.

"I have something to say to you."

"Okay." She drew it out, trying to buy time to get her balance. "Come in. I was just going to get some juice. You want something to drink? Eat?"

"No."

But he did follow her into the kitchen. As she got the juice from the refrigerator and poured a glass, she heard him shifting from foot to foot behind her.

She wasn't going to get her balance, not any time soon, and the waiting was worse. She put the container away, took a long swallow from the glass, then faced him.

"Okay, Rob, what is it?"

"You're not skiing tomorrow. The repor —"

"What! What are you talking about?"

"I'm pulling you from the race."

"You can't."

One long stride brought him practically toe to toe with her.

"I can, and I am." He took her by the shoulders, then just as abruptly released her. "Listen to me. There's a reporter nosing around — the jerk from your news conference. Remember him? He was at Nan's, too, trying to stir up trouble with her. But he hasn't stopped at that. He's asking questions and getting some answers. So far they aren't the right answers, but they're too damn close." He told her what Stephen had relayed.

"So?"

"So? This bastard, with no great ethics in the first place, has got his teeth into you. How long do you think it'll be before he takes a bite out of you? And once he does, the others'll be all over you. Even the ones who maybe believe you're entitled to a private life won't have the option to let you have one then. It'll be all over. I won't expose you to that."

"I can't believe I'm that big a story. Even if I am, I've worked too long for this, I've trained too hard to let your misguided gallantry —"

"Maybe if you hadn't been training so damn hard, it wouldn't have happened."

She felt as if he'd pushed her off the side of a mountain. She was falling, trying to grab on to anything. But nothing made sense. She'd expected disdain for allowing herself to get pregnant, but he blamed her for the miscarriage, too? She hadn't expected that blow.

"You son of a bitch –"

She pushed at his chest, trying to gain room. He took a quick step back as if her touch had scalded him.

"Yeah, I am. And I have to live with knowing that if I hadn't been pushing, you wouldn't have been training so hard. There's not a damn thing I can do about that now, but I'm not going to let you take chances."

The last words hung in the silence for a long moment, then he turned and started out.

"No! Wait." She automatically held on to his arm, hardly aware of it, trying to get her mind to deal with what her ears told her – he blamed himself? But – No, she didn't have time to sort through this. Not now. She had to convince him to put her name on that race roster first. She had to think of a way . . . Words that would make him see. Words that would get through to him.

His own words.

"What you said, Rob. You said it. About being a coach."

"What? What are you talking about."

She had it now, the calm she felt on the hill, the absolute rightness of meshing with the ripples and curves so there was no separation between them and her skis, between her skis and her mind.

"You said that the coach has to look at what's best for the team. That's what you said when you put Marilynne in for Polly instead of me in the Super-G. That the coach can't look at the individual skier first. That your decision wasn't about me, it was about the team. Can you still say that?"

He looked away, staring at the refrigerator.

"I won't ask you to put me in the slalom because it's what I want. But you can't keep me out because you feel guilty for pushing me in training." Was she right about that? If she wasn't he'd think she was crazy. If she was, she'd only add to his hurt. But she had to make him see.

She drew in a breath, forcing the oxygen deep into her lungs, holding herself still.

"All I ask is you make this decision on what's best for the team, Rob. As a coach."

✧ ✧ ✧ ✧

ROB MET STEPHEN Carlisle outside the room where they would turn in the official entry list and receive the skiers' start numbers and bibs. Carlisle exchanged handshakes with two officials from the Swedish team, receiving congratulations on the silver medal won by Brad Lorrence that afternoon. The American team, men and women, was performing quite respectably. The head coach almost smiled.

"Everything all ready?" he asked Rob.

"Yes."

"You have the start list?"

"Yes."

He looked at his assistant, the near smile gone. "Anything I should know about before we go in there?"

"One thing. I'm quitting as soon as these Games are over."

Stephen looked him up and down. "You have a contract through the season. We will talk about your idea of quitting when the season is over and your contract is done. But I will tell you now, you're too good a coach to quit."

"I want to be something more than a coach, good or not."

"Like what?"

"Like a man."

✧ ✧ ✧ ✧

"ENTRIES FOR THE United States of America?"

The silence made the race official look up at Stephen Carlisle. Carlisle nodded toward the man seated next to him.

The race official looked at Rob Zemlak's face and began to worry. Everything had been going so smoothly . . . Then he gave a mental and very philosophical shrug. No event ever went perfectly smoothly. It was impossible. But what problem could this man pose for a simple race official? And how would the race official deflect the problem to someone else?

"Dorrie Garrison." The official's head dropped as he wrote Rob's words with great relief. "Jennifer Lee Tracy."

The official looked up, concerned at this new hesitation. "A third entry?"

"Nan Monahan."

Again the hesitation, again a look from the official. "Please? And the last?"

"WELL?"

"Put this down to dry somewhere, Kyle." Nan handed her the damp scarf she'd just unwound from her head. "I didn't have a hat and it's snowing. They're saying it'll –"

"Nan, don't give me a damned weather report. Did you get a copy of the start list."

"Sure. Here."

There it was in black and white. Kyle Armstrong. Starting eighth.

She was going to get her chance. Her last chance.

DAY 14 – FRIDAY

FOR THE NUMBER of people in the lodge it was surprisingly quiet. There was little conversation in the section set aside for the athletes. Some forty women from their late teens to their late twenties scattered about, reading books, listening to music on earphones, four quietly playing a game of cards, a few apparently napping, one knitting steadily. And most trying not to look out the floor to ceiling window too often or too anxiously.

Kyle did look out the window, watching the snow swirl toward the ground it had already layered with fresh white.

She'd given up trying to read the book she'd brought when the marks on the page stopped translating into words.

In the easy chair across from her, Nan sprawled, apparently totally at ease, eyes closed, a pair of earphones playing an audio book. Every once in a while, though, her fingers contracted into a fist, a twitch of muscles that should have been holding a pole right now.

Voices slightly above the general murmur pulled Kyle's attention to the far side of the room. Through an archway she saw an assortment of coaches huddled around a single official. Rob was there, but not part of the group barking at the official – from his expression he'd rather bite than bark.

The official escaped and, after a few more words among themselves, the coaches came through the archway and spread across the room in search of their athletes. Kyle watched Rob stop for a few minutes with each of the other U.S. entries before making his way to where she and Nan sat by the window. She didn't mind the delay. She already knew what he was going to say.

He touched Nan's arm to get her attention. While she turned off the player and slid back the earphones he crouched on the floor between their chairs and stared straight ahead at the snow beyond the window. He was near enough that Kyle could have touched his hair where it curved on his neck behind his ear just by stretching her arm.

"They're delaying the start another hour."

"There's no way they're going to get this run today. Look at it out there." Nan was disgusted. "Why are they screwing around with this?"

"Because they really want to run it today. Because —"

"Because TV wants it run today," interrupted Nan.

"That's probably a factor, but that's not all of it. With just two more days left, they don't want to run out of time. One day left, really, because they don't want to run the race Sunday and conflict with the Closing Ceremonies."

"Well, their schedule and their TV can't change that it's snowing like a bitch out there."

"No. It can't, but they say they keep hoping it'll let up and —"

Nan's snort stopped him. "And even if it stopped dead right now, they couldn't get the course in shape in time to have us all go two runs before dark. Why don't they let us get out of here?"

"You don't have a hot date, do you, Nan?" Kyle's quiet entrance into the conversation drew Nan's and Rob's eyes to her. "No, I didn't think so. So what difference does it make if you sit here and wait or go back to the apartment and wait? There's no sense giving anyone a hard time. The officials are just showing that they're trying their best to get the race in. If they'd called the race at nine this morning like we all know they could have, people would have been all over them for giving up too easily. So we'll sit here another hour, then they'll delay another hour, then they'll finally give up and we can go. There's no sense getting worked up about it."

She felt the speculation in Rob's eyes without meeting them.

"That's right," he added. "You only hurt yourself by getting worked up about it, Nan."

"Besides," Kyle went on, "there's a more important question:

What's the forecast for tomorrow."

"Clearing. Snow should let up about sunset today."

"Good, then they'll have plenty of time to work the course and we should go off on time tomorrow."

"It'll be a different course tomorrow, Kyle." He was staring out the window, but his frown showed in profile.

"So?"

"So, a soft course isn't your best."

"You always say a soft course's a great equalizer."

"Not for you. When it was slick, that was one thing, but –"

She leaned forward and spoke very low. "I'm skiing, Zemlak."

When he turned his head to look at her, they were so close she could see the slashes of dark and light that wove together to form the gray of his eyes, she could feel the rhythm of his breathing, she could see the way the skin stretched lighter over the bump on his nose where he'd broken it.

She straightened her back, drawing away from him. No panic, no hurry, yet a deliberate retreat.

He said nothing. He simply stood in one easy motion, and walked away.

✧ ✧ ✧ ✧

MIDWAY THROUGH THE first period, Rikki was still wondering why she'd done this to herself, coming to the arena to watch the United States play for the bronze medal in hockey. To watch Lanny Kaminski.

By late in the third quarter, she'd stopped thinking about it. So what if she'd sworn she'd stay away. So what if she winced every time he tried to bend or twist. So what if it hurt that this game meant more to Lanny than she had. The U.S. team's 2-1 lead had turned into a 2-2 tie, and it looked rattled.

As they set for the faceoff, Rikki saw the head coach say something to Lanny, and from the way he held his head so stiff, she knew he didn't like it. He said something, and the coach cut him off with a gesture. Lanny turned toward the clock.

Two minutes thirty-eight seconds. If they could hold on for one hundred fifty-eight seconds against the German team, they'd go to overtime, and then there'd be time to sort out whatever it was the coach had them doing that Lanny didn't agree with.

Just hold on, Rikki prayed.

Bodies formed a logjam in front of the net. She could see Lanny shouting something, then give that up and try to push two German players out of the way. Trying to clear the goalie's sight. She saw it half a second before it was too late. One against two, Lanny couldn't clear the screen the two German players created. Their teammate, chased by three American players, swooped around the side of the net, took his stick back and connected with the puck.

Goal.

Noise erupted all around the pocket of silence where American flags abruptly stilled. Down a goal with twenty-three seconds to play.

She hadn't even absorbed the fact of that when she saw Lanny shouting at his teammates, pointing them to positions, in the case of Tonetti shoving him and jawing at him until the younger player's head came up and he nodded once.

The official dropped the puck, and the clash of sticks and skates was so intense it seemed to churn the ice. The players swarmed, shoving and maneuvering with as little finesse as starving men after a single loaf of bread.

Out of the melee, Rikki saw the puck squirt loose. And just as quickly, Lanny had it corralled.

Sixteen seconds.

He deked one opposing player, advancing down the ice with the others following. A German defenseman slid into place between Lanny and the goalie while he was still forty feet away. But Tonetti had eluded his defender, and found a spot to Lanny's right, with a clear path to the goal.

Before anyone else recognized that, Lanny rocketed the puck to Tonetti, the defenseman following the path with open-mouthed horror. Tonetti's stick connected with the puck and sent it toward the goal.

It was going to make it. It had to. The line was straight and true. Both the goalie and the defenseman had pulled to the opposite corner to stop Lanny's threat. It had to. Please . . .

The defenseman, stick outstretched, hurled himself along the ice. He was too late to stop the puck, but the tip of his stick nicked it, altering its path by inches. The few inches that redirected the black disk from inside the net to a collision course with the pole at the mouth of the goal. The puck ricocheted wide, a German player pounced on it. The buzzer sounded. The game ended.

And Lanny Kaminski finished his hockey career.

He stayed where he was. Bent at the waist, one mitted hand braced on his thigh, the other holding his injured side, staring down at the ice. A still figure amid his opponents' frenzied celebration.

It hurt to watch. Rikki couldn't take her eyes off him.

He straightened his back a vertebra at a time. Remained still a moment, then skated directly to Tonetti, forlorn in a deserted patch of ice. With his helmet on – she wished he would take it off so she could read his face – Rikki couldn't tell if Lanny said anything, but he put his arm around Tonetti's shoulder and gave the younger player's back a hard thump. They stood there alone an infinite moment before another player, then a third and fourth came up to Tonetti, stragglers rallying to their unit after an ambush.

Lanny led the line of benumbed Americans through the formality of exchanging handshakes with the Germans.

Sitting at one end of the bench with a gap between him and the next disconsolate figure, his back to the American fans, his head down, Lanny finally removed the helmet. And Rikki prayed he'd put it back on.

All she could see was the back of his neck, and even that was too vulnerable. His hair was matted and wet with sweat, drawn straight at the bottom by rivulets slipping down the sides of his broad neck.

An assistant coach made his way to Lanny's isolated position, said something that drew a nod, then clasped him on the shoulder. After that, players came by, one by one, before they made their way out of the box and headed to the locker room. Many, like Mikey Sweet,

ment. She wanted him, wanted to be with him, but not in a hotel this time. Maybe her room in the apartment seemed less impersonal, or maybe she wanted some sense of being in her territory.

Inside the room, he placed the shopping bag she hadn't asked him about on the floor, and as deliberately took her in his arms. There was the same, unhurried ease as two nights ago, yet different. As if he'd needed to go slow before, but now he wanted to.

Kissing her, he slipped off the suit jacket and skirt she had worn to appear the perfect coach for the TV cameras. He unfastened her blouse a button and a kiss at a time. When that joined the skirt and jacket over the arm of the easy chair, he bent to slide one hand along her calf, down her ankle and under her shoe. A hand on his shoulder helped balance her as she stood on one foot and allowed him to remove her shoe. The other followed as easily.

Rising, he gestured for her to sit on the edge of the bed, and she did, not quite certain what to expect from him, even less certain how she felt about that uncertainty.

He dropped to his haunches before her, resting his hands on her knees. His touch turned the outdoor chill that had clung to the delicate fibers of her hosiery into soft warmth. Slowly, he slid his hands up, bringing his body forward, between her legs, until he held her hips cupped in his large palms.

Still except for the movements of breathing, he looked at her a long, long moment. She could not be certain of what she read in his eyes. She'd once put her trust in what she'd thought she read in his eyes, and she'd paid.

"All right, Tessa."

Barely a whisper, she didn't know what it meant. Then she didn't have time to wonder, because he hooked the band of hosiery and panties alike, and was sliding them off her.

Freeing her toes, he rose easily and laid the bits of nearly translucent material on the chair. He faced her from two feet away, as he pulled off his clothes and disposed of them with considerably less care than he'd shown hers. In a fully lit room, with her slip covering more than many a "little black dress" would, watching him strip down to jeans was disturbingly erotic.

Perhaps it was the vulnerability of wearing no panties. Or the unrelenting impact of his look. Or . . . It didn't matter. When he touched her, she would burn.

"Now, dessert."

He released her look at last, pivoted and picked up the bag.

When he turned back his eyes held the secret amusement that so seldom touched his mouth, though she thought there might also have been some sadness.

"Dessert?"

He held the bag higher. "Dessert."

He plumped the pillows against the headboard and when he gestured for her to sit against them, she numbly complied. From the bag, he drew a bottle of wine, two plastic glasses, a small round of cheese, a packet of plain crackers and a box of local pastries.

"I hoped we would have dessert in private, so I provided," he explained as he poured wine.

She teetered between an urge to giggle and a desire to sweep every bit away – including his jeans and her slip – and drag him down to the mattress.

She accepted the wine glass.

And she accepted the cheese and the simple, conversational questions. She never quite remembered when his quiet questions opened a spigot in her, releasing a gush of half-completed sentences and jumbled thoughts about Amy's program, her own skating, the rink, the conflicting tugs of teaching beginners and coaching a champion, her past career, Amy's future.

Certainly not until the torrent had slowed to a trickle and they sat side by side with his arm around her shoulder, her fingers skimming the tickling wire of his chest hair and the remains of their dessert picnic littering the bedspread.

"I don't know why I'm bending your ear about all this."

"Bending my ear?"

"An expression." A little shyly, she tugged on his earlobe. "Bending your ear, talking your ear off, spilling my guts."

He smiled. "You need to do that. To talk with no guard on your words."

Maybe understanding only comes in flashes, pinpoints of revelation in the puzzles other people present. Like the moment in the hallway after he'd helped Xi Ling escape her keepers, when she'd glimpsed a fragment of the constraint of his life as a Soviet athlete. Like now, when another flash of empathy or imagination displayed the isolation of being an outcast from his world.

"And don't you, Andrei? Don't you need that, too? To talk with no guard on your words."

"I do not know how."

So simple, so sad.

"Oh, Andrei." She laid the back of her hand against his cheek. "I am so sorry."

For pain, for opportunities denied, for dreams lost.

"It is past." He brushed his lips against hers, soft and demanding. "Now, Tessa . . . Now is . . ."

She met his second kiss with parted lips, and his tongue delved into her mouth. Kisses layered on caresses and the slow burn from earlier caught fire with urgency.

He slid the straps of her slip and bra down her shoulders to explore her breast with his mouth. She freed herself of the entangling straps to smooth and stroke the muscle and flesh of his shoulders and back.

She gasped when he slid his hand under her slip, cupping her and dipping inside. He encouraged in jumbled Russian and English when she opened his jeans to cradle his heat.

He swept the bed clear. She stripped away the last of their clothes.

"I love you, Tessa."

The lights still blazing, he thrust into her, and the surge of his desire and the power of her passion would not allow the words to hold still to be examined. The drive was too strong, the words were left behind in the rush, the undeniable rush to release.

The shudders, the spasms, the shivers that in everyday life reflected horror or pain came at last, and they lunged for their pleasure.

But in the quiet afterwards, his words came back.

He slept holding her. She lay awake surrounded by his warmth, their scent.

He couldn't just come back into her life after all this time and expect her to rearrange it to make room for him. He couldn't just come back into her heart after all this time. He couldn't.

ROB SKIED UP as Kyle prepared to start her inspection of the slalom course. He must have been up early to be among the first to check the course; he hadn't bothered to shave.

"I don't like it Kyle. The conditions –"

"Are hardening up every minute. It's not nearly as soft as you thought it would be. It's only going to get harder."

"Maybe. But the course is tighter than I expected. There are four, six hot corners. You aren't sharp enough. You could go off at any one. I can't let you –"

"I'm going to ski, Rob."

He shook his head.

"Kyle, you have the talent, you have the ability. You don't have to prove anything by skiing today. Not to me, not to the world, not to anybody. It's not worth the risk."

"It's worth the risk to me." She took a breath and met his eyes. This was tougher than she'd thought. She'd spent so long hiding her emotions from him. "I'm not going to win any medal today, I don't fool myself about that. But I can still earn myself something no amount of my daddy's money can buy me."

"Kyle, you don't –"

He was going to apologize for those words, try to take them back, and she didn't want that. She laid a hand on his arm to stop the words, the first time she'd intentionally touched him in fifteen months.

"I need to earn that."

Random snowflakes fell, rag-tag followers of yesterday's storm. One hit her cheek, the sting first feeling hot before the cold registered. Around them voices muttered in memorization, rose to call an observation and sank again to a mumble of curses.

"Shit, Kyle."

A bubble of laughter hit her, unexpected and unstoppable. Such a heartfelt curse, and such an appropriate way to acknowledge that Kyle Wetherington Armstrong was going to ski in the Olympics.

"Thanks, Rob." She started away from him, then looked back. "See you at the bottom."

✧ ✧ ✧ ✧

ANDREI REACHED THE corner into the corridor that held his room just as a man turned away from his door.

He recognized the man. He was surprised, but masked it. There were too many reasons in this world for one man to see them all. The reason for this would be revealed if he were patient.

"You are looking for me, Lanny Kaminski?"

"Uh, yeah."

Andrei watched the younger man scan the stubble of beard on his face, the subtle disarray of his clothes that had started the previous day fresh.

"Looks like neither one of us made it home last night," Kaminski said. He swept an ironic hand at his own disheveled appearance. "I sure as hell hope you had a better time than I did."

"You came to discuss this?" Andrei asked as mildly as he could. His night with Tess was too precious – and too raw – to discuss.

"No. I came . . . Uh . . ." Then Andrei saw the pain in the other man's eyes. "I guess I came to ask you how the hell you stood it when you couldn't skate anymore."

Andrei looked at the solid figure in front of him and felt much older than the eight or ten years difference in their ages.

He got out his key and opened the door.

"Come inside."

✧ ✧ ✧ ✧

WHEN NAN MONAHAN took the lead with her first run, the celebration at the top of the course was jubilantly restrained. First, there was another run to come. Second there were still a good number of racers to go on this run – including Kyle.

She felt like a thoroughbred being prepared for the big race by all the stablehands. The ski tech checked her edges a second time, or maybe a third. The boot rep asked again about the feel. The goggle rep polished without asking. The physiotherapist rubbed at her legs, keeping her muscles loose. The slalom assistant coach adjusted the shin pads and arm pads that warded off blows from the gates.

None of it reached beyond her surface attention. None of it got to where she truly existed at the moment, where it was only her, the mountain, the snow and the half a hundred gates that held her back from what she wanted.

I can still earn myself something no amount of my daddy's money can buy me.

The assistant coach began relaying messages on the condition of the course, first from another assistant a third of the way down, then Stephen Carlisle two-thirds of the way down. Rob would be next from the finish.

"Is she there? Kyle?"

Instead of Rob, it was Nan. Kyle looked at the assistant coach for permission, and took the receiver when he shrugged.

"Nan! Great run."

"Thanks. Now, listen to me. About the course –" She was so no-nonsense, so un-Nan-like in her instructions that every one listening in looked at Kyle as if expecting an explanation. Kyle looked back at them without any. "– and it runs real rutty right before the last section, so be prepared for that. Two people have wiped out there. Don't try to push it through there. Be careful. And –"

"Sorry, Nan. Got to go. Time to get to the start house." She clicked off, though she wouldn't be called for a couple more minutes. But she didn't want to hear Nan's concern for her. She didn't want to know if Rob wished he could pull her from the race. She didn't want anything, but the mountain.

And then it was time.

Standing in the start house. The count down.

Planting, pushing off. Going . . . Going . . . Speed and rhythm. Balance. Inside ski to inside ski, left, right, left, right. The smell of blue sky and cold air. The texture of shouts, cheers and horns. The communion of snow-packed ground and computer-designed fiber-glass, wood and composite.

The rhythm slipped slightly, the gates came faster, not quite where she wanted them. She batted them out of her way with her arms and legs. Rob was right, the turns were tight. *Light on your feet, Armstrong. No fishtailing. Hold your line straight.*

Her pole plant was a little late, but she survived that gate, caught up a little on the next, and was back in sync by the fourth. Just in time to hit the rutted section Nan had warned her about. With Nan's forewarning, she weathered the ruts, not fighting them, not letting them throw her off track.

Then into the last section, quick cutting turns down a steeper grade, picking up speed for the short dash to the finish line.

And it was over. Too fast. All that effort, all that training, all that worry, all that fighting with Rob and herself, and it was over in a blink.

The clock flashed her time and her first-run placement: eleventh so far, though that probably would drop with seven more skiers behind her.

It didn't matter. It didn't matter that it had been only a blink. It didn't matter that it was over.

She grinned as she pulled off her headgear and released her skis.

It was worth it.

✧ ✧ ✧ ✧

LANNY FELT AS if his scalp moved independently of the rest of his head.

"I think it's a good thing we've got lunch coming. I'm not used to drinking vodka before noon."

Andrei Chersakov, occupying the room's only chair, opened a second bottle, filled the short tumbler the hotel had meant for water and pushed it across the night table to where Lanny could reach it from his spot on the bed. "It is not a good thing to become used to."

"Guess not." Lanny took a drink, then eased into the pillows jammed against the headboard and considered the remaining liquid in the glass. Without looking up, he asked, "Did you? Become used to it? When you couldn't skate?"

"Yes. For a brief time."

Lanny nodded. He'd heard Andrei's story over the first half bottle.

He'd told his over the bottom half. "Life sucks."

Andrei gave no answer to that, but silently took a sip from his own glass.

"You spend your whole life trying your damnedest to be something, to be as God-damned good at it as you can – and then it's over. And you never even had a chance to show what you really could have been. Because of knees or because the Bruins had too many good, young defensemen ahead of you or because of politics or . . . And then it's over."

He turned the glass around in his fingers, fast at first, then more and more slowly. "All over. And what do you do? What the hell are you supposed to do?"

Abruptly, he drained the glass, feeling heat but no warmth down his throat and into his gut.

"And women are totally fucked," Lanny added. "Who the hell knows what they want."

"Ah."

Sitting up from the pillows, Lanny demanded, "What does that mean? That 'Ah' crap? You sound like some damned psychiatrist. If you're thinking something, have the guts to say it."

"It means," Andrei said with such precision that Lanny thought maybe he wasn't the only one with a strange-feeling scalp. "Women are totally fucked."

THE WAIT WHILE they set the new course for the second run was too long.

Nan's time had stood up as the best in the first run, but only by five one-hundredths of a second. Kyle's time was fourteenth. The top fifteen from the first run would go off first in the second run, starting with the fifteenth, then the fourteenth and working back to Nan. Then the first-run finishers from sixteenth on would ski.

Kyle supposed she should be thankful she wasn't among that group, whose wait would be even longer. But with Nan trying to sound as if she didn't have a care in the world all the time her fingers fretted at whatever they met, this wait was plenty long enough.

Even having Tess, Rikki and Amy around didn't distract Nan enough. When Nan excused herself to go to the bathroom, Kyle made her escape.

"I've got to get away by myself for a while." She turned back after two steps, and grinned at Rikki. "You might tell her you're a little concerned about me."

Rikki nodded. "I just might do that."

✧   ✧   ✧   ✧

ROB WATCHED KYLE head to the lift that would take her to the top of the mountain, gauging her movement, checking for signs of pain or discomfort. He'd been watching for her. She often did this between runs, seeking out a spot where she would be left alone.

Alone. That's the way Kyle dealt with things. Only in her emotionally and physically weakened state after the miscarriage had she accepted his help.

She wouldn't accept it any longer, that was clear. She'd come down that mountain this morning and she would come down it again too damn soon for him, all to prove to herself and the world that she could do it alone. To prove she didn't need anybody, not anybody to help her, not anybody to worry about her, not anybody to love her.

To her, that was worth the risk.

✧   ✧   ✧   ✧

IT CLICKED WITH the first gate. She felt it that fast. And from that moment, Kyle knew she had this run, had this course. It was hers. The whole mountain belonged to her.

She'd liked the layout on inspection, but you never know for sure until you push off and start feeling the beat of the course, the timing of the gates.

This one was perfect.

Part of her mind knew she was going fast, but it didn't feel that way. The time between the gates spread into balletic slow motion, the planting of her pole, the shift from inside foot to inside foot, the switch in balance, the sweep of the gate out of her way all a flow of mind, body and mountain.

Into the flats. A transition into the next movement. But the underlying theme remained and she picked it up, carrying the speed, so sure on this gate that she could look to the next one, set up her approach perfectly. And head into the next section flying.

Attack. Keep the line.

God, this was beautiful. This was the perfection she'd sought, she'd dreamed of from the first time she'd seen a human on boards take on a mountain.

Around a corner, and the finish line came in sight.

She didn't look at the mass of humanity lining the course here, but she sensed them. And then she heard them. She couldn't pretend it was her and the mountain, alone, not anymore.

For a flash too short for even the most sophisticated timer to measure she just wanted to slow, to extend her moment. But training – and pride – wouldn't allow it.

The weight of tears squeezed the bridge of her nose. But training and pride wouldn't allow that either.

Out of the last gate, she pushed for the final millisecond of speed and crossed the finish line.

Arms raised and grinning widely, she pivoted to a stop. But she kept her head down until the tears retreated.

She'd done it. She'd worked for it, she'd earned it and she'd done it. Just her. Out on the mountains, where the Armstrong name didn't mean a thing. She'd skied in the Olympics. And she'd skied damn well.

Only then did she look at the time. And the grin grew. There'd be no medal, but accomplishment could be felt well beyond the top three.

She smiled at the wall of spectators cheering. A special clamor drew her attention to the Monahan crew, swelled by the addition of Rikki, Tess and Amy. She waved to them and the noise increased.

Polly Tresher, on crutches, greeted her with a hug made awkward by skis, poles and crutches, but still heartfelt.

"That was great, Kyle! Wait till you see the tape on that. Perfect! They'll use that run for years as a how-to – and mine in the giant slalom as a how-not-to! If they ever let me see the thing. They keep saying I should wait a while to see it. I keep telling them, hey, I was there!"

Kyle laughed, but that didn't diminish the warmth she felt at her teammate's generosity. Polly had had Olympic medal dreams, and they'd crashed around her, too. The circumstances were different, but the emotion wasn't.

Kyle glanced at the enclosure for coaches and competitors.

"Uh, Rob had something to, uh, take care of," Polly said, following the direction of her look. "He saw your run, and said, um, how happy he was. He should be right back. I know he'll want to see you."

"No reason he should," she responded coolly.

Polly looked miserably uncomfortable, and Kyle was about to take pity on her with some bland phrase when a great, empathetic groan went up from the crowd. Both skiers turned to the video screen in time to see the young Norwegian skier who'd followed Kyle lose the balance she'd been fighting for, hook a tip in a gate and go down, poles and skis twisting her body as she skidded along the slope, taking several gates with her and plowing up the snow.

Kyle felt the tension in the crowd, the stillness, the waiting.

"Maybe I don't want to see the tape of my fall after all," Polly murmured beside her.

Attendants reached the downed skier almost as soon as she came to rest. She sat up, and the spectators first let out their breaths, then a cheer.

"She's not hurt too bad. Looks like she might have twisted an ankle," Polly said, watching the screen carefully. Then she turned to Kyle. "But she did a number on the course. It'll take them a while to get re-set. This would be a good time to get changed without missing anything. I'd go with you, but it takes so long for me to get anywhere on these things, I'd slow you down."

"Good idea. I'll see you when I get back."

Kyle had gotten about thirty yards when she heard her name called.

She turned automatically. It was that reporter, leaning over the back corner of the barrier. The one with the sneer and the oiled hair from her news conference. The one Rob had said was nosing around. The one who'd almost caused Rob to pull her from the race.

The man levered himself over the low barrier and pushed past the last two people separating them. An official started toward them, to shoo him off, though technically he was allowed to be in the open area between the enclosures and the lodge. Kyle waved away the official. She would handle this.

"A couple questions. *Le Mot*, Paris."

The way he identified himself raised her eyebrows, but she answered civilly, "The medalists' news conference will be inside when the race is over."

She started to turn away.

"I said I've got a couple questions. For you. I think you'll want to hear these."

"Your questions don't matter. I don't choose to answer."

"Yeah? You want me to print what I know?"

"Do you think you know anything, Mr. Narlin?"

His head retreated toward his neck and his eyes narrowed. She wasn't sure if it was her tone or the fact that she knew his name that made him uneasy. Well, the tone wasn't going to change, and with the facts she still had to fire at him, he'd retract that sneering face like an unpleasant turtle.

But not yet. He wouldn't give up so easily.

"I know you went to the town hospital the night before the combined started and were treated for an attempted suicide. I've got sources to confirm that. And I'm going to print that. What's your comment?"

She didn't blink.

"My comment, first is that you have paid your source too much – it is just one source, isn't it? Yes, I thought so. The ambulance driver who cares a little too much for brandy. A most credible source. Or perhaps you paid him too little. Perhaps if you'd paid him more, he would have produced five or six athletes in the hospital that night. Or any other night of your choosing."

She leaned forward, not letting him look away from her. "Second, I would comment that if you were foolish enough to submit this fiction and your editors desperate enough to print it, both of you would be looking at a formidable array of legal talent. The Armstrongs don't take their name lightly.

"Third, even before the wheels of justice could start grinding you into something even smaller than you are, I would make every effort to let the public know your background. Ah, yes, I see that interests you. Your fast track started to derail when that paper in Wisconsin fired you over your coverage of hospital administrations –"

"It was a crusade and that limp-wristed editor didn't have the balls for it –"

"Crusade? I heard it was a witchhunt. Another firing in Missouri for falsifying sources. Then, losing the libel suit in Oregon – you've really come down in the world since then, haven't you? I'm sure the networks who might ask my response to your report would be interested in all that. If necessary, I would take out full page ads in every metropolitan daily newspaper to tell these facts. And I suspect there is more. My investigators are thorough, unlike you, and my sources are credible, unlike yours."

"Are you trying to blackmail me into sitting on this story?"

"There is no story. Moreover, how could I blackmail you if you've done nothing wrong?"

"Blackmail, intimidate, whatever you want to call it."

"Apparently I choose my words more carefully than you do. For example, *Le Mot* fired you last April, yet you just identified yourself as working for them."

He went red. Not just his face, but his neck and his ears. "I didn't –"

"And I would say that you are trying to intimidate me into giving you information that is none of your business. And I would say that you have attempted to bribe supposed 'sources' to lie to give you a 'story.' A 'story' no one has a right or a need to read. And the last thing I would say to you – the last thing, you understand? – is that now you understand the consequences if you proceed."

She looked at him steadily for a moment, letting him see her determination. And her ability to follow through. She nodded once and walked away. He wasn't worth a goodbye.

She almost collided with Rob on the path to the lodge. He gripped her arm to steady her, then released her as soon as she had her balance.

"What did he want?"

He was looking over her shoulder, in the direction she'd just come. "Who?"

"You know damn well who. That scum."

"It's all taken care of. No need to worry about it."

His eyes came back to her face, and for an instant she thought she saw emotions tumbling through them. Then everything shut off – his eyes, his face. Even his voice slid into neutral.

"I see."

The wind kicked up, piercing the minimal protection of her race suit. She shivered despite herself.

"Here –" Rob thrust a bundle of clothes at her. "I brought your warm-ups."

"Thanks."

Another stop to the conversation.

"You going into the lodge?"

"Yes. I thought I'd change and get something quick to eat while I watch the others."

"Yeah, okay. When you're done, come out here." He tipped his head toward the coaches' and competitors' enclosure. "I want to talk to you."

Without waiting for an answer, he strode away.

It didn't do much for her appetite. She hurried through changing, downed a bottle of mineral water, grabbed an apple and headed back out.

She'd missed two runs. There were ten more to go before Nan.

She spotted Rob, standing on the second row of bleachers at the back of the enclosure, but it took some effort to work her way through the crowd. Most of them wanted to tell her how great her second run looked – what a shame she'd been under the weather early in the Olympics, but she was obviously back on track.

She took a handshake from the last one, an assistant coach with the Swedish team, said thanks, turned and met Rob's concentrated look. He immediately looked away.

She climbed the two steps and stood by his side. "You wanted to talk to me?"

"Yeah." She followed his gaze to the screen showing an Austrian skier's run.

"Well?"

He glared at the apple she pulled out of her pocket. "That's what you're going to eat?"

"I wasn't very hungry." She took a healthy bite as if to refute what she'd said, and he turned away. "Zemlak, what did you want to talk to me about?"

"How are you feeling?"

"Fine."

He didn't respond, and she looked over at him, only to find him staring at her as if he had X-ray vision that would pick up lies, or pain, if he just looked at her hard enough.

"I'm fine, Zemlak."

Abruptly, he turned back to the screen. "How'd you like the slalom today?"

"Fine." He slashed her a look, and she relented. "It was good. Fun. More fun than I remember it being. Why?"

"I think you should talk to Stephen about skiing it more in World Cup. You like it, it would probably help your combined, you could pick up some points, move up in the overall standings."

Talk to Stephen? Why not talk to him?

"Instead of the GS?"

He shrugged. "Maybe. Sometimes. Sometimes in addition to." Another lightning glance at her. "Think about it a few days."

"Okay, I will."

That seemed to be that, and she was down the first step when his voice stopped her.

sought out her family.

In sudden isolation, Kyle and Rob stood side by side. When he turned to her, he was grinning.

"She did it. You were right, Kyle. She skied fucking out of her mind." Then his face tightened with some thought she couldn't follow. "You were right, Kyle. About everything."

He stepped off the bleachers and headed toward Nan, leaving her alone.

✧ ✧ ✧ ✧

THE OFFICIAL MEDALS ceremony was scheduled for evening, so they returned to the apartment to change for the nighttime temperatures. Afterward Amy and Tess planned to meet the Yosts to watch the exhibition by the figure skating medalists, while Kyle and Rikki celebrated with Nan.

Nan rushed in, hugged everybody, cried and laughed – as if she hadn't already done all three several times over at the finish line. Then she changed to her Team USA outfit, and rushed out to meet her family before the ceremony.

Tess was in her room, sorting through papers at the desk, when Rikki came to the door. "Where is everybody?"

Tess smiled, and gestured her to a seat. "You must have heard Nan's exit. Kyle's in the shower now, because she couldn't get ready until Nan finished. So it'll be a while. And Amy's gone ahead to the cafeteria. She said it was to find a table, but I suspect she's meeting Denny Kittrick for a private farewell. He's a nice enough boy, but I'm very grateful he lives three time zones away from Amy. Teenage hormones are a force to be reckoned with."

Her smile dimmed, and she met Rikki's eyes.

"Adult hormones, too. I suppose we both learned that."

"Yeah, I suppose. You and Andrei –?"

Tess shook her head, occupying her hands with taking papers from her purse and putting them in a file.

"That's too bad. He's a nice man."

Tess looked up. "I could say the same to you."

Rikki tried for a wry smile. "Guess we both learned that sometimes the head's right and the heart's full of it, huh?"

Tess's hands stilled in the act of replenishing the supply of business cards in her purse.

. . . Sometimes the heart knows what it's doing before the head has any clue. I'm not saying the heart's always right when it falls fast. But it's not always wrong, either . . .

. . . If I just skate from inside myself like you said, Tess, it's just me, alone. But if I can skate from all of them, too, then I have a lot more to give back . . .

. . . That one time you skated above your talent because Andrei loved you. Maybe he gave you that night, not took away something all the other nights . . .

Kyle appeared at the door. "Ready. Sorry to keep you waiting."

"No problem." Rikki stood and pulled on her parka. "Tess?"

Tess stared at the business card in her hand.

"Tess, are you okay?"

"What? Oh, yes. I'm fine. Just thinking. About skating." She slipped the card in her pocket.

✧   ✧   ✧   ✧

AFTER DINNER, RIKKI and the others headed across the Olympic Village to the central medals ceremony platform.

Rikki saw Lanny standing at a corner, scanning the faces in the crowd. Her lungs and heart felt as if they'd been snatched by a huge hand with a mean grip. She kept walking.

"Rikki, there's —"

She didn't break stride. No expectations, no disappointment, "I see him, Tess, just keep going."

He looked awful. A day's worth of beard stubble. Hair haphazard. Clothes a mess.

"Rikki!"

His voice was raspy. But his grip was plenty strong enough when he grabbed her arm. She tried to pull away. He held on, pivoting her around to face him.

"Rikki, I want to talk to you."

His eyes were as darkly intense as ever, and a little grim. She stared back a second then glanced at her friends.

"Go ahead, I'll catch up with you. I'll be right there," she added with emphasis. This dealing with Lanny Kaminski wouldn't take long. There wasn't much left to say.

Up close, he looked worse. Grooves by the sides of his mouth showed through the stubble. Dark patches spread under his eyes. The shirt that showed beneath the half open jacket had a blotch of something gray on it.

He said nothing.

"Well?"

"Be patient, I'm feeling my way here."

"You smell like a distillery."

"I'm not as drunk as I smell. In fact I'm not drunk at all. Not any-more. I got close last night, but I was only really drunk for a while this morning in Andrei's room when we finished the first bottle of vodka –"

"Andrei? Andrei Chersakov?"

"Yeah. But we slowed down after that and then when we ordered lunch and –"

"*First* bottle? You spent all day drinking with Andrei Chersakov?"

"No. You're not listening. We spent the morning drinking. We tailed off around lunch."

"Glad you spent your first morning out of training in a worthwhile pursuit."

He prevented her from turning away by taking her arm again.

"Wait. I've got a question."

She tugged; his hold didn't ease. "What do you want?"

"You said something about falling in love with me, didn't you?"

"I said something about you being an asshole."

"Yeah, I'll get to that." One side of his mouth lifted, then all hu-mor vanished. His look was a blatant challenge. "First, answer the question. Did you or did you not say something about falling in love with me?"

"I said it."

He let out a breath, slowly. "Okay." He seemed to weigh the wary word, and find it needed more. "Okay."

"You asked your question, let me go."

He shook his head. "That was a preliminary. What I really want to know is what you meant by that." She gave him a disbelieving look. "I mean, I could take that a couple of ways, see? 'Falling in love.' If I'd paid attention to that grammar the nuns tried to teach us at St. Andrew's, I'd probably know the name for that tense or case or whatever it is. But 'falling in love,' that could be you're just starting the process. Like a breakaway developing, and you're at the point where you've still got a choice – you can keep driving for the goal or you can pull back and dump the rock off to a teammate. Or it could mean you're past that point, see? 'Falling in love.' Could mean you're already committed – to the play, I mean. So you might as well wind up and slap that baby, because if you pull up now there's no chance at all. At least if you shoot, you might score."

His eyes narrowed, the thick lashes almost meshing. But she felt the power of his dark eyes trained on her.

"See, it makes a difference. In my thinking, I mean. Now that hockey's over, I've got to look at other things. I know lots of people wouldn't think an old, broken down hockey player had much of a future, but I have it on the best authority that this broken down player is the exception. So, starting now I'm looking at the future – a little late, but I'm doing it – and I'm trying to figure if it's going to be solo or –"

She closed her eyes, and his words cut off. Did she have the courage to be pushed by Lanny Kaminski for a lifetime? Did she have the courage to push herself?

"We're too different, Lanny. We see things from totally different angles."

"Maybe together, we see all the angles. If we work as a team." Dogged, stubborn – she listened to his voice and could see him on the ice. "If you meant what you said about loving me."

In the darkness behind her eyelids, she faced the black depths of fear. But in these past two weeks she'd learned about going for broke. She'd learned from the best. She opened her eyes, and looked into his.

"I love you, Lanny. Committed. Past the point of holding back. All the way."

She expected him to say something about her not sounding too happy about it – she wasn't. He didn't.

He swallowed hard and the fire in his eyes ignited.

"Good." He nodded solemnly. "Now I can start working on a plan with the two of us. See, I figure we've got a lot of catching up on getting to the small stuff about each other. Build a good base so we don't have trouble again. We should spend time together. I have this one idea –"

"Wait a damn minute, Kaminski!" Despite herself, a laugh crept into her voice. "That's it?"

Suspiciously bland, he looked at her. "What else?"

"For one thing, there's still the asshole factor –"

"Yeah." He nodded. "But see, I figure we can make use of that. You tend to pull back on giving everything you've got, and I can make sure you don't do that." He shot her a look under his brows. "Sort of a coach."

"Oh, God!"

"Hey, you said I'd make a good coach."

"What I said was you'd make a great coach – if you had a touch of humanity. But not for me."

"Why not?"

"Besides all the other things, and on top of the facts that I couldn't afford a private coach and I don't know how many more years I might compete so this would not be a long-term career for you, look at what's happened with Rob and Kyle, and he's a lot easier-going than you."

"I don't think Brad Lorrence would agree with that. But I'm not talking about coaching you full-time. More like keeping an eye on you. As a sidelight."

"A sidelight? To what?"

"If I coach, hockey's the most logical thing, right? And I know a lot about international-style play. But I don't exactly see eye-to-eye with the men's head coach, so that wouldn't be much of a possibility."

"There are other places. College or –"

"The head of U.S. women's hockey association and I've had some interesting discussions."

"I thought you wouldn't talk to them."

He actually looked a little sheepish. "Well, they were pretty one-sided conversations. They did most of the talking. But I listened." He took a breath. "So, you think I could be a good coach?"

"I know you can be a great coach if –"

"If maybe I had somebody to remind me I'm dealing with people not machines, keep me from getting too tough, like I could keep you in line the other way?"

"Maybe," she conceded. "But there's the question of how you feel about me."

"That's no problem." Sneaky quick, he engulfed her in his arms and lowered his head until they were nose to nose.

"How I feel about Rochelle Lodge is that you're the best, brightest, happiest thing that's happened to me. No gold, silver or bronze can hold a candle to you. I hope to God you'll marry me and help me look beyond the next game."

She took the words into her heart, wise enough to know she'd see them more often in his eyes than hear them from his lips. And knowing that, she felt no compunction about prompting for more.

"Because?"

"Because what?"

"Why do you feel all those things."

"Because I love you." A hint of impatience at her slowness was replaced by a dawning smile. He repeated, "Because I love you."

He bent his head and flicked his tongue along her bottom lip, the moisture slick on the chilled skin, the pressure a kind of warmth. She parted her lips, and he kissed her. Open-mouthed, deep and slow. Tongues enacting the dance their humming bodies craved.

"Let's go back to your room."

She wanted to. But, "Nan's medals ceremony . . . I want to be here."

"I want to be inside you."

Her determination slipped. "Shower and shave first," she bargained.

"Some women want everything. I did brush my teeth before coming after you." He touched fingertips to the delicate skin by the corner of her mouth that his beard had already rubbed red.

"Noble, but I still say: shower and shave."

"If you'll shower with me."

He kissed her again, deep, long, delving his tongue into her mouth, until she wondered if some of the vodka lingered and now intoxicated her, darting into her bloodstream, dizzying her head.

"After the medals ceremony," he said, the words unsteady.

She must be dizzy; she couldn't follow a sentence.

"Shower after the medals ceremony," he clarified. "We'll do both. First, medals ceremony, then your room."

She laughed. "Deal."

After four steps she stopped, pulling on his hand until he turned back to face her.

"What?"

"I just want you to know I don't do things like this."

"Like what?"

"Like fall in love."

His eyes went dark, his mouth lifted slightly. "Shit, me either, Rikki. Me either."

✧ ✧ ✧ ✧

THEY STOOD TOGETHER, pressed close by the crowd now, linked indelibly by the crucible of the past two weeks, and watched Nan Monahan receive her gold medal.

Kyle looked at the now-familiar faces. They'd each dreamed of being on that podium, bending to receive the flowers, the congratulatory kiss and the ribbon bearing a precious gold circle.

Lanny, whose years of effort had brought him close enough to touch the dream, only to have it stay just out of reach. Rikki, whose dreams had always been so distant, so outlandish she'd never allowed them full life. Lanny took her hand. He was learning new dreams. She was learning to bring her dreams into the light; that was the only way to reach them.

Tess, whose dream had come true, but for years was dimmed and distorted by memories. Amy, whose dream would need dedication, determination and luck to nurture it over the next four years. Tess had confronted the past, now Amy had the future.

Kyle had thought it would be her on that platform. Her eyes following the slowly lifting flag. Her flag, her event, her triumph. Her lips forming the words of the anthem. As Nan's did now.

And the disappointment that it wasn't her couldn't be denied. Worse, she'd never know if she could have done it.

But in a way it didn't matter. This was Nan's. She *had* done it and nothing would ever take that from her.

And Kyle had a victory; she'd won her race. She'd earned something no money had every bought.

Oh, say can you see by the dawn's early light . . .

Kyle looked down the row of these familiar faces, felt a tightening of emotion in her throat.

What so proudly we hailed . . .

DAY 16 – SUNDAY

"I WANT YOU to come with."

Kyle sat on her bed, pillows cushioning her back from the wall, arms wrapped around drawn-up knees, and watched her friend and roommate prepare for another celebration. No – considering the time they'd gotten in last night, more like a continuation of the earlier celebration. Nan deserved it. Kyle smiled at her.

"Maybe I'll catch up with you later, at the Closing Ceremonies," she lied.

"You'll have missed half the day by then."

"I thought I'd start packing. We do leave tomorrow."

Nan waved that away. "Plenty of time to pack. After the celebration this afternoon and the Closing Ceremonies and the post-Ceremonies party and the post-party party. I'm going to party this town to its knees – to its *knees!*"

"I thought you did that last night."

Nan snorted. "That was just a preliminary. If they thought I went wild with bronze, wait until they see me with a gold in my pocket, too!"

"The bronze was none too shabby you know," Kyle commented dryly.

" 'Specially not for someone with enough scars on her knees to make a road map of Colorado. Don't I know it!" She hummed a little to herself as she buttoned her silk blouse, considered it in the mirror, then undid the top two buttons. " 'Course, I probably could have won the gold in GS, too, if I hadn't spent all that energy worrying –"

268 PATRICIA McLINN

"Oh, no you don't! You aren't going to say you were worrying about me and otherwise you'd have taken the gold in the giant slalom. No way, Monahan." Lord, it felt good to joke and banter again.

"I only said –"

"I know what you said, and I can just bet what you were about to say. And I'll have you know that future sports historians will surely determine that you took that gold – probably the bronze, too – because for once your mind was occupied enough with something else to relax and follow your instincts."

Dimples flashed, then instantly gave way to seriousness.

"Maybe so, but in that case you'll have to share the credit. Because you weren't the only one occupying my mind. You weren't the only one I was taking care of and worrying about." Nan tilted her head in contemplation of her image and undid another button, but Kyle thought at least some of her attention was devoted to her listener's reaction.

"What do you mean?"

"You two are really a pair, you know it?"

"Who – What do you mean?"

The subtle change was wasted on Nan. Hands on hips, she faced Kyle from across the room.

"You know exactly who, Kyle. Your coach and mine, Rob Zemlak. And don't go pokering up like that. It isn't going to stop me from saying what I want to say, so don't bother. Between the two of you, I've seen enough people go pasty white and look like they wanted to toss their cookies in the past two weeks to last me a lifetime."

"What do you mean?"

"You know damn well what I mean for your half of it. As for Rob, I mean before each of your runs yesterday, he lost it but good. I thought he was going to puke on my boots. And I hear on good authority it was nearly as bad for the second run."

"That's ridiculous. I saw him after my run. I talked to him. He wasn't sick. I would have noticed."

"First off, I don't think he had anything in his belly to pitch or it would have been gone in the morning. And second, when was the last time you really looked at him? You two skitter away from each other like opposite magnets."

"I don't . . . Why would he feel sick?"

Nan grinned with savage pleasure as she advanced on the bed. "It's about time you asked that. In fact it's about time you asked yourself a lot of whys about Rob. Like why he's so scrupulously careful never to touch you when he roughhouses with the rest of us. Like why his eyes follow you until you look at him, and then he shutters down faster than a shack in an avalanche. Like why – Oh, hell, you'll just have to figure out the questions for yourself, along with the answers."

She poked a finger against her roommate's collarbone. "But I can give you the answer to that first one. I'd say it's because he's been in love with you for months and he was worried sick – literally – that you'd fall off that mountain and kill yourself."

KYLE FACED THE closed door in the anonymous hallway and marshaled every trick that had ever gotten her out of the chute. Knocking on this door was much worse than any mountain.

Especially when the thuds her knuckles produced faded into silence with no result. The room inside seemed as deserted as the hallway behind her. Everyone had gone off to celebrate with Nan. What made her think Rob hadn't, too. He was probably sitting in the middle of them all, grinning and joking the way he did with everyone except her.

The thought made her second knock sharp, emphatic.

She heard a muffled sound, a scrape, and the door yanked open. "Don't you understand English? I said I wasn't go –"

He stood there, the anger and impatience draining from his face. She waited for the barrier to come up as it always had. She thought perhaps he tried to summon it. If so, he didn't succeed.

Wariness. Uncertainty. That's what she saw. God, could Nan be right?

He looked tougher than usual. He wore jeans and an unbuttoned shirt. The beard stubble from yesterday, now more pronounced, gave an edge to his boyish looks.

"May I –"

"Come in."

They spoke simultaneously, but it drew no easy laughter. He held the door wider, and she walked in.

The bed had once been made, but showed signs of someone lying on top of it. Someone restless.

"Are you okay?" he asked before she could turn to him.

"Yes – quit asking me that! I'm fine." His mouth clamped shut. *Great start, Armstrong.* She softened her voice. "I, uh, I wanted to thank you. For everything."

"I don't want any thanks."

"Well, I want to give them, so shut up and listen for once."

He shut up, his jaw tight beneath the stubble, his eyes narrowed and unrevealing. Under the weight of the silence she'd demanded, she lamely repeated, "I wanted to thank you. For everything you did for me."

"No need."

Temper rose like a flare. "No, of course, it was no more than you would've done for any other team member."

Perhaps wisely he remained silent, dropping into a chair and gesturing for her to sit on the bed. The flare sputtered to darkness.

She cleared her throat. "Well, anyway. I wanted to say thank you. And –" Before he could repeat how unnecessary that was, she hurried on. "– I wanted to explain."

"You don't owe me an explanation."

"No, I don't owe you anything," she snapped. The belligerence faded as she saw an easing in his eyes that might have indicated something close to humor. She swallowed and tried again. "But you've been very, uh, kind to me these past few days." That seemed miserly. "The past week, really. Two weeks. Ever since. . . Ever since the miscarriage." Swallowing was harder. "Well, I wanted you to understand. I wanted to try to make you understand . . ."

"I think I do understand."

"Do you?"

"Yes, I think I do. You went to him —"

"God, I didn't even go to him. I didn't even make that active a choice. I just let it happen. I let it all happen."

"All right, you let it happen because you needed love."

"Love?" She pushed the hair back from her face. "Love had nothing to do with it." She amended that. "Love had nothing to do with what happened with Brad. More like loneliness, I guess. And other emotions bubbling up under it." She shifted one shoulder. "Most of all, I let it happen because he wanted me."

She looked at his face then, and saw it.

That knife-edge of control he balanced on. Like that moment the skis start to get away from you, hurtling down a mountain full-speed. Not gone yet, but teetering, precariously teetering in a breath-held microsecond between regaining command and losing it.

And then he had it back. He was going to listen to her.

"My parents . . . Well, I guess you know, I don't have a loving, close-knit kind of family. I used to console myself that everybody's family was really like mine. It was only on TV that anybody had a family like the Waltons. But the Monahans . . . The Monahans are like that. And they took me in, made me part of the group, made me feel wanted. I love them for that.

"It's very seductive being wanted." Dreamily, she seemed almost to talk to herself. "Even in the limited, surface way Brad wanted me. I hadn't had that in a long time. I —"

The guttural sound that tore from his throat could only have been a curse, but it didn't scare Kyle. Any more than she feared the scraping sound of his chair tipping over as he lunged across the space to take her by the shoulders and yank her upright, tight against him.

For the first time she saw the danger, the fury that had been his competitive trademark. She should have been frightened of him. Terrified. But her heart rate had nothing to do with terror.

Oh, God, please . . . She couldn't complete the prayer, but she figured He knew.

"Wanted? Weren't wanted? It wasn't enough for you to be wanted every minute, with every breath? It wasn't enough for you to torment me with being right there and so damn far out of reach? To be what I wanted more than anything in this world."

She faced him, and gave back the question he'd asked her in the clinic. "Why didn't you tell me?"

His hands eased on her shoulders, and a flash of humor dry enough to spark tinder crossed his eyes as he repeated her answer. "You were the last person I wanted to have know."

"Why?"

"I was the coach. You were my athlete. I had an obligation to be as impartial as I could humanly be. An obligation to every member of the team. I blew that obligation once, blew it big-time. I wasn't going to let myself do it again."

She looked at him, waiting for more, waiting for the fullness of the truth.

His hands slid across her shoulders to her neck. His fingers circling behind, his thumbs tracing the delicate line at the front.

"I had an obligation to you. Not to use my position to . . . to influence you. To make you think you cared for me more than you did."

"I loved you last winter."

He winced, perhaps at the past tense. But he didn't hesitate to grab onto her words to make his point.

"You'd had a crush. Even if I hadn't seen it, you told me so. And I had a duty to not take advantage of those feelings. I screwed that up, too. You had a right to want to carve me up with a wax knife. I knew that, even if you didn't. There's nothing I can do to make that right. The backup I've given you here – when I wasn't giving you a hard time – doesn't make a dent in it. So, for God's sake, stop thanking me."

All the times he'd refused her efforts to thank him – often begrudgingly . . . Now she understood.

But he didn't seem to recognize that small self-revelation. He tightened his hold fractionally, and looked directly at her.

"You had me all mixed up with the Olympics and glory and winning. All the things you craved, all the things you thought would make

"In one month I will meet you at the World Championships, Tess Rutledge. I promise that. One month, I give you, and then we will talk of the future. The past will not disappear, but we will look away from it to the future. You understand me."

He waited. She said nothing, didn't move, but what he found in her eyes must have satisfied him. His mouth stayed solemn, but some of the secret amusement slipped into his eyes, heated and softened by other emotions.

"And if you try to hide, if you do not come to the World Championships, I would find you, Tessa. Always."

FLAG BEARERS CAME first, led by Greece. The solemnity of the opening was gone; even the honored individuals carrying the flags smiled and waved to the crowd and each other, the standards of their countries dipping and swaying.

The teams followed on to the track, with no semblance of lines now. Freed from the organizers outside the stadium, the masses of like-colored jackets and parkas broke into smaller groups, mixing with others until the blocks of colors became sprinkles. Each athlete sported some touch not part of the official uniform, a scarf traded from another team, a cap purchased in town, a pair of gloves given by a new friend. They not only waved and mugged for camera and crowd, they carried their own cameras, recording a memory. And they carried each other – Amy perched on Mikey Sweet's shoulders, Nan had a better view thanks to Scott Stanicek.

Some athletes had already left, clearing out as soon as their events ended, spurred by dismay or practicality. But for those remaining, the mood was giddy. They had formed a bond that crossed sex, race, nationality, event.

Win or loss, triumph or disappointment, they had shared the moment.

The moment.

Rikki Lodge looked at the man next to her and marveled at the power of a moment. That's all it had taken for Lanny Kaminski to enter her life, and to change it. They had shared their moment. Now they were ready to go for broke – to face the challenge of sharing a lifetime.

A lifetime.

Kyle Armstrong wondered if even that would be long enough to absorb all the lessons taught in these sixteen days. Probably not. But she had mastered one. She'd learned luck was not her only companion. She had friends, and she had the belief in herself that would allow her to turn to them. She had the strength to love Rob. She would not try to face all the lessons in her life alone as she had in the past.

The past.

Tess Rutledge had watched the past come alive, had fought it and, finally, had faced it. Like any living thing it had changed, would continue to change. How that would change her, she couldn't know. But she accepted that in these sixteen days Andrei Chersakov had strode from her past to her future.

. . . I proclaim these Winter Olympic Games closed . . .

The flame dipped, spurted once more toward the sky and disappeared. A sigh filled the sudden dark, then a gasp at the flame's seeming resurrection, as a burst of fireworks, spangling the sky with a thousand flashes of color. Enough for each of the athletes dancing and singing across the floor of the great stadium, and for millions more dreaming thousands of miles away, to capture a spark.

. . . And in accordance with our tradition, I call upon the youth of the world to assemble four years from now to celebrate with us the Winter Games.

✧   ✧   ✧   ✧

If you enjoyed the story, I hope you'll consider leaving a review of The Games to let your fellow readers know about your experience.

For news about upcoming books, subscribe to Patricia McLinn's free newsletter.

www.PatriciaMclinn.com/newsletter

Don't miss any of the Caught Dead In Wyoming series:

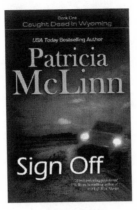

SIGN OFF

With her marriage over and her career derailed by her ex, top-flight reporter Elizabeth "E.M." Danniher lands in tiny Sherman. But the case of a missing deputy and a determined little girl drag her out of her fog.

Get SIGN OFF now!

LEFT HANGING

From the deadly tip of the rodeo queen's tiara to toxic "agricultural byproducts" ground into the arena dust, TV reporter Elizabeth "E.M." Danniher receives a murderous introduction to the world of rodeo.

Get LEFT HANGING now!

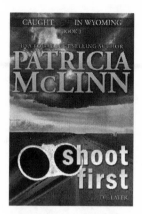

SHOOT FIRST

Death hits close to home for Elizabeth "E.M." Danniher – or, rather, close to Hovel, as she's dubbed her decrepit rental house in rustic Sherman, Wyoming.

Get SHOOT FIRST now!

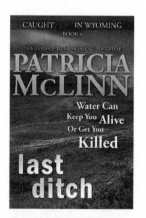

LAST DITCH

A man in a wheelchair goes missing in rough country in the Big Horn Basin of Wyoming. Elizabeth "E.M." Danniher and KWMT-TV colleague Mike Paycik immediately join the search. But soon they're on a search of a different kind – a search for the truth.

Get LAST DITCH now!

What readers are saying about the Caught Dead in Wyoming series:

"Great characters" … "Twists and turns" … "Just enough humor" … "Truly a fine read" … "Exciting and well-crafted murder mystery" … "Characters and dialogue were so very believable" … "Couldn't put it down" … "That was fun!" … "Smart and witty"

For excerpts and more on the Caught Dead in Wyoming series books, visit Patricia McLinn's website.

If you particularly enjoy connected books—as I do!—try these:

A Place Called Home series

Wyoming Wildflowers series

The Bardville, Wyoming series

The Wedding Series

Explore a complete list of all Patricia's books

patriciamclinn.com/patricias-books

About the Author

USA Today bestselling author Patricia McLinn's novels—cited by reviewers for warmth, wit and vivid characterization – have won numerous regional and national awards and been on national bestseller lists.

In addition to her romance and women's fiction books, Patricia is the author of the Caught Dead in Wyoming mystery series, which adds a touch of humor and romance to figuring out whodunit.

Patricia received BA and MSJ degrees from Northwestern University. She was a sports writer (Rockford, Ill.), assistant sports editor (Charlotte, N.C.) and—for 20-plus years—an editor at the Washington Post. She has spoken about writing from Melbourne, Australia to Washington, D.C., including being a guest-speaker at the Smithsonian Institution.

She is now living in Northern Kentucky, and writing full-time. Patricia loves to hear from readers through her website, Facebook and Twitter.

Visit with Patricia:

Website: patriciamclinn.com

Facebook: facebook.com/PatriciaMcLinn

Twitter: @PatriciaMcLinn

Pinterest: pinterest.com/patriciamclinn

www.PatriciaMclinn.com/newsletter

ISBN: 978-1-939215-59-8

61857036R00172

Made in the USA
Middletown, DE
16 January 2018